'A narrative that is never less than throat-grabbing. . .
You can't help turning the pages hungrily to see what
happens next.'

— *THE TIMES*

'A cracking thriller from a rising star in British crime
fiction.'

— *IRISH INDEPENDENT*

'Sharply written and wonderfully wrought, this crime
thriller sings with every twist and builds to a more-
than-satisfying bang.'

— *PUBLISHERS WEEKLY*

'It's impossible not to root for the feisty, flawed Kate.'

— *DAILY MAIL*

ALSO BY ROBERT BRYNDZA

STAND ALONE CRIME THRILLER

Fear The Silence

KATE MARSHALL PRIVATE INVESTIGATOR SERIES

Nine Elms

Shadow Sands

Darkness Falls

Devil's Way

The Lost Victim

DETECTIVE ERIKA FOSTER CRIME THRILLER SERIES

The Girl in the Ice

The Night Stalker

Dark Water

Last Breath

Cold Blood

Deadly Secrets

Fatal Witness

Lethal Vengeance

COCO PINCHARD ROMANTIC COMEDY SERIES

The Not So Secret Emails Of Coco Pinchard

Coco Pinchard's Big Fat Tipsy Wedding

Coco Pinchard, The Consequences of Love and Sex

A Very Coco Christmas

Coco Pinchard's Must-Have Toy Story

STANDALONE ROMANTIC COMEDY

Miss Wrong and Mr Right

ROBERT BRYNDZA

A **KATE MARSHALL** THRILLER

THE LOST
VICTIM

Raven Street Publishing
www.ravenstreetpublishing.com
Copyright © Raven Street Ltd 2024

Cover design by Henry Steadman

eBook ISBN: 978-1-914547-25-6
Paperback ISBN: 978-1-914547-26-3
Hardback ISBN: 978-1-914547-27-0
Audiobook: 978-1-914547-29-4

Robert Bryndza is the author of the international number #1 bestselling Detective Erika Foster and Kate Marshall Private Investigator series. Robert's books have sold over 6 million copies and have been translated into 30 languages. He is British and lives in Slovakia.

For Heather and Les

Go where we may, rest where we will,
Eternal London haunts us still.
— Thomas Moore

PROLOGUE

FRIDAY, 23 DECEMBER 1988

The air was bitterly cold as Janey Macklin hurried down the dark street that ran behind King's Cross St Pancras station, past a stretch of lock-ups on the left side of the road, opposite the high brick wall running along the train tracks. Hunger gnawed away at her stomach, and the pound coin and fifty-pence piece her mother had given her to buy cigarettes were hot in her hand. The rumble of a goods train passing on the other side made the pavement vibrate.

Janey zipped up her thin jacket, almost as thin as her pleated blue school skirt, as she crossed the street with her head down against the cold. She passed the Golden Fry chip shop. The big picture window was steamed up, and the colours from its flashing Christmas lights caught in the condensation. It was busy inside, and a young mother sat at the table against the window, holding out chips to a little girl.

The hot smell of frying fish hit Janey's nostrils as she passed the door, and then it was gone, replaced by the cold, sharp smell of drains and pollution. The smell of London.

When she reached the bright street lamp outside Reynolds newsagent, Robert, the young assistant of the owner, Jack, was outside. He was packing away the empty newspaper stands, whilst being watched over by a solemn little brown dog with greying whiskers who sat patiently by the door. Janey liked dogs; she had always wanted one, but the high-rise flats where they lived didn't allow them. She put out her hand, and the dog sniffed and gave it a hot little lick.

A stooped old man wearing a pork-pie hat and a long frayed sheepskin coat stepped carefully out the door and onto the pavement. He had a large brown paper bag, which Jack gave his customers for their top-shelf porno mags, under his arm.

'Evening, love.'

'Evening,' said Janey. Through the brown paper, she could just see the faint image of a blonde woman with huge, pale breasts.

'Come on, Whisky,' he said. The dog looked up at him and blinked as a lone swirling snowflake landed in his eye. 'Looks like it's going to freeze tonight. Mind how you go, darlin'.'

It didn't feel much warmer inside the newsagent's, and a smell of mould and cleaning products were fighting against each other to be the dominant scent. She passed a man with his back to her, looking at the top-shelf magazines. Jack was hunched over a giant ledger with curled pages at the counter, totting up figures with a chewed-ended biro and fingerless gloves. A small three-bar electric heater was on in the corner. Janey felt the warmth on her bare legs.

'Twenty Lambert and Butler, please,' she said. Jack looked up at her through rheumy eyes. Janey was tall for her age but thin and birdlike, and she loved to dance. She was flat chested and hadn't hit puberty yet, so she would never pass for sixteen, but Jack ran the kind of shop where this didn't matter, as long as he knew who you were. He nodded, reached around, plucked a packet of cigarettes off the tall display behind him, and put them on top of a pile of *Sunday Sport* newspapers bound in twine.

'One forty-five,' he said. Janey placed the pound coin and fifty pence in his grubby gloved hand.

'Can I please have the change as a five-p coin?' He sighed, as if this were a great inconvenience, and fished around in the open cash-box, muttering until he found a new, gleaming silver five-pence piece. He put it down on top of the right naked breast of the model gracing the front of the *Sport*. 'Thanks.'

If Janie was lucky, her mother would let her keep the change to play on the *Space Invaders* table machine when she returned to the pub. And often, when her mum saw she was playing it and keeping her little sister, Maxine, occupied, she'd buy them a glass of Coke and a bag of crisps.

Janey stuffed the box of cigarettes in the pocket of her coat. The shop was now empty, and Jack followed her to the door, where Robert was collecting his backpack. He was a few years older than Janey, with thick, greasy, shoulder-length black hair and small brown eyes. Janey and Robert stepped out the door, and Jack closed it behind them and turned the sign on the door to 'Closed.' The light under the awning went out, and they were plunged into darkness.

It was now snowing heavily, and the cold seeped across Janey's back through the thin material of her coat.

'Do you want a lift? I've got my van,' asked Robert, eagerly, indicating a big white van parked opposite. Janey hesitated. The unlit section of the road with the lock-ups now seemed longer. It was a ten-minute walk back to the pub, and she wanted to be in the warm with salt-and-vinegar crisps and a game of *Space Invaders*. 'It's okay. Where are you going?' Robert always seemed nice when she came to buy cigarettes. But his desperation was off-putting.

'The Jug.'

'Are you a little boozer?' he said laughing. He had tiny, sharp teeth. Like his baby teeth still hadn't fallen out.

'My mum's waiting for these,' she said, holding up the box of cigarettes. Janey could feel the weight of the wet snow landing on the top of her head, and a rogue snowflake found its way under her collar, smarting as it hit the skin between her shoulder blades.

He laughed again. 'I can drop you outside? I'm driving that way.'

The door to the newsagent opened again, and Jack stepped out with a folder under his arm. He was now wearing a thick woolly hat and a scarf over his long grubby coat.

'Haven't got homes to go to?' he muttered with an unlit cigarette in his mouth.

'I've offered Janey here a lift, but she's worried I'm a stranger. I'm not, though,' said Robert.

4

'He's stranger than most people,' said Jack, flashing a rare smile, pleased with his joke. 'No. He's fine.'

There was something about the way Jack said *fine* which seemed like an insult.

'Merry Christmas, boss,' said Robert.

Jack peered at him. 'What? Oh. Yeah, same to you.' He gave them a vague wave, then turned and walked away. The colossal gas towers loomed above him in a cloud of swirling snowflakes.

'So? I can give you a lift, yes?' asked Robert. Janey bit her lip. Her shoes were now soaked, and she was shivering.

'Okay. Thank you.'

They crossed the road to the van. There was a layer of dirt and grime on the paintwork, and the sides were covered in a grey, frozen slush.

'Do you want to sit in the front or back?'

'I'm old enough to sit in the front.'

'It's a van. There's no back . . . It was a joke.'

'Front,' said Janey, now irritated by him.

Robert unlocked the passenger door and helped her up the small step. The smell of fried food and stale cigarettes hung inside, and the plastic seats were freezing cold. It took a couple of attempts to start the engine, and then Robert had to let the windscreen wipers work to clear the accumulated snow on the front window. Janey didn't know how to fill the silence, and was glad when they pulled out into the road. They passed the Golden Fry chip shop. He didn't slow down as the lights in the windows of The Jug came closer.

'That's the pub,' said Janey.

'Do you fancy going for chips?'

Janey watched as they passed the swinging sign above the pub door.

'The chip shop's back there,' she said, beginning to panic as the glow from the pub receded in the passenger-door mirror. 'My mum is waiting for me.'

At the end of the road, Robert took a sharp left, barely slowing down, and then they were in the derelict area, speeding towards the canal and the giant gasworks.

Janey tried to open the door, but the handle only flapped uselessly.

'Let me out. Please.'

Robert switched on the radio, and 'I Wish It Could Be Christmas Every Day' by Slade boomed out.

'What do you think? Boom box speakers! Don't they sound awesome?' he shouted above the music.

Janey wanted to be back inside the warm pub with her mum and sister, even if she spent the night hungry and bored with clothes stinking of smoke. She scrabbled at the door lock, trying to pull it up, but Robert slammed on the brakes. Janey wasn't wearing a seat belt, so the abrupt stop threw her against the windscreen.

'Why are you trying to get out?' Robert cried. His face was now red and angry. 'I'm going to take you for chips. I'm being nice!'

He put on his hazard lights. Janey, in shock from the force of hitting the window, now lay in the footwell of the passenger seat. The side of her head throbbed, and when she put her hand to her temple, it came away with blood on it.

'Shit. You've cut yourself,' said Robert. The opening bars of 'Merry Christmas Everyone' started to play. He turned down the volume and then leant over. Janey flinched as he helped her back up into the passenger seat. He pulled the seat belt across her and fastened it with a click.

'Please. Let me out,' she said, clutching her temple. There was quite a lot of blood. Robert opened the glove compartment. It was filled with old crisp packets, paperwork, and a red scarf. 'Is that my scarf?'

'Yeah.' He smiled and handed it to her. There was a small printed label on the end of the thin material with her first name.

'Why have you got my scarf?' she said. She held it up to her bleeding cut.

'You dropped it a couple of weeks ago when you came to Reynolds.'

'Why didn't you give it back to me?'

The sound of the hazard lights blinking ticked loudly in the silence. They were now by the canal, with the gasworks directly in front of them. The round towers obscured the light, so everything glistened black, like tar.

'I like you, Janey. I thought you liked me?'

Janey could hear her heart hammering in her chest. She was confused. Robert looked hurt.

'I do like you.'

'You must be hungry? Why don't you let me take you to get chips?' Janey took the scarf away from her head. The bleeding had slowed a little, but her temple still throbbed. She eyed the lock in the door-frame under the window. If she pulled it up quickly, could she get the door open and run for it? Robert flicked on the fog lights, illuminating a wall of snowflakes that had begun to whirl across the canal path.

'Why don't we go to the Golden Fry?' said Janey. She knew if they went back, she could run for it. The Jug wasn't far.

He laughed. 'If I do that, you're going to run off, aren't you? You're a cheeky monkey.'

'No,' she said in a small voice. She was really very frightened now.

'The chip shop near where I live is much better than the Golden Fry. When you taste the chips, you'll agree. They're the best in London.'

When Janey dared to look at Robert, his face had changed. He looked like a hungry wolf. His brown eyes burned in the glow of the headlights, and his tiny razor-sharp teeth glistened. The snow was now falling thick and fast, obscuring the windows with a blanket of white.

'Look at that,' said Robert. 'Jack Frost is giving us some privacy.'

1

Thirty Years Later
THURSDAY, 27 DECEMBER 2018

Private Detective Kate Marshall stared at the wide channel which had been carved into the earth by the rainwater run-off from the previous day's storm. It cut a swath through the empty static caravans dotting what had been a grassy slope down from the main road above.

'It's good it didn't take out the caravans,' said Tristan Harper, Kate's partner in the detective agency. He took a photo of the wide earthy trench where water still poured down from the road.

'Is it? We could have claimed on insurance for new ones,' replied Kate. Tristan crouched close to the edge of the channel with his phone to take another photo, and the soil started to crumble. He jumped back just as another chunk of turf broke away and fell into the channel with a splash.

'It's a good job no one was mad enough to stay in the caravans over Christmas,' he said, shaking the mud off his wellington boots. He took a picture of the silver vintage-style caravan which sat closest to the trench, next to a small brick building that housed the communal toilets and showers.

Kate had inherited the caravan site, and a small building which housed the campsite shop, and the offices above for their struggling detective agency, from her friend Myra. Kate and Tristan had spent the past few years working hard to make the agency a success, and the caravan site provided a much-needed income to fill the gaps. However, they often felt more like caravan site managers than private detectives.

A cold breeze was coming off the sea, making Kate's eyes water. It was midmorning, but storm clouds hung low in the sky, and the town of Ashdean's lights, a few miles away, glowed on the horizon. Kate's house sat just below the campsite on the cliff edge, where waves pounded the beach. Thurlow Bay was a hamlet of six houses; four of them were owned by people from London, who used them for only a few weeks a year; the fifth had been abandoned several years ago and was in a state of disrepair; and Kate owned the sixth.

'Come on, let's have a cuppa. We should get these photos sent off to the insurance company, and I've got something else I need to talk to you about,' said Kate.

They followed the trench back down to the road running parallel to the cliff, where the water was leaving a muddy slick over the tarmac and pouring onto the beach.

'How has Olivia enjoyed Christmas in Thurlow Bay?' asked Tristan. 'The south coast of England must be a culture shock compared to all those palm trees in Los Angeles.'

Olivia was Kate's son Jake's girlfriend. Jake had met her whilst studying at university in California.

'She joined me for a swim on Christmas morning.'

'How did she get on?'

'Her lips went blue.' Kate gave a snort of laughter. 'Sorry, I shouldn't laugh.'

'Olivia must be serious about Jake.'

'We'll see about that. He's taken her today to visit the Crystal Path Mine Experience – that's what they've rebranded the Ashdean Caves as. I don't know what a tour in a damp cave in December will do for their relationship.'

Tristan laughed. They went up the steps and into the agency office. Kate switched on the space heater under the windows looking out to sea and stood in front of it, warming her hands. Tristan went into the tiny kitchen which faced the road, opened the blinds, and put on the kettle.

Their office had been the large studio flat where Kate's friend Myra lived when she ran the caravan site. They'd kept the 1970s yellow-and-green-squared carpet and Myra's old drop-leaf dining table, which now sat in the middle of the room as a communal desk. One side of the room had a filing cabinet and an IKEA bookshelf filled with case files and reference books. The other half of the office was designated for the campsite, with staff cleaning rotas on the wall, another filing cabinet, and six neat piles of clean bed-sheets, towels, and pillowcases, ready for when the campsite reopened in the spring.

Despite the clutter and the feeling sometimes that it wasn't a proper office, Kate liked it. The space heater quickly filled the room with warmth, and when Tristan lit the gas burner and put the kettle on, it was almost cosy.

A DHL envelope sat on the desk with some paperwork and a copy of a true crime tabloid called *Real Crime* magazine. Tristan picked up the magazine and saw it had a coloured tab marking a page.

'What's this?' he asked.

'It's what I wanted to talk to you about. I had an email yesterday from a creative agency who want to hire us to investigate a cold case. They're very keen. They couriered that over this morning.'

'Ah. I see why,' he said, opening it to the marked page, where the article headline read:

THE LOST VICTIM - DID THE NINE ELMS CANNIBAL KILL JANEY MACKLIN?

'Yes. A case a little close to home,' said Kate. Jake's father was Peter Conway, an ex–police detective who was serving multiple life sentences for the murder and mutilation of five young women in and around the Nine Elms area of South London. Kate, then a police detective, had worked out that the reason the 'Nine Elms Cannibal', as he became known in the press, had evaded the police for so long was because he *was* the police. To muddy the waters further, Kate had been having an affair with Peter Conway when she cracked the case.

And after surviving his attack, Kate had discovered she was four months pregnant with Jake. The ungodly mess of it all had caused Kate to have a breakdown and turn to alcohol. She'd lost custody of Jake when he was six, Kate's mother had stepped in to look after him, and this was the point when

Kate had sought help, entered rehab, and rebuilt her life, first as a university lecturer and later when she started the private detective agency with Tristan. This whole saga had been tabloid fodder for many years, and it had been written about many times in the press.

'Janey Macklin went missing in 1988, just before Christmas,' said Tristan, reading through the article. 'She was last seen in King's Cross on December 23, getting into the van belonging to a guy called Robert Driscoll. Driscoll was tried and convicted for her murder in 1989; however, Janey Macklin's body has never been found. . . Driscoll was convicted of her murder based on a history of stalky behaviour towards young women, and Janey's scarf, with her blood, was found in his flat. He went down for eight years, until a retrial in 1997 acquitted him due to lack of evidence. . . That's quite rare, isn't it? A murder trial going ahead without a body?' asked Tristan, looking up from the magazine article.

'It is. But the UK is one of the countries with the most successful convictions in murder cases without a body.'

'How is Peter Conway involved?'

Kate leaned over and turned the page. 'Thomas Black is a child-killer serving life in the same prison as Peter Conway. For many years, he corresponded with a woman called Judith Leary. She died last year, and the letters between her and Thomas Black were auctioned off as part of her estate sale. Serial killer letters are big business for a certain kind of collector.'

'I bet they are.'

'Thomas Black told Judith Leary in one of these letters

that Peter Conway had been seen hanging out in the pub near where Janey Macklin vanished, and he was seen grooming young girls in the weeks leading up to her going missing,' said Kate.

'And the client who sent all this is a creative agency?'

'Yes. I get the impression they want to produce some kind of true crime project, a book or a podcast, based on what we could discover.'

Kate took the cover letter out of the DHL envelope, and handed it to Tristan. The kettle on the stove began to whistle and she went to make the tea.

'Do you think they want access to Peter Conway?' asked Tristan.

'I presume, yes,' said Kate, returning with two mugs of tea. 'Jake tells me that Peter is in a bad way, health-wise.'

'Does Jake visit Peter?'

'No. Peter calls him once a month.'

'What if you have to dredge up the past? After . . . After everything you've been through with Peter Conway?'

'Tristan. I've been clean for twelve years. I go to regular AA meetings. I have a good handle on the past. It's the investigation that interests me. We have some contract work lined up for January and February, but now, with that happening,' said Kate, pointing in the direction of the caravan site, 'we could really do with the money.'

2

The following morning, Kate and Tristan caught the early train from Exeter St David's to London. It was the quiet week between Christmas and New Year, so the carriage was only half-full, and they managed to bag seats at a table. They'd split up after their conversation the previous morning, and done some research into the case.

'This is the King's Cross area where Janey Macklin went missing,' said Kate, taking out a printed map and putting it on the table between them. 'It's unrecognisable now, from how it was in 1988. There were grimy lock-ups and derelict buildings. It's now been supergentrified with new office and apartment blocks, and people drinking cappuccino on fancy piazzas.'

'On the night Janey went missing, she'd been at a pub, The Jug, with her mum and sister,' said Tristan, tracing his finger along the map. 'It's on St Pancras Road, which runs behind King's Cross St Pancras station. She left the pub just before 6pm to get some cigarettes for her mum at a newsagent farther along the road, and never came back.'

'I found a photo of Robert Driscoll,' said Kate, holding up a printout of a Facebook profile. 'After he was acquitted, he went back to live in the same flat where he grew up, a mile away from King's Cross on the Golden Lane Estate.'

Tristan peered at the photo of a large man in a black T-shirt sitting on a plastic garden chair, holding a cigarette and a can of lager. His pale face was toad-like, and his shoulder-length hair was dotted with grey. He wore a T-shirt with the logo of the band *Nirvana*.

'He looks a bit wild. What does he do now?'

'I don't know. It says in the *Real Crime* article that he worked in the newsagent on St Pancras Road where Janey went to buy the cigarettes. His Facebook profile is set to private. There isn't much stuff online from when she went missing, 1988 being pre-internet, but I did find some stuff about his appeal, which was in 1997.'

Kate looked through her pile of papers and pulled out an article she'd printed from the *Independent*: **IS ROBERT DRISCOLL IN PRISON FOR A CRIME HE DIDN'T COMMIT?** Underneath the headline was a picture of an elderly woman with messy black, curly hair, who shared Robert's toad-like features. She stood on a small balcony wearing a melancholy look on her face and a flowery housecoat, next to a row of pink geraniums in bloom. Behind her was the London skyline.

'This is Barbara Driscoll, Robert's mother. She campaigned heavily for his release, hired a new barrister, and got legal aid,' said Kate. She pulled out another article, this time from the *Daily Mail*: **MAN ACCUSED OF KILLING SCHOOLGIRL JANEY MACKLIN RELEASED AFTER SENSATIONAL RETRIAL**.

'The original murder trial hinged on the fact that Janey Macklin had dropped her red scarf in the newsagent a few weeks before she went missing. Robert Driscoll had picked it up and kept it, and it was found by the police in his bedroom two weeks later, covered in blood. They matched the blood with Janey's. It was one of the first uses of DNA testing in early 1989. It also says he had a previous criminal record for violence and harassment against a young woman, but the article doesn't give details.'

'That's what's scary about jury trials,' said Tristan. 'He went down for murder without there being a body.'

'It sounds like he had awful legal representation in the first trial, and the prosecution had the blood-covered scarf and his past record. It says that when they put him on the stand in the first trial, he was angry and belligerent. He played into the prosecution's hands. In the retrial he was the wronged victim.'

'And Janey Macklin has never been found,' said Tristan, looking back at the map of the King's Cross area. 'What do we know about Peter Conway in 1988?'

'He was still training to be a police officer at Hendon Police College in North London. It's where I trained, a few years later.'

'How long was your training?'

'Four months.'

'So Peter Conway was in London at the same time as

Janey Macklin went missing. Was he active as a serial killer in 1988?'

'It's possible. He used a white van to abduct his victims, the ones he was tried for as the Nine Elms Cannibal. Dumping their bodies in parks and wastelands. The King's Cross area was very seedy and dangerous back in 1988, and parts of it were a huge wasteland with abandoned buildings and warehouses.'

'What about Thomas Black? He named Peter Conway in these letters, but where was he in 1988?' asked Tristan.

'He was living in London. He went down for abducting young boys and girls, some of them Janey's age. He drugged them, and then raped and murdered them.'

'He could have killed Janey?'

'Yes. And Thomas Black is banged up with Peter. Has been for the past three years.'

Tristan tapped his finger on the map. 'There's been so much reconstruction in the King's Cross area. If Janey's body had been dumped close by, they would have found her when they were digging.'

'Or she's still there, buried under tons of new concrete,' said Kate with a shudder.

3

'How was your journey? You've come so *far*?' asked Fidelis Stafford. The Stafford-Clarke Creative Agency had their offices in a small terraced house just off Kensington High Street.

'The fast train takes about two hours,' said Kate. She sat with Tristan on a small IKEA sofa in the shadow of Fidelis's huge desk, which filled the bay window of her cramped office and looked out over an old George V postbox on a leafy avenue.

'Good Lord. I didn't know that. Did you know that, Maddie?' Fidelis turned to a tall, thin, nervous middle-aged woman with glasses and long honey-blonde hair, who wore a blue knitted pullover with stirrup leggings. She'd joined the meeting shortly after they arrived, and the only place left to sit was a small leather pouffe. Fidelis's assistant, a young woman who hadn't yet been introduced, sat at the back behind a tiny desk, partly obscured by a pile of boxes.

'Yes. Claudia gets that train often. She has a lovely

weekend cottage in Bude,' replied Maddie. Whoever Claudia was, they weren't going to offer up any more information, thought Kate. Fidelis was old-school upper class. Her shiny black hair was cut in a severe bob, and she wore glasses with a thick black frame and a beautiful cap-sleeved dress with big pockets.

'Well. Thank you for coming in during the Christmas holidays! I'm still feeling the effects of overindulgence. It's lovely to meet you both,' said Fidelis.

'Yes. We appreciate your time,' agreed Maddie. Her nose crinkled with the smile, giving the impression she was indulging them.

'Is your son spending Christmas at home?' asked Fidelis.

'My son?'

'Jake? Yes?' asked Fidelis, peering over the top of her glasses. 'He's the son of . . . er . . .'

'Peter Conway,' finished Kate. There was a chilly little silence.

'Is it correct that Jake is studying in America, at UCLA in Los Angeles?' said Maddie, tottering a little on the tiny pouffe. She hitched one leg under the other.

'I don't understand why you're asking me about Jake.'

'Oh, we just did some background research on you. Both,' said Fidelis, waving it away as if it were a trifling matter.

'Background research?' repeated Kate. Fidelis smiled. It was the first time Kate had seen a smile make someone look less likeable.

'Yes. We've done background research on you both and this case. Nothing obtrusive. So much about you is already out there,' Fidelis added, fixing Kate with a keen stare.

'Jake has just finished studying film and media at UCLA, and he's now an intern at the Jeffery Blakemore Agency,' said Kate.

'Jolly good for him. And you, Tristan?' said Fidelis, turning her keen stare to him. 'You started out as a research assistant at Ashmore University?'

'Ashdean,' said Tristan, sitting up and gripping his legs. Fidelis nodded and smiled. 'Yes. That was ten years ago.'

'And how did you find your way into that?'

Tristan hesitated. 'Er. It's quite a funny story. I was supposed to be interviewing for a cleaning job at the university that day, and at the same time Kate was interviewing for a researcher. But she thought they were all a bit . . .' Tristan hesitated. Kate had thought that all the applicants were stuck-up posh kids with no imagination.

'I wanted someone smart, savvy, and keen to learn, which I found in Tristan,' said Kate, jumping in. She noted that Tristan was playing down his West Country accent. He glanced over at her and smiled gratefully. 'And I hope your background search shows we now run one of the most successful private detective agencies in the south of England.'

'*Absolutely!* You have quite an impressive body of work,' said Fidelis. 'Five murder investigations, three of them historic cold cases. And you also do work for the public sector?'

'Yes. As well as our private work with individuals, we have several local government contracts and contracts with multinational firms.'

'What do local governments ask you to do?' said Fidelis.

'It's often a deep background check on individuals. All

employers conduct a CRB check, criminal background check, and/or a DBS check, Disclosure and Barring Service . . .'

'Yes, we're aware of the terms as an employer ourselves.'

'Of course. Sometimes, if an employer hires for sensitive roles, they'll want to know more,' said Kate.

'We've also taken local government contracts which involve surveillance on an employee suspected of stealing or fraud,' said Tristan.

'*Gosh.* It all sounds so stimulating. Well done, both of you,' said Fidelis. She smiled, but her eyes remained reserved, watching. Kate didn't return the smile; she sat back on the sofa. They hadn't come all the way to London to sell themselves and pitch for a job. Stafford-Clarke wanted *them*.

'Let's talk about this project, potential investigation,' said Kate. 'We're intrigued, but the details still seem a little vague.'

Maddie looked to Fidelis. 'Well, we've purposely kept things vague.'

'What exactly does Stafford-Clarke do? You are a creative agency. Is that another word for a literary agency?'

'Yes. That's been our bread-and-butter work since I founded the agency many moons ago,' said Fidelis. 'But the publishing industry is constantly evolving, and so is the area of online content – audiobooks and podcasts, true crime podcasts in particular . . . Maddie, do you want to continue?'

'Absolutely,' replied Maddie, still trying to accommodate her gangly legs on the tiny pouffe. 'We would be interested if you could investigate the disappearance of Janey Macklin in 1988 to see if there is a possible link to Peter Conway. *Or* if something else happened to her. We're not asking you to be involved in this potential creative project. You would be taking the roles of investigators. And when your investigation has concluded, we would then have the information to move forward and potentially create something like a book or a true crime podcast . . . We may ask you to make sound recordings, which may or may not end up in the podcast.'

'And it would all be subject to you signing nondisclosure agreements,' added Fidelis. 'We know you are both entirely qualified to . . .' She seemed to grope for the right words.

'Investigate and present your findings,' added Maddie.

'Yes. But a "name" writer or performer or presenter would be better placed to front an eventual book or true crime podcast.' Fidelis said the word *podcast* with disdain, as if she would prefer to be working with Pulitzer Prize winners.

'That's what we thought,' said Kate, looking to Tristan, who nodded.

'What's our timescale?' he asked.

'Six months. Find out as much as you can. In addition to your fee, there is a "Brucie Bonus,"' said Fidelis, rolling her *r* on *Brucie*. 'If you solve the case.'

'If for any reason you don't solve the case, we could still proceed with an "unsolved true crime case", which ironically often makes things more creepy,' said Maddie. 'You are based in the West Country, and we appreciate that you can do a certain amount of work remotely. However, we have a small flat available to accommodate you, if you need to stay in London.'

'It's a snug little box, but it should be perfectly adequate. It belongs to the company. And it's in King's Cross,' said Fidelis.

Kate looked across at Tristan. That was very interesting.

'Your letter mentioned that you would like access to Peter Conway?' Kate asked.

A look passed between Fidelis and Maddie.

'Yes. If we *could* get hold of a recorded interview with Peter Conway, that would be like gold dust,' said Maddie.

'But we are aware of reporting restrictions, and the restrictions of recording an interview with a serving, er, prisoner for commercial purposes. If you *did* gain access to him, we could have an actor record and recreate the interview based on a written transcript,' said Fidelis.

'There is the option to license archive material of Peter Conway,' said Maddie, seeing the look on Kate's face. She added hopefully, 'Do you own any recordings of him?'

'No.'

'Right. That's okay.'

Kate looked around the office. There was a bookshelf on the wall behind Fidelis with English-language and foreign editions of their clients' fiction books.

'How did you come to find this case, Janey Macklin? I've never heard the name, and I don't remember it being a high-profile investigation when I was a police officer in London in the 1990s,' she said.

'Maddie's partner, Forrest, is a features writer,' said Fidelis. Her tone suggested that she thought being a 'features writer' was akin to shovelling shit for a living.

'The Forrest Parker who wrote the magazine piece about Janey Macklin?' asked Tristan.

'Yes,' said Maddie with a bashful smile. 'Forrest was

friends with Judith Leary, who had the correspondence with Thomas Black.'

'Well. She was more of an acquaintance, Maddie. Yes?' said Fidelis with a look of dismay.

'Yes. Acquaintance, but they did know each other quite a long time,' said Maddie.

'How did Judith come to start writing to Thomas Black?' asked Tristan.

'Forrest met Judith when they were at drama school together. Many years ago. One of Judith's acting jobs involved going into prisons and doing drama workshops with the prisoners, and that's how she met Thomas Black.'

'Do you have copies of the letters?' asked Kate.

'Yes. Forrest took copies, before he sold them on behalf of Judith's estate,' said Maddie.

'Does Forrest work for *Real Crime* magazine? Or is he an actor?' asked Tristan.

'Neither. He's a freelance writer,' said Maddie. There was a long, awkward silence. And Kate thought Fidelis was enjoying it.

'We're very interested in working with you both,' said Fidelis, breaking the silence. 'My job as a literary agent and in the creative sector is to curate great stories and shepherd them to, gosh, I don't know what you'd say for a podcast – shepherd it to the air waves?'

'A podcast is downloadable, not broadcast,' said Maddie.

'Yes. I know,' Fidelis snapped. 'My point is I can see a good story, a great story, that needs a bit of excavation. We have a fantastic location: King's Cross, and old London, which *thrums* with history and intrigue. We have an unsolved disappearance or a murder with young Janey Macklin. A miscarriage of justice with, er . . .'

'Robert Driscoll,' said Fidelis's assistant, speaking for the first time behind her desk.

'Yes, of course – Robert Driscoll. And we have Peter Conway and Thomas Black, two of the most notorious bastard, if you excuse my French, serial killers. This could be a blockbuster . . .' Fidelis smiled and checked her enthusiasm. 'So. That's where we are. What do you think?'

'I agree. It all sounds intriguing. What exactly are you willing to pay us?' asked Kate, going in for the kill. She saw Fidelis and Maddie recoil a little at the mention of money.

'That can be negotiated,' said Fidelis.

'Okay. Let's negotiate,' said Kate.

4

Tristan stared at the laminated map above the seats as the Tube train shook and shunted its way from South Kensington to King's Cross on the Piccadilly line. In his backpack was the cardboard folder of information they'd been given by Fidelis's assistant. He was excited at the prospect of an investigation, especially one which could mean spending time in London. They had negotiated a good deal, and Tristan felt relief that their financial future was secure for the next few months.

'We need to see a contract,' said Kate for the fifth time, when he caught her eye.

'I know,' he said. 'But the meeting was good. They want to hire us.'

Kate nodded, but she didn't know if *good* was the right word. The meeting had been interesting, but there was something about it all that she couldn't put her finger on; was it all too good to be true?

The Tube train was busy on this Friday afternoon, mainly

with shoppers taking advantage of the post-Christmas days off, and it was standing room only.

'Where did you live in London, when you were in the police?' asked Tristan.

'Deptford Bridge.'

He studied the map. How the hell did anyone find their way around London? The Tube map was a grid of coloured, snaking, angular lines radiating out from a hub which looked like a bottle of stout lying on its side. Kate reached up and pointed to one of the train lines made up of two thin blue lines.

'Here. Deptford. Close to the end of the Docklands Light Railway. I was twenty minutes from the centre, and when I lived there, there was a lot of new construction, new flats. The DLR was a new train line.'

Tristan thought back to what he knew about the night Peter Conway attacked Kate; it had been at her flat in Deptford. And as far as he knew, it was the last night she had lived in London. She'd been hospitalised and then moved back to live with her parents when she was pregnant with Jake.

'Yeah. That's where it happened,' said Kate, seeing what Tristan was thinking.

'Did you own the flat in Deptford?'

'I wish. It would be worth an absolute fortune by now.'

'And the flat the agency have offered us is . . .' The Tube train pulled to a stop at Holborn, and the doors opened with a whoosh. To Tristan, it was all so bright and vibrant. The platform was crammed with people, and passengers with bags and a lady with a pushchair flooded past them against the tide of more passengers boarding the Tube. A recorded voice asked them to mind the doors and the gap.

'It's in King's Cross. Percy Circus. A short walk from the main King's Cross station,' said Kate as she moved to one side to let a couple of nuns pass.

'What did you think of Fidelis and Maddie? They're very posh.'

'Yes, they are. And maybe not in a good way.' Kate wondered why it was bothering her. Her own feelings of inferiority? The middle-class chip on her shoulder?

Tristan did a double take as the nuns moved past. One wore a hot-pink handbag over her shoulder, and the second had scarlet lipstick and big false eyelashes.

'Fancy dress, I presume. I hope. Or they're from a very forward-thinking order,' he said. Kate laughed.

'Where do you want to go first?' she said, looking back up at the map.

'We should have a look at the area in King's Cross where Janey went missing. And let's find somewhere to have a coffee and look at those letters between Thomas Black and Judith Leary.'

When they reached King's Cross, there was a crush of people waiting, crammed on the platform with shopping bags and thick coats, and it seemed chaotic.

'Bloody hell, this has changed since I was last here,' said Kate when they emerged from King's Cross underground station and into a paved plaza.

'Isn't that the hotel where they filmed the Spice Girls video for "Wannabe"?' said Tristan, pointing to their right at the enormous red-bricked splendour of the Midland Hotel, now called the St Pancras Renaissance. The courtyard out front was busy with people, and a bellboy pushed a pile of suitcases inside.

Kate smiled.

'Yes. When I was a copper in London, this whole area was horrible. The train station plaza was all enclosed in a dingy, squat building, which always seemed to have scaffolding wrapped around it. Drunks, prostitutes, and drug dealers hung around along the side of the road in the doorways and windows, and the Midland Hotel there was boarded up, with piss-stinking doorways. In my first year on the beat, I was called out here so many times to deal with trouble. Mainly drugs.'

Tristan turned and looked around. Christmas lights and decorative silver stars and gold snowflakes formed a canopy above the road, red buses roared past amongst the traffic, which included an open-top bus filled with tourists peering down and shivering in the weak sunshine.

'Look at all this,' said Kate, turning to their left to face the glass-and-steel skyscrapers. A crane swung slowly to the left with a load of concrete blocks. 'This place is unrecognisable from when I was last here in 1995. How will we find anyone who saw or knew anything about Janey?'

Kate was quiet as they walked past the hotel. A group of tourists posed for selfies in front of a red phone box, and the smell of roasting chestnuts and mulled wine wafted over from a food van parked on the edge of the piazza. They took a left down Pancras Road. The click-clack of the trains behind the high brick walls was the same as she remembered, and so was the smell: diesel mixed with the cold air which hit the back of your throat. Kate recalled Pancras Road's grimy lock-ups under the brick arches. The brick arches were still there, but they were now occupied by designer shops and posh restaurants, and much of the brickwork had been sand-blasted, removing the black stain from a hundred years of London smog.

They stopped outside a smart-looking gastropub with shiny copper lamps and red-painted window frames. A chalkboard with a flowery hand announced that they served ales from a microbrewery and champagne by the glass.

'Look,' said Tristan, indicating the sign above them, swinging in the breeze. It read 'The Jug.'

'Bloody hell. The Jug is still here. I bet they didn't serve champagne by the glass back in 1988,' said Kate.

They carried on walking. Amongst the shops and restaurants, the arches also housed modern warehouse-style offices. They were all closed for Christmas, but many of them had left their lights on, and in a couple, Christmas trees twinkled with fake presents neatly wrapped underneath. Kate felt dismay. This whole area had been scrubbed clean. The past erased, 1988 might as well have been 1888. A few minutes later, they reached a small crossing with a tiny Starbucks on the corner.

Tristan took out his phone, scrolled for a moment, and looked back up at the familiar sign. Inside it looked cosy and inviting, and a small Christmas tree stood by the counter.

'This was Reynolds newsagent's,' said Tristan.

'I should have guessed. Of *course* it's now a Starbucks,' she said. 'Let's get a coffee. I need caffeine, and time to think.'

5

Kate sat in one of the high seats in the window, and Tristan left his backpack and went up to the counter to order coffee. They'd found a photo of Reynolds newsagent, taken in 1990, and Kate looked at it on her phone. There was a ripped awning in faded red-and-white stripes with 'REYNOLDS' written in black. The picture window where she now sat was filled with what looked like wanted ads – the kind of little postcards that you could use to place an ad to buy or sell. The pavement out front was filled with metal racks containing all the daily newspapers and magazines. And a small metal Wall's ice cream sign stood next to a tall revolving rack with greeting cards.

'I asked the barista if he lives locally,' said Tristan, coming over to the table with two coffees and chocolate croissants. 'He looked at me as if I were mad. He commutes an hour to get here every day.'

It was a shock to be back in London, and to realise how

provincial she'd become. She sipped her coffee; it was hot and strong and just what she needed.

Tristan opened his rucksack and took out the slim folder they'd been given by Fidelis and Maddie. It was blue, and written across the front and then crossed out was ~~Booker Prize long lists 1990–2000~~. Printed underneath was MATERIALS FOR KATE MARSHALL DET. AGENCY.

There were only a couple of A4 papers inside fastened with a paper clip, and a tiny black USB key. There was a typed note on a compliments slip:

These are the letters from Thomas Black to Judith Leary where Janey Macklin is mentioned. The USB key contains all letters. Please keep safe. Maddie x

'Is that a London thing, signing off with a kiss?' asked Tristan, holding up the compliments slip and raising an eyebrow.

'Not when I lived here,' said Kate. 'Maybe it's a publishing thing.'

Kate put the first letter between them, and they read.

Friday, 29 October 2010
3948562 HMP Wakefield

Dear Judith,

Despite what you might have read in the media recently, I spend twenty-three hours a day in my cell. It's true; I am lucky to have access to my reading and writing materials and a small television,

*but I would give anything to have true freedom.
Please, my dear, understand that you have true
freedom. You have a degree of financial
independence, your own flat, and the luxury of time.
You wrote in your last letter that you woke up with
nothing to do. You took the train into London and
wandered around Regent's Park in tears at your lack
of acting work. Oh, what I would give to wake up,
leave my cell, and walk through the city unchecked
from place and time!*

*I have no doubt that you have been reading the
newspapers. Peter Conway has been returned to
incarceration after his escape attempt ended in
tears. We are back at the circus, with media and
staff gawking like we are all monkeys in a zoo. He'll
be kept in solitary for a few weeks, so I won't have
the misfortune to bump into him. There's a certain
vulgarity about Conway, I've always thought. It
seems he had a fan on the outside who helped him
escape, and there was a promise to reunite him with
his 'common old mum', Enid. The rumour is that the
two of them were screwing. Old Ma has been having
her way with him since he first filled out his
trousers . . .*

'Are you okay with continuing to read this?' Tristan
asked Kate. She felt a tightening in her chest when she
saw the date of the first letter. When Peter Conway

escaped on 27 October 2010, his plan had been to abduct Jake and for them to flee to Spain with Enid. She shuddered at the thought of how close they had come to reaching their aim.

'Yes. We need to read it.'

Tristan nodded, and they turned back to the letter.

No doubt he'll be using up all of his prison stamp allowance to write to dear old Ma, who is (apparently) being held in HMP Downview, down south, until the CPS decides what to do with her. I think she'll only get a few years.

My path crossed with Conway's a few times on the outside. Back in the day, when he was a copper, he pulled me over late at night for driving with a faulty headlight. Even then, I thought it was odd for an officer to be out on the beat, on his own, at 2am, dealing with such mundane tasks. He was quite dashing in his uniform that night, and the only reason the encounter sticks in my mind is that I saw him a week or so later, drinking at The Jug in King's Cross. Back then, The Jug was delightfully seedy. Peter Conway was there on his own that night, and I don't know if he recognised me, but he didn't let on if he did. Conway seemed to be watching the younger women in the pub quite closely. I thought he was on surveillance until he bought a young girl who couldn't have been more than fourteen or fifteen a double vodka and then another, before asking her to join him. It only stuck in my mind because a month or so later, it was all over the papers that a girl had gone missing in King's Cross . . .

Tristan looked up at Kate.

'Hang on. Thomas Black says Peter Conway stopped him at two am for having a faulty brake light, and this was five weeks before Janey went missing. That would make it mid-November 1988.'

'It means Peter was impersonating a police officer,' finished Kate. 'He didn't graduate from Hendon until early 1989.'

'It doesn't say if Peter Conway was in a police car or plain clothes.'

'Plain clothes officers have ID,' said Kate, troubled. They read on:

I later heard on the grapevine – grapevine is a much more pleasant word for it, I won't subject you to that, my dear – that Peter Conway was the one who kidnapped Janey Macklin. He'd got to know her in the pub weeks before she vanished, so she was happy to get into a car with him. He also might have been wearing his police uniform when she got into his car.

I don't know if I'll get the chance to bring this

up with Conway. I'll let you know. But back to how I started, please try to enjoy your life out there. You are an outstanding actress. I'm a monster, and many people would think my endorsement of your talent isn't worth a fig. However, I believe it's worth its weight in gold. I have no reason to lie to you, my dear.

Keep your pecker up.

Yours, Thomas

Tristan sipped his coffee, and Kate took out the second photocopied letter. This was much longer, but the short section about Janey had been highlighted.

You wrote in your last letter, dated Sunday, 31 October, which itself was in reply to my letter dated Friday, 29 October 2010, that you felt burdened by me telling you about a girl named Janey Macklin, whom I believe could have been an early victim of Peter Conway. Just to reiterate, Judith, my dear, the screws open and read every one of my God damn letters. So they've probably read every word I've ever written to you, and God knows who else. Rest assured, you don't need to do anything with the information I've given you. It's now known by the higher-ups, whomever they may be. I still haven't had the chance to ask Conway about this, and I don't know if I will have anytime soon. He's being *kept in solitary confinement under strict supervision.*

Kate looked up from reading. They had only been in the coffee shop for half an hour, but already, a fog had descended on the road outside, and the light was fading.

'What do you make of Thomas Black?' she asked.

'He thinks he's an intellectual. He's displaying a lot of the classic serial killer traits: smooth-talking but insincere, egocentric and grandiose.'

Kate nodded. 'Yes, he needs excitement. He likes to manipulate. He's writing this letter and openly acknowledging that the guards read the letters. It would be interesting to see the kind of letter he writes to someone else. Which could tell us what his relationship was to Judith.'

'The most important thing is that he says he saw Peter Conway at The Jug buying Janey a drink.'

'That's Black's assumption, but it could have been another girl – he didn't positively identify her as Janey in the letter.'

'Sorry, yes. That's his assumption. But can we trust what he's written to Judith? Peter Conway and Thomas Black were both hanging around in the same area of London around that time. Thomas Black was part of a paedophile ring. Two of the young girls Peter Conway killed were under the age of consent. Maybe their paths crossed in other ways.'

Kate looked around at the busy coffee shop. A group of young girls chatted in one corner, and another group waited to collect their orders from the barista. They were all oblivious to the history of where they stood, which was a good thing.

'We're really close to Victoria House, where Janey lived. Do you want to check it out?' asked Tristan.

Kate finished the last of her coffee, and as they left the Starbucks, she saw the sign for The Jug lit up far down the road. A cold breeze shifted the hair on the back of her neck, and despite the bright Christmas lights and people on the streets, she had the same feeling of fear and revulsion she remembered from the seedy, dangerous side of the King's Cross of her early years in the Met Police.

6

'It feels . . . intimidating,' said Tristan.

'It's called brutalist architecture,' said Kate.

They stood on the street in front of Victoria House, a ten-storey concrete block of flats five minutes from the Starbucks. The flats were set back from the road with a large courtyard lined with a low concrete wall, similar to the central reservation of a motorway. Grass and dead weeds peeped up through the cracks in the concrete slabs of the courtyard.

'*Brutal* is a good description.'

In a few of the windows, Christmas lights twinkled and flashed, adding a splash of colour. As they crossed the courtyard, a fake Santa on a small roped ladder hung out of a second-floor window. Kate wondered if Santa was trying to get in or trying to escape.

'What's that supposed to be?' asked Tristan as they passed a giant ugly statue, again in concrete, sitting on a low plinth. 'It looks like an eight-sided dice, or a weird Rubik's cube.'

As they passed, they saw someone had sprayed 'FUCK OSTERITY' high up on one of the sides of the dice facing the front entrance.

'Interesting spelling of *austerity*,' said Tristan. Dusk seemed to be clinging on, along with a faint mist in the air. The concrete surfaces of the building were stained with watermarks and mould. It all felt very damp and miserable.

A curtain of glass panels had been built across the main entrance. On the other side, a concrete staircase was open to the air. Kate wondered whether the entrance had been open when they built Victoria House in the 1950s and if the glass panels were put in later as a security measure. There was an entry intercom panel, and the numbered buttons listed the surnames of some of the residents. There were fifty flats, and a neat square with **MACKLIN** printed on it was under the number 50.

Kate was just working out what to say when they rang the bell, when a young man walked up in a hurry with two bags of shopping. He placed a card on a sensor, and the door popped open. He wasn't interested to see Kate and Tristan enter behind him, and he took the stairs.

A urine-stinking lift creaked and groaned its way up to the tenth floor. When they got out, a long corridor, open to the air, ran alongside a neat row of front doors painted with a rather garish pillar-box red. All but one of the windows to the right of each door had blinds or net curtains.

They walked along the corridor. Orange sodium lights were stationed between each door, casting their faces and the concrete in a sickly pallor. The view from the tenth floor was panoramic. Kate could see the full extent of the development around King's Cross, with glittering high-rise flats and two parks, and the gas towers by the canal had been repurposed into a square illuminated with floodlights.

'What do we say to Doreen if she's in?' asked Tristan. 'I feel like we're stumbling in a bit blind here.'

'The truth. We've been asked to look into her daughter's disappearance. Her reaction will be worth noting, and what if she talks?' Kate felt a little overwhelmed by being back in London, which she hadn't expected.

They passed a window where they could see into a small kitchen where pans boiled on a stove, and another where they heard shouting from behind a set of glowing blinds.

When they reached the last door, Tristan rang the bell. They heard it jangle deep inside the flat. The blinds in the window were down, and it looked dark inside. He rang it again. They heard a door open, and a white-haired older lady stepped out from the flat next door. She folded her arms over a cosy green woollen cardigan and wore a pleated skirt with a tartan check, thick leggings, and a rather moth-eaten pair of fluffy slippers.

'Are you from Bellingham's?' she asked hopefully.

'No,' said Kate. She rang the bell again.

The older lady went to the concrete wall, peered down to the ground, and then looked back at them. 'She's not in.'

'Doreen Macklin?' asked Tristan.

'Yes. Are you debt collectors?'

Kate wondered what about them made the older lady think they were debt collectors.

42

'No. We're actually private investigators.'

A yell came from inside: 'Close *the door*!'

Kate took out their business card and handed it to her.

'Ashdean . . . That's up in Scotland, isn't it?' she said, peering at it.

'No, other direction. Down south,' said Tristan.

'What's Doreen done to warrant *two* private detectives?'

'We're investigating her daughter's disappearance,' said Kate. There was a small silence and a shift in her attitude.

'Oh. Yes. Janey.'

'Did you live here when Janey went missing?'

'Yes. We've been here fifty years. We knew Janey and her sister, Maxine. It's terrible what happened. I saw her on the morning of the day she vanished. She was looking forward to Christmas.'

'Do you know when Doreen will be home?' asked Kate.

'No. She just won the lottery, would you believe it. Won a hundred and fifty grand on a scratch card a month before Christmas. We haven't seen her since . . .'

There was another yell from inside the woman's flat. She sighed.

'I thought you were the carers for my husband, Stan . . . They seem to show up whenever they want.' The woman looked Tristan up and down keenly. 'You're strong. Could you lift my husband out of his chair and onto the bed?'

'Er,' said Tristan.

'He's not nude or nothing. He broke his hip before Christmas and is having to sleep downstairs until it all heals. I'm Betty Cohen. I could tell you more about Doreen and Janey.'

'Okay,' said Tristan, looking at Kate, who nodded. They followed her inside. The entrance led past a small kitchen into a big, high-ceilinged living room with lots of bookshelves and cheese plants, and a balcony looking out over the London skyline. An older man, dressed smartly in tan slacks and a roll-neck jumper, sat in a high-backed chair. He had a shock of white hair and giant glasses with thick lenses, which made him look rather mad and kind at the same time. Next to him were a single bed, a walking frame, and a tall, scrawny Christmas tree, which had now shed most of its needles onto the carpet.

'Stan. This is Tristan and Kate. They're private detectives, and they've come to help you into bed,' said Betty.

'Is The Corporation sending private detectives now!' Stan grinned.

'No. They're here about her next door . . .' Betty tilted her head.

Stan's enormous eyes widened. 'Doreen the Dreadful.'

'Stanley. No!' she said sharply. *'Janey.'*

'Ah. Yes. Terrible business,' Stanley said, shaking his head.

'Tristan, if you can help Stan onto the bed.'

Kate stood back as Tristan, under Betty's guidance, hooked his arms under Stan's, lifted him from the chair, and deposited him gently on the single bed.

'Thank you, dear boy,' boomed Stan. 'I lost my balance on the crossing out in front of the Midland Hotel, of all places. Bloody embarrassing, it was, with ambulances and "well-wishers" who thought I was some clapped-out old duffer . . . I still work, you know!'

'What do you do?' asked Tristan.

'I'm in antiquarian books. Betty, would you?' he said, indicating a sideboard covered in books and china figurines.

'Why can't the carers lift you like that?' said Betty, opening an old cigar-box and taking out a business card. She handed it to Stan and put two pillows behind his back. 'Last week, they sent this tiny little woman. Why send someone so *feeble*? She could barely knock the skin off a rice pudding, let alone lift my Stan. Here, sit down; you've earned a cuppa.'

Kate and Tristan sat on a large sofa opposite, and Betty went to the kitchen, leaving them with Stan.

'Who's hired you to find Janey Macklin? Is it Doreen, now she's flush?' he asked keenly. Kate hesitated. They hadn't technically been hired, and without a contract, they didn't know the level of confidentiality. Stan raised an eyebrow. 'Or is it Robert Driscoll wishing to prove his innocence?'

Betty came gliding back into the living room with a tray of tea things. 'What have I missed?'

'I'm trying to wheedle it out of them who they're working for, but they don't want to tell me. Come on, who is it?'

7

'Our client is a writer who wants us to research Janey Macklin's disappearance for a potential book,' said Tristan, glancing at Kate. *Good one, Tris*, she thought.

'He's not related to the Macklin family, and it's envisaged as a respectful piece of journalism,' Kate added, bending the truth even more.

'Ah. Right. A journalistic endeavour,' said Stan. Betty set down the tray with a lovely pale-blue china tea-set. She poured them each a cup. When Kate took a sip of her tea, it was deliciously strong.

'Is it okay if I take notes?' asked Tristan, pulling out his notebook and pen.

'Of course,' said Stan. He looked quite excited at the prospect of someone making a record of their conversation.

'Our starting point has been this article in *Real Crime*,' said Tristan, taking it out of his bag and turning to the correct page. Stan took the magazine and peered at the article through his giant spectacles.

'Good Lord,' he said, looking up at them. 'It says here that Janey could have been an early victim of the Nine Elms Cannibal.'

'A cannibal? What cannibal?' shrilled Betty.

'You know. That case, years ago – South London, wasn't it? It was a police officer who bit chunks of flesh out of those girls, killed them, and dumped their bodies.'

Betty got up and moved over to peer at the magazine. They were silent as they studied the article. Kate noted that Betty's lips moved slightly as she read.

'Doreen used to clean at The Jug and told some stories about the kind of men who used to go there. Men who liked young girls, if you know what I mean. There were also a lot of drug dealers. Dodgy types. But not *serial killers*,' she finished, tapping the magazine.

'Doreen was at The Jug with her daughters on the night Janey went missing in 1988?' said Kate.

'Yes. The girls used to go and meet her there after school on a Friday. Doreen used to like a few jars after work. She was the one who sent Janey off that night to buy her some cigarettes. I don't think she ever forgave herself.'

'Why did Doreen let her young girls come to The Jug?'

Betty shook her head. 'I don't know. It was a different time, and you never think the bad stuff is going to happen to you, I suppose, do you?'

'Are you friends with Doreen?'

Stan looked over at Betty with a raised eyebrow. She came back to sit in her chair.

'Let's just say we have a healthy respect for each other. We've been neighbours for a long time. This place was built after the war. This whole area around King's Cross was bombed in the blitz. My mum got herself on the list for a council flat, which is what these were. We bought ours. Doreen moved in next door with her mother in the same year. Hers is still a council flat.'

'What does Doreen's other daughter, Maxine, do?' asked Kate.

'She managed to escape,' said Betty. 'Maxine was twelve when Janey went missing. It must have been a terrible time. Watching Doreen lose herself in the drink. Social services almost took Maxine away from her. Doreen would go off on one of her benders and go missing for days. We looked out for Maxine. She used to come here and sleep on our sofa.'

'Did Maxine ever talk about what happened the night Janey went missing?'

'Not really. And we never wanted to question the poor girl.'

'She had enough to contend with in life without things being dragged up,' said Stan, sadly.

'She finished school, got her GCEs and her A levels or whatever they're called, then got a summer job working at a kids' camp in America and fell in love with a bloke. Troy, his name is. They got married, and she's been in the States for twenty-three years. Maxine sends us a Christmas card every year with a letter.' Betty got up and went to a set of shelves by the entrance to the hall. She picked up a card and brought it back to Kate and Tristan. It was a personalised Christmas card with a picture of a family on the front dressed in identical reindeer pullovers and Santa hats, posing around a

Christmas tree. *HAPPY HOLIDAYS FROM THE DAWSON FAMILY* was written in sparkly letters above. 'She's Maxine Dawson now.'

'And she has *five* kids?' asked Tristan.

Maxine's husband was a large man, but Maxine was very slight, and their five children, four boys and a girl, were tall and athletic and looked to be in their twenties and late teens. Kate glanced at the photo of the smiling mother with a short, glossy bob of brown hair. She had the same eyes and heart-shaped face with a slightly pointed chin as Janey. The address was in San Luis Obispo, California.

'Do you mind if I take a photo of this on my phone?'

'Take it. I've got enough photos of them all; they send one every year,' said Betty.

Stan looked at them keenly. 'How long have you been conducting your investigation?' he asked.

'We just started,' said Kate.

'Most of the people around here think Robert Driscoll was responsible for Janey's disappearance, but of course, the body has never been found. There are . . . rumours. Theories of what happened.'

'What are they?' asked Kate.

'One of the last people to see Janey alive, apart from Robert Driscoll, was Jack Reynolds. He owned Reynolds newsagent over on Pancras Road.'

'Which is now a Starbucks?'

'Yes. Driscoll was Jack's newspaper boy, and he was working that evening when Janey showed up to buy cigarettes for Doreen. The rumour is that Driscoll took Janey off down by the canal in his van and killed her, or did all kinds of other things before he killed her.'

'Did you know the police found Janey's red scarf in Robert Driscoll's flat? And it had her blood on it,' said Betty.

Stan looked irritated at the interruption.

'Yes, of course they do, it's in the article . . . What's *not* in the article is that, apparently, after Robert killed Janey, he hid her body in the drain in the yard behind Reynolds newsagent.'

'How do you know this?' asked Tristan.

'The police! They searched the area a few days later, with scent dogs, and they traced Janey's scent into Reynolds *and* into the drainpipe in the yard out back. The theory is that her body was put there and then moved a few days after she died.'

'How soon after Janey went missing did the police search Reynolds?' asked Kate.

'I couldn't tell you exactly—'

'A few days?' finished Betty. 'It was all we could talk about here on the Estate. We have a social club downstairs, and the gossip was rife.'

'Did the police arrest anyone else?'

Stan put down his empty teacup and leaned forward, his eyes relishing the gossip. 'I know they spoke to Jack Reynolds, and the two lads Robert Driscoll hung around with, Roland Hacker and . . . what was his name?'

'Fred Parker,' said Betty.

Stan nodded. 'Both lads were elsewhere that night, they had alibis, so Robert Driscoll was on his own. The rumour is that Driscoll managed to find somewhere more permanent for Janey's body and he moved it the night before the police brought in the dogs.'

'Where did he move it to?' asked Kate. There was something a little too theatrical about how Stan told the story, and there was that word again, *rumour*. Stan sat back and raised an eyebrow.

'If we knew that, she'd no longer be missing! One theory is under the concrete in the huge underground garages in the Golden Lane Estate, where Robert Driscoll lives. They were being dug up and fixed around the same time. Another theory is that her body was buried on the wasteland around Regent's Canal or in one of the warehouses that were all around here, lying empty and filled with squatters in the 1980s.'

'I don't think so,' said Betty, shaking her head. 'The police dug around there when they did the massive regeneration project in King's Cross and found nothing.'

'Ah, but they could have buried her deep,' said Stanley, holding up his gnarled index finger.

Tristan frowned and rubbed at his eyes. 'Did the police question Jack Reynolds?' he asked.

'Yes, but he had an alibi. He closed up the newsagents shortly after Janey bought the cigarettes, and ten minutes later he was here ordering a pint in the social club downstairs. He stayed there until closing drinking with a load of his mates. They arrested Driscoll, based on the red scarf and his past conviction of violence towards another woman, charged him, and then he went to trial and was found guilty,' said Stanley.

'What happened after Robert Driscoll was released in 1997?'

'Nothing. As far as we know, the police never reopened the case. Whoever is responsible for Janey's disappearance is still out there.'

8

Betty offered them another cup of tea, but Kate saw it was approaching 5pm, and they had a train to catch.

After such a productive day, the journey home was a nightmare. They took a wrong turn on their way back to King's Cross St Pancras station and ended up in a busy piazza filled with bars and restaurants. When they reached the underground, it was heaving with people wringing the last out of the holiday cheer, and they only just made it to Paddington to catch the last fast train back to Exeter St David's. Kate wanted to talk to Tristan, but the carriage was packed, and they hadn't reserved seats, so they ended up standing separately in the hot carriage for most of the journey.

Tristan dropped Kate off at home shortly before nine, and they agreed to catch up the next morning. When he'd driven away, Kate stood by the dark caravan site for a moment, and breathed in the cold fresh air. The stars were bright in the sky, and the silence was punctuated by the soft roar of the waves breaking far down on the beach. She was glad it was dark and she couldn't see the flood-damage trench running through the campsite, which still needed to be dealt with.

The door to the garage was open, and Jake and Olivia were gathering wood from the woodpile and putting it in a basket. Olivia's nose was bright red from the cold, and Jake's hair was windswept and soaked with salt spray.

'Hey, Mum. We were just going to light a fire on the beach.'

'I could do with some fresh air after the train journey I've just had.'

'How was London?' asked Olivia.

'Good. It was an interesting day. Jake, could I talk to you?'

'Sure,' he said, dropping a piece of wood into the basket.

Olivia looked up at Jake. 'I'm actually a little chilled. I think I'll skip the fire, and take a hot bath.'

Kate was pleased that she seemed to sense the mood. 'There's clean towels in the airing cupboard on the landing,' said Kate.

'Okay. I'll keep my phone on. Call me if you need anything,' said Olivia, reaching up on tiptoes to kiss Jake. 'I made pasta, Kate. We left you some,' she added.

'Thanks, love,' said Kate.

'I think you make her nervous,' said Jake when Olivia had gone inside.

'She said that?'

'No. I can sense it.'

Kate liked Olivia, but she felt pleased the girl was a little intimidated. Power was everything in the game of future mother-in-law, especially when it's your only son.

Kate grabbed a bottle of fire lighter fluid and a couple of old newspapers off a shelf and slung them into the basket. They each took a handle and carried it out of the garage, alongside the house, and down the sandy slope to the beach. On the other side of the dunes was a concrete ring, which had washed up during a storm a couple of years back. Kate had it dragged up the beach, and they now used it as a fire pit.

They worked silently to build the fire, clearing away sand accumulated on the old ashes and unburnt wood. They were both flushed and sweating by the time the fire caught and the beach and dunes were bathed in the glow of the flames.

Kate knew they had a good blaze when it felt too hot to be so close. Jake went and fetched a couple of rusting deckchairs from inside the dunes. She removed her gloves and sat back, holding her bare hands towards the heat.

'I think I know what you want to talk to me about,' said Jake.

'Yeah. What do you think about this approach we've had to investigate this missing young woman? Peter Conway could be involved.'

'What do I think? It's a job for your agency.'

'It's more than just any old job, Jake. It's Peter Conway.'

'Do they want you to talk to Peter?'

Kate was pleased he didn't say *Dad*.

'Yes. I don't know if he'd talk to me.'

Jake smoothed over the sand with his feet, and seemed to consider this. 'Mum. Can I ask you something?'

'Sure.'

'Did you love him, Peter?'

Kate sighed.

'I knew Detective Chief Inspector Peter Conway as one person. My boss. Colleague. A decent, if sometimes difficult, policeman who was popular and handsome. Is it important to you that I did love him?'

'No. I don't expect you to. Olivia's family don't think I should carry any shame being the son of a serial killer.'

'That's good of them.'

'They didn't mean it like that.'

'Do you feel shame?' asked Kate, curious and nervous at him talking about this.

'Not when I'm there, in California.' *Ouch,* thought Kate, but she let him carry on. 'Olivia thinks who my father is is very interesting, almost like an asset. Like I've been born with this rare life experience. Her family are fascinated by it all.'

'What if you two ever get married? Will they want to invite him to the wedding?'

'Very funny. And we're just having fun. Well, it's more than fun. It's just nice. Has she said anything to you?'

Kate laughed. 'No. Don't worry.'

Jake smiled. 'I like her, and I like living in LA. The American positivity and the attitude that you can do anything with your life and be anything is incredible. I'm only an intern at this huge talent agency, and there's this agreement, almost like an unspoken agreement, that if I work hard enough and put in the hours and learn, I can someday be a writer or a film producer. Can you imagine if I tried to do that here in the UK? The first question would be, *What school did you go to?* And if I didn't go to the right school, I'd have to be let into the club in another way. I'd have to be a "northern writer" or a "working-class writer", whatever the fuck . . . Sorry, whatever the hell that means.'

This made Kate feel very sad.

'Are you writing anything now?' she asked, changing the subject.

'Yes. But don't panic. It's not some *Daddy Dearest*.'

'You know, someone will ask you to write that book at some point.'

'I'd have to be really desperate to do that. No. I'm writing a science-fiction screenplay.'

'Really? Can I read it?'

'When it's ready. Maybe.'

Jake was silent as the fire crackled. He got up and threw on another log, and they watched in silence for a moment as it spewed a shower of sparks up into the dark sky.

'When did you last speak to Peter?' asked Kate.

'Beginning of December. I call him once a month. He gets thirty minutes. He's not great – he's having major problems with his teeth.'

'The irony.'

'I told you he was beaten up pretty badly by another prisoner last January?'

Kate nodded, staring into the flames. Peter Conway had been hospitalised after the attack. He'd ended up with a fractured eye socket, cheek, and jaw, and he'd had to have six teeth removed. 'And then his mum died at Easter. My grandma, I suppose.'

'That woman was many things; she wasn't fit to be called your grandmother,' said Kate.

'It's okay. I agree. Sorry I used the *g*-word.' Kate felt a flash of anger at the subject of Enid Conway. If ever there was a mother-in-law you didn't want, it was her. 'He said you sent flowers.'

'It took a great deal of control not to write *yippee* on the card.'

Jake laughed.

'When I talk to him on the phone, it's weirdly normal. I don't think about what he did. He's just, like, a nice—'

'—old man?' finished Kate.

'I'm sorry.'

'Stop saying sorry. Don't you *dare* be sorry,' said Kate, putting a hand on his. 'There's no proper, correct way through all of this. Having him as your father. That's why I wanted to ask if it's okay if I pursue this investigation. The facts of the case and the horrific things Peter did will, most likely, be dredged up again.'

'Have you spoken to Grandma – your mum, Grandma – about this?' asked Jake.

Kate's mother had come to stay for Christmas Day, then travelled back to Whitstable to spend Boxing Day with Kate's brother and his family.

'Not yet.'

'You should. Grandma deserves to know and to give you her opinion.'

'Yes. Grandma loves having her opinions,' said Kate.

Jake jokingly waggled a finger at her. 'Don't be cheeky, Catherine,' he said, imitating Kate's mother with surprising accuracy. The fire was burning hot and fast. Jake got up, chucked on another log, and then returned to his chair, shifting it closer to Kate.

'You should take the investigation, Mum. If there's another girl's death he's responsible for, you'll be the one to work it out. You're a bloody good private detective.'

'Thanks, love.'

He leaned over and rested his head on her arm. 'Love you, Mum.'

'Love you, too.'

9

Kate had a long sleep, and woke up just before midday. Jake had sent her a message to say he'd gone to the cinema with Olivia. It was a bright, clear day, and after a long drink of water, Kate pulled on her wetsuit, hooked her goggles over her arm, and left the house through the kitchen door, which led to a small terrace and a sandy path down to the beach.

The remnants of the fire she'd made with Jake were now covered in sand, the tide was out, and the beach was littered with plastic debris, seaweed, and a collection of smooth white cuttlefish bones. Jake used to love finding them when he was little because he thought they looked like tiny surfboards. She dropped her towel a few metres from where the surf broke onto the shore, and she stepped into the water. In the summer, she swam in her swimming costume, but her wetsuit kept her warmer in the winter. There was still that awful moment, though, the slight delay before the cold water infiltrated her wetsuit. The six-inch scar on her abdomen, the souvenir left by Peter Conway on the night he attacked her, was always the first place to feel the sting.

At this time of year, the sea pushed more sand onto the shore, and the shelf was steep underfoot. Taking a deep breath, she put on her goggles and dived under a big wave. The feeling of total immersion in the cold water always woke her up and made her feel alive. Kate swam out strongly to where the waves stopped breaking, and the swells of water moved underneath. Despite a good night's sleep, she felt tired and floated on her back, looking up at the slate-grey sky. A flock of cormorants passed overhead, their black wings and graceful long necks standing out against the sky. She turned over and dived down. In the summer months, on a clear day with the sun shining, she could see down to the black rocks on the sea bed. Today, however, the water was gloomy and filled with the silt churned up by the rougher sea. She hung for a moment in the murkiness, listening to the strange clicks and bangs from the deep.

She thought of what Maddie had said at their meeting yesterday: 'If we *could* get hold of a recorded interview with Peter Conway, that would be like gold dust.'

Gold dust.

It was the people who'd never experienced the true horror of a serial killer or a violent individual who valued interactions or trophies from them. Would Peter talk to her? Or Tristan? The only person who had phone access to him was Jake. And did she want to involve him? She looked back at the cliff. Her house sat on the end in blissful seclusion. It was paradise to watch the sea every day and be so close to nature, living on her own terms. It had been a shock to be back in London, amongst the hustle and bustle. The feeling that you had to be somewhere, doing something, or the sand would run out of the hourglass. She had so much sand here, a whole beach at her disposal.

Her fingers and toes were now numb, so she swam back to the shore, rode the breaking waves onto the sand, and then hurried back up to the house, shivering.

After a hot shower and some buttered toast, Kate went to her bookshelves and found the book she was thinking of. *No Son of Mine*. It was the tell-all autobiography Peter's mother, Enid, had written back in 2000, and she'd been given a lot of money to write it.

The cover image was a split-pane photograph. On the right was a picture of a sixteen-year-old Enid Conway wearing a long, flowing dress, standing outside the front entrance of an unmarried mothers' home in Scotland, cradling baby Peter wrapped in a large blanket. His eyes were wide and staring at the camera, while Enid looked down at him adoringly. Through the window directly behind was the blurred image of a nun, staring out at them stony faced.

The other half of the cover was Peter's police mug shot, taken on the day he gave evidence at his preliminary trial. His eyes were wild and pupils dilated. This was before he'd started on the cocktail of drugs to deal with his schizophrenia and dissociative identity disorder.

Kate opened the book. On the title page, the dedication from Enid was there, the ink a little faded:

Rot in hell you bitch,

Enid Conway

She'd never understood why Enid had felt the need to sign her surname and her first name.

Kate flicked to the index in the back. There were only two mentions of Peter during 1988 and 1989. The first was when he was accepted to Hendon Police College to train as a police officer, and the second was when he passed out, or graduated, in February 1989.

Kate closed the book and sat back. Peter had spent so much time trying to hide that he was a copper. During the original Nine Elms Cannibal case, he'd made sure there was virtually no link between his professional life and the murders he committed. Why would he have risked everything back in 1988 by pretending to be a police officer, whilst he was in training, to lure victims? Thomas Black wrote that Peter pulled him over for having a faulty brake light, but what if this was a lie?

And what about Thomas Black – what was *he* doing at the time of Janey Macklin's disappearance?

10

On the other side of town, Tristan woke late and then had a mad dash to cook a roast chicken lunch for his sister, Sarah, her husband, Gary, and his one-year-old nephew, Leo. After they'd eaten, Sarah sent Gary out for a walk with Leo strapped to his back, which was ominous. It meant she had something she wanted to talk to him about.

'Tristan. Why didn't you tell me you missed a mortgage payment?' said Sarah, getting right to the point as she rinsed and stacked plates in the dishwasher.

'This is why I want a bank account at another bank. Isn't snooping through customers' accounts illegal?' said Tristan.

'Not when I work at the bank, as a credit analyst. It's part of my job.'

'Why don't you write me a letter? Or get one of the gorgons who work in your call centre to ring me,' said Tristan, scraping the burnt potato from his new roasting dish.

Sarah took a deep breath. 'Why did you miss a payment? Is everything okay?'

'Everything is fine,' said Tristan. It was almost true. The run-up to Christmas was always a bit tight with cash. 'It was an accident, a timing issue with payments coming from the agency. It was only a day late.' Tristan could feel his hands starting to shake, and he didn't know if he was angry or scared. Sarah always made him feel stressed when she talked about money.

'That day-late payment goes on your credit score . . . That's a very nice roasting dish. Le Creuset?'

Now it was Tristan's turn to take a deep breath. He put the pan down on the kitchen worktop. 'It was a Christmas present from Ade.'

'Where is Ade?'

'He's gone away for Christmas and New Year to Australia.'

Sarah tore off a length of tinfoil and tucked it around the remains of the roast chicken. 'So he can afford Le Creuset pans, if he's jetting off for the winter.'

'Do you know how long their stuff lasts, Sarah? Ade has a huge Le Creuset Dutch oven from his mum, which is still good after thirty years.'

'Well, maybe you can borrow it from him to live in when you miss another mortgage payment and this flat gets repossessed!'

Tristan took another deep breath. Sarah always seemed to live in a state of high alert, thinking the worst and waiting for it to happen.

'I'm fine for money. We're just about to take on a new case in London.'

'London?' said Sarah. As if he'd said *Timbuktu*. 'How is that going to work with you being here?'

'The client is giving us the use of a flat in King's Cross.'

'Who is the client?'

'A creative agency.'

'Is that a real thing?'

'Yes. They're like a literary agency.'

'*Like* a literary agency, but creative. What's not creative about literary agencies?'

'Things are changing with streaming and podcasts. Literary agencies do more than just books.'

'Sounds a bit vague to me.'

'It's not vague,' said Tristan, struggling to hide his frustration. 'Why don't you come up and visit?'

'Me? Come up to London!'

'Yeah. I can meet you at King's Cross, and take you to see platform nine and three-quarters, and then push you off it.'

'Why do you think everything is a joke?'

'The agency is making money. We have several lucrative government contracts . . .' Sarah opened her mouth to speak. 'Let me finish! And they pay quarterly. That's why November was a bit quiet. For payments.'

'Tris. I could get you an overdraft.'

'I don't want an overdraft.'

'That's what I thought. Listen. A colleague at work is looking for a place to stay, short-term, in Ashdean. I told him you had a spare room that you rented out.'

'I don't want another lodger. Not after Glenn.'

Glenn had been Tristan's lodger for a year, a glowering, moody chap who cast a grim atmosphere over the flat when he was in, and he'd left hair everywhere. Tristan had vowed not to have another housemate while he could afford to live independently.

'Adam isn't weird. He's from a very well-to-do family. And he's not at all hairy. The bits of him that I've seen.'

Despite their argument, Tristan laughed. 'Why would a well-to-do guy with minimal body hair need to rent a room in my flat on Ashdean seafront?'

He stepped out of the way to let Sarah rinse a handful of knives and forks in the sink.

'He's going through a messy divorce. They're waiting for their house to sell so they can split the assets. He's willing to pay a lot more than Glenn paid. And it could be perfect if you'll be up in London for the next few months.'

'I don't know how long and if we'll be up in London. We're still waiting for the contract.'

Tristan regretted it the moment it came out of his mouth.

'Oh. This London job isn't definite? Then you should seriously think about it.' Sarah wiped her hands on a tea-towel and rummaged in her purse on the end of the kitchen counter. 'I promised Mum I would look after you, as your older sister.' She went to the fridge and slid a business card under the turtle fridge magnet, which kept the local Indian takeaway menu in place. 'Give Adam a call. You could make a few grand without really having to do anything.'

'I'll think about it.'

'Good. What are you doing for New Year?'

'Probably going to The Boar's Head. What are you doing?'

'I have a fifteen-month-old and a full-time job. I'm going to be in bed by nine thirty.'

———

When Sarah and Gary left with Leo, who was asleep on his dad's shoulder, Tristan went to the spare room he used as a workspace. He looked around at the neat desk with his laptop, the squishy armchair, and the filing cabinet. His steadily growing collection of true crime and crime reference books half-filled the low bookcase. The window looked out over the beach and the promenade – he preferred to sleep in the bedroom at the back, which was quiet. They had the agency office in Thurlow Bay, but he loved having this space at home.

He sat down at the desk and logged in to the agency network. Kate had just uploaded all the Thomas Black letters and created a file for the case. There was also an email from Fidelis at Stafford-Clarke with a contract.

He started to type up the notes he'd made at Stan and Betty's flat, and something made him stop and take a closer look.

Kate rang a little while later. 'Did you see the contract?' she asked.

'Yes. It looks good. I've just found something odd. Stan said that Robert Driscoll hung out with two guys called Roland Hacker and Fred Parker. I haven't been able to find anything online about Roland Hacker, but Fred Parker, he changed his name to Forrest Parker when he became an actor,' said Tristan.

'Maddie's boyfriend is Forrest Parker. The guy who wrote the article in *Real Crime* magazine.'

'It's the same guy. He's an actor, and he's represented by

Charkham Murray Associates, which look like quite a posh actors' agent, and they have some big-name actors on their books,' he said. 'He doesn't seem to have done that much work recently, but he went to Cambridge University, which, as we know, means a lot. And then he went to RADA, the Royal Academy of Dramatic Art. On the council tax register dated last year, he's registered as living at the same address as Maddie, which you would expect if he's her partner.'

He had Forrest's acting head shot on the screen. Forrest had a very high forehead and thinning hair. He had pretty, delicate features and pursed lips, which might have been called rubious when he was younger, but he looked to be in his late forties now, and the intense stare coupled with the pursed lips and his head at an inquisitive angle made him look quite camp and waspish.

'How did you make the link?' asked Kate.

'He's got a Wikipedia page. It says he was born Fred Parker, and that he grew up in the Golden Lane flats. I think he might have written the Wikipedia article himself, because he's bigging everything up. It's mentioned that the flats are a 'Grade One listed building.' He's also the same age as Robert Driscoll.'

'Is that why he wrote the article for *Real Crime* – because he knows about the case?'

'Possibly. And why didn't Fidelis and Maddie tell us about the link when we met with them?'

'This case has just got all the more interesting,' said Kate.

11

The New Year came and went, and 2018 became 2019 with little fanfare. Jake and Olivia left to fly back to Los Angeles on 2 January, and the next day, Kate and Tristan set off for London.

They arranged to meet Maddie outside a flat in Percy Circus in the early afternoon. Kate was surprised at just how central to King's Cross they were, only a few hundred metres from King's Cross station. Percy Circus was a circle of smart white Georgian townhouses built around a garden surrounded by black railings, which must have been beautiful and lush in the summer months, but now the large trees were bare. Despite being so close to everything, it was tranquil on this sleepy January afternoon. The sun was shining, but the air was very crisp and cold, and despite it being later in the day, there was a layer of frost on the windows of cars parked on the street.

Maddie waited for them by the black railings outside number 34. There was something very whimsical about how she was dressed, in pink UGG boots; a multicoloured, long, baggy duffel coat; and a big squashy handbag in the same duffel material over her shoulder. She wore a pink beret at a slightly jaunty angle on her head. Her long honey-blonde hair was plaited in pigtails, and her nose was bright pink from the cold.

'Hello! It's lovely to have you here,' she said, opening her arms wide to hug each of them. It felt completely at odds with why they were there, and Kate assumed Fidelis wouldn't have been so touchy-feely. 'Happy New Year!'

Kate and Tristan both wished her a happy New Year in return.

'This will be your accommodation,' said Maddie.

'Is it this whole building?' asked Tristan as he tilted his head to look at the four stories above them, all with white sash windows.

'Goodness, no! You'll be in the ground-floor flat. This entrance is shared by four flats.'

Maddie opened the door to a tiny, musty-smelling hall with no windows. A light flicked on. A door was to the left, and a small enclosed staircase led to the upper flats. Kate noted that there was something rather exciting about having a small flat for their use.

The front door opened into a small hallway with scuffed herringbone parquet floor. Straight ahead was a bathroom, and then a door at the end led into a living room with bare walls and high ceilings. The furniture was all IKEA and a little shabby. There was a big television, and one wall was packed with hundreds of DVDs.

'It's not a palace, but there are two double bedrooms, a

good kitchen, and because you're on the ground floor, you also have access to a small courtyard through the kitchen,' said Maddie, adding, 'If either of you smoke, then you'll need to do it outside.

'Fidelis apologises she can't be here. She's in contract negotiations with an author.'

The doors to the kitchen and bedrooms led off the large living room. Kate and Tristan poked their heads through each; it all looked a bit tired, but clean. Tristan tried a door next to the DVD shelves in the living room, but it was locked.

'That's our Airbnb cupboard, as we jokingly call it,' said Maddie. 'We keep all supplies in there – bedding, toilet paper, and the like.'

'Does Forrest work with you running the Airbnb?'

'Yes. He's a Superhost . . . and a super host,' she added with a laugh. She beamed at them, but Kate thought underneath the smiles, Maddie was a little twitchy.

Her glasses had steamed up, and she took them off to clean them with a grubby tissue. Without her glasses, Maddie looked like a blind little mole. She slipped them back on, and normal service resumed.

'Would you like a coffee? I don't have to be back at the office for an hour.'

'Yes, it would be good to have a quick chat,' said Kate.

'Right,' said Maddie, then she recovered her composure and went to the kitchen.

Kate and Tristan each chose a room. They were similar sizes and had the same view. As Kate put her bag down and pulled out her phone charger, she stared out over a dingy little square of concrete backing onto the building behind, which was a warren of windows and gutter pipes. She was suddenly glad she had so much space back in Ashdean – views out over the sea, and acres of beach.

Maddie was waiting for them with three steaming mugs of instant coffee. The living room window looked out over Percy Circus, and Kate could see a chunk of the frost outside thawing in the gaze of the rising sun. Maddie still had her coat on.

'I've just put the heating on. There's a folder on the kitchen table with all the instructions for the appliances, et cetera. And the Wi-Fi password.' There was an awkward little silence. Kate and Tristan sat on the sofa opposite Maddie. Kate took a sip of the black coffee and tried not to recoil. 'Where do you think you'll start? Did you have the chance to read Thomas Black's letters with Judith?'

'We did,' said Kate.

'Interesting, aren't they? I do think that Thomas is remarkably intelligent and manipulative. And the fact that his path crossed with Peter Conway, who could have abducted Janey . . .'

Kate could see Maddie was keeping her voice light, but her eyes shone keenly, and maybe she was a bit afraid? Kate couldn't quite read her, and she tried to frame the next question as informally as she could.

'Why didn't you tell us about Forrest being a friend of Robert Driscoll?'

There was a crashing silence. Maddie stared at them, caught in the glare of Kate's question.

'Oh.' She gave a tinkly little laugh, like broken glass. 'He wasn't . . . Robert's friend, per se.'

Tristan took out a printed article from the *Big Issue* magazine, and held it up.

'Forrest's Wikipedia page mentions that his name was Fred Parker, and that he grew up on the Golden Lane Estate. We dug a bit deeper, and we found this article from March 1988. Fred, Robert Driscoll, and another lad called Roland Hacker all went to the same youth club on Old Street. They're all named in this article about a spray-painted mural they helped to design.' Tristan took out a photocopy of Forrest's acting head shot photo from the early 1990s, and put it next to the *Big Issue* article on the coffee table. The article showed a colour photo of Robert, Fred, and Roland standing in front of the mural.

Maddie put up her hand. A look of panic danced across her face, and then it was gone.

'Just hold on a moment here . . .' She hesitated and then flashed her smile, which was a blaze of everything but happiness. 'I . . . We at Stafford-Clarke are the client. I don't think it's your job to investigate me – us. Myself and Forrest have been together for almost seven years. We're actually engaged to be married.'

'You do understand that we have to ask questions?' said Tristan.

'Yes. I just didn't expect to be ambushed.'

'Is this an ambush? Forrest is also directly connected to Judith Leary, who knew Thomas Black. Why mention one connection and not the other?'

'Because, Tristan. It really isn't relevant. Forrest had nothing to do with Janey Macklin. He was *horrified*. He walked away from that friendship when Robert was arrested. That's all far, far, far away in the rearview mirror.'

Kate stared at Maddie and felt shocked at her naivety or her denial – she wasn't sure which one it was.

'In light of this, we need to talk to Forrest.'

'Of course. I'm sure that would be fine. He thought you would want to talk to him anyway about the piece in *Real Crime* magazine.' Maddie stood up abruptly and rummaged in the pocket of her coat. 'I should really be getting back to the office. These are your keys. The main entrance, front, and the back door leading out into the courtyard.' She placed two sets of keys on the table. 'I'll ask Forrest to call you. As I say, he'd be happy to talk to you, whenever. Now, if you'll excuse me.'

A moment later, the front door slammed. Kate and Tristan sat in shock for a moment, and then both got up and went to the window. They watched Maddie emerge from the outer door and cross the road with her head down. She was already on her phone, speaking animatedly to someone. She looked like a completely different person. Strident and sure of herself.

'What the hell was that?' said Kate.

'I think that meeting went as sour as this coffee,' said Tristan, holding up his cup. 'How did she think we wouldn't find out about Forrest?'

'Thank God we've signed the contract. I think we need to arm ourselves with more information. Take a trip to the Golden Lane Estate. Pay Robert Driscoll a visit.'

12

The midafternoon sun slanted down through the gap in the four walls above the exercise yard at HMP Wakefield, dubbed Britain's 'Monster Mansion.' Peter Conway stepped through the secure doors, moving slowly, leaning heavily on the walking stick he had to use.

He was due to see the dentist the next day, but he hadn't been able to eat or sleep because of the pain in his infected gums, and his body was weak for it. The two guards accompanying him had helped him walk down the corridor from his cell.

Since his hospitalisation, he'd noticed the shift in how people treated him; he would be fifty-nine in a few weeks, and in this frail state, weak and toothless, he felt like a lion who had lost his roar. He was no longer taken to the general exercise yard for his daily dose of fresh air, and he was now in a smaller yard he had never seen before. Another inmate, the child-killer Thomas Black, was sitting in his wheelchair.

Despite the weak sunshine, Thomas Black wore huge

shades over his eyes with a woolly hat. Black had been a big, muscular man, both on the outside and during his first ten years of incarceration. In the past two years, his body had been ravaged by cancer, and he was now unrecognisable. He glanced at Peter as the door was closed, shutting them in the courtyard for thirty minutes. The only view was a square of clear blue sky high above them, which had to be viewed through a thin mesh net. An orderly was stationed to watch them through a window.

The thought of being incarcerated for the rest of his life no longer terrified Peter. It was the knowledge that he would get old and die in prison. There was a level of celebrity and notoriety being a high-profile prisoner. You were feared. You were treated differently – not better, but differently. You had respect. Everyone was a little tense around you. But now, Peter could see he was sliding into old age and wasn't going gracefully. He remembered one of his colleagues, back in another era when he was a police officer, talking about growing old: 'You have your thirties, your forties, and in your fifties, you either turn to vinegar or wine. It's up to you.'

'Is this where they send us, before the knacker's yard?' said Peter, hobbling over to Thomas.

'This *is* the knacker's yard. We just don't know it yet,' said Thomas. 'They've taken my bladder and bowels. And from what I've heard, they've taken your teeth.'

'They're taking the rest tomorrow.'

Thomas flashed a Halloween Horror Night smile.

'Got the shit kicked out of you good and proper by Henry Yates, didn't you?' Thomas was making a hissing sound as his shoulders shook.

'Is that a stage three or a stage four laugh?'

'Stage four. Everything I do makes a little bit of pee come out, but I have a bag to catch it.' He wiped his finger under his sunglasses and recovered his composure a little. 'You should thank me. I was the one who called for the guards.'

'You waited a few minutes and watched before raising the alarm.'

Thomas broke down, hissing again. 'You made the mistake of not staying up on your feet. Whatever happens in a fight, staying on your feet will stop you from getting your face rearranged.'

'How long have you got left to live?'

'Six months, they say.'

Thomas looked like he had less time than that, and you could never describe him like fine wine. He was vinegar to the core.

'I'll make a note in my diary,' said Peter. There was a beat of silence. He looked around at the pathetic yard, and it seemed almost a joke for him to start walking in a circle. It was so small that he'd look like a dog getting ready to lie down. Thomas adjusted his woolly hat and squinted up at him keenly. Peter knew everyone's story. How they got caught. Thomas Black had been stopped by the police over a set of faulty brake lights. They found a half-dead young girl wrapped in a tarpaulin in the back of his van. He'd been forty-two.

There were always hysterical pieces written in the newspapers, saying that the worst of the UK's serial killers were kept in a life of luxury in prison – fed better than hospital patients with access to their own televisions. While that may be true, it was in old age that serial killers got their comeuppance. Peter could see it was happening to him. He was turning sour, his body withering and shrinking. Black was now an old biddy, too frail to be feared. What would happen to him when he could no longer walk? When he was at the mercy of carers to wipe his bum and feed him? That's what terrified him.

Thomas reached up and with a skeletal hand dotted with black bruises like ink-stains, he removed his giant sunglasses. He smacked his dry, cracked lips and glanced at the window, where the orderly was working at a screen, disinterested in the two elderly monsters.

'Here. Come closer,' said Thomas, holding out his hand.

'I'm not pulling your finger,' said Peter. Something about Thomas made him feel ill, like the skin off the top of the custard hanging off a saggy carcass. He licked his lips again. His tongue was like a dried-up lizard.

'You heard about my letters being auctioned off,' he said, pride in his voice.

'The pervy ones you sent to that dried-up old cow on the South Coast?'

'Fuck you, Conway.'

'Sorry. Only her cunt was dried up; the rest of her was perfectly acceptable.'

'That's it. You've had your chance,' he said, trying to attract the attention of the orderly through the glass.

'Wait, wait. I'm just playing . . . I'm sorry. I know she was . . .'

'She was,' said Thomas, pursing his lips.

'What about the letters?'

Thomas slowly scratched his nose and then put his shades back on. 'I mentioned something in one of them about you and an unsolved murder case in your old stomping ground.'

'Our old stomping ground,' said Peter.

'It seems some company, a literary agency or something in London, have been sniffing around. They've contacted my solicitor about the copyright on my letters. And your boy's mother is apparently involved.'

'Kate?'

Thomas nodded.

'They'll want to talk to us. They might pay. Money . . . or even better, we can exert some leverage. And as we both know, we can only spend a few quid inside in the tuck shop. Leverage is where the gold is.'

'Who?'

'Who what?'

Peter looked up at the orderly, but he was still absorbed elsewhere.

'Who is the unsolved murder?'

'Young girl.'

'How young?'

'Fourteen. Janey Macklin, she was called.'

'Never heard of her,' said Peter, quickly, but he thought, *Had he?*

Thomas put up his hands and smirked. 'Me neither, me neither. We both know how it works. Someone on the outside wants to know stuff. We know the stuff.'

'Spoken like a true poet,' said Peter. He shifted his weight from one leg to the other and leaned on his stick. Thomas waggled his withered finger again.

'You're scared to lose your dignity, Peter. I can see it. You don't have much left to bargain in your old age. This could be bargaining material. You could get a transfer. Better facilities, a private shower and toilet. A place to slide into old age gracefully and not this hell-hole.'

'And what's in it for you?'

'I want to have my chemo in a hospital. A proper hospital for ordinary people. I can't die in this hell-hole, in one room with nurses and doctors who hate me.'

Peter looked at him. He understood.

'What do you know about this Janey Macklin?'

'Same as you. Never heard of her,' he said, tapping his nose and flashing that gruesome smile again.

'Okay. What do we do?'

'My solicitor said it should be soon, someone will want to talk to us.'

13

The Golden Lane Estate sat near the Barbican Centre. Kate remembered visiting the Barbican a few times when she lived in London. It was a complex with apartments, cinemas, concert halls, and a hub of restaurants, which had been expensive, even back in the early nineties. The Golden Lane Estate sat across the road from the Barbican and was sandwiched between high-rise office buildings. It was a brutalist structure, like Victoria House, and seemed a bit plonked, even though it was older than most of the buildings it sat amongst.

The main entrance had a wall of glass panels with an entry phone system similar to the one at Victoria House. Robert Driscoll's home phone number was listed on 192.com. He'd answered their call, and seemed happy to talk.

'All right. It's the second floor,' answered a gruff voice through the intercom when they rang his bell. There was a crackle as the phone hung up, and then the entrance door buzzed and popped open. Kate looked up and saw a security camera above the door.

It was another smelly lift ride, much like at Victoria House, but the block of flats was only three stories high with a long concrete courtyard.

Robert Driscoll was waiting for them with the door open. He looked much like his Facebook profile photo. His greying hair was longer, and he was a short, large man. His torso seemed to blend into his chin with little in the way of a neck. His eyes were beady and brown, and he wore plain grey tracksuit bottoms with a plain blue T-shirt.

'Hi, I'm Kate Marshall, and this is my colleague, Tristan Harper,' said Kate.

He squinted at them keenly. 'Kate Marshall? The bird who caught the Nine Elms Cannibal?'

'Yes, I'm the bird,' said Kate, her heart sinking slightly, both at the fact he knew who she was, and that he called her a *bird.*

'Sorry. *Woman,*' he said with a chuckle. He put out his hand, and they all shook. 'Come on in.'

They followed him into a small living room with a bland set of grey furniture and black shelving units which were filled with DVDs, and hundreds of VHS cassettes, labelled with neat blue writing. A huge window at the end of the living room looked out onto a landscaped piece of grass and more tower blocks.

A flatscreen TV was on the wall, and underneath was a low table with so much tech: two DVD players, a video recorder, and other boxes for pay TV. A small coffee table in between the grey sofas was piled neatly with scores of magazines.

Robert indicated they should sit down. He took a grey, high-backed recliner in the corner, which Kate got the impression was his chair, and they sat opposite on the overstuffed sofa.

'What's going on with Janey Macklin after all these years?' he asked. He seemed genuinely interested.

'We've been hired by a creative agency who want to make a potential true crime project about the case,' said Tristan.

He looked between them. 'Project? Like a TV show?'

'We're just doing background research for them,' Kate added. 'It could be a book or a podcast. It's not up to us.'

'Well, as you know, I didn't do it. And the last time I heard, a court acquitted me of any wrongdoing.' He shrugged. 'End of.'

'But no other arrests have been made since your acquittal?' said Tristan.

'Not that I've heard.'

'The mystery has never been solved.'

'When you put it like that, I suppose . . .' His voice trailed off. He shrugged. 'I just want to live my life.'

Kate looked around the small living room which seemed to focus on watching TV. There were no photos or plants. She wondered what kind of a life he was leading.

'Thank you for meeting us. We really appreciate your time,' said Kate. 'Our investigation was sparked by an article in *Real Crime* magazine. Which contains a theory, or potential evidence, that Peter Conway, or another serial killer called Thomas Black, was responsible for Janey Macklin going missing.'

Robert put his hands on his knees and looked between them.

'Okay,' he said.

Kate opened her bag and removed a photocopied page from one of the Thomas Black letters.

'This is a letter from Thomas Black to a woman called Judith Leary dated Friday, October 29, 2010,' she said. She handed it over with a section highlighted:

I later heard on the grapevine – grapevine is a much more pleasant word for it, I won't subject you to that, my dear – that Peter Conway was the one who kidnapped Janey Macklin. He'd got to know her in the pub weeks before she vanished, so she was happy to get into a car with him. He also might have been wearing his police uniform when she got into his car.

Robert scanned it, and then looked up at them. 'This is the theory of a serial killer?'

'You've never heard this theory?' asked Kate, watching him. 'The magazine article was published in *Real Crime* magazine.' She took out a copy of the magazine and handed it to him.

'Judith Leary died a few months ago, and she was friends with a man called Forrest Parker . . . As well as writing the article there, he brokered a deal to sell the correspondence between Judith and Thomas after she died.'

Kate observed Robert at the mention of Forrest. His face remained impassive.

'None of this means anything to you?'

Robert put the magazine article and the photocopy of the letter down on the table. 'You know it does. I don't see Fred – Forrest – anymore,' he said.

'So, you admit you were friends?' asked Tristan.

Robert looked annoyed. 'Admit? I haven't denied anything. We were friends. 'Course we were.'

'Do you know why Fred changed his name to Forrest? He's been quite evasive about the connection between the two of you.'

'He probably wanted to escape being associated with me for the rest of his life.'

'Can you tell us about your relationship?' asked Kate.

'*Relationship?* It weren't nothing like that.'

'Sorry. Friendship.'

'We grew up here. Forrest . . . Fred used to live here on the estate, on the top floor, with his mum.'

'Does his mum still live here?'

'No, she died when I was inside. I put in a request to go to the funeral, but it was denied.'

'Do you mind if I take notes?' asked Tristan.

'Go ahead. I've got nothing to hide.'

Tristan took out his notebook and pen and turned to a blank page. Robert eyed it, and there was a long pause.

'This is just for our reference.'

Robert hesitated and nodded. The sky was darkening

outside, and thick fog had descended, but Robert didn't switch on a light. A row of lamps flicked on in the courtyard.

'You and Forrest were friends with another lad, Roland Hacker. Are you still in contact with Roland?'

'No.'

'Where did Roland live?'

'Over in Stanley Cohen House, across the courtyard.'

'Where is he now?'

'No idea. Roland disappeared. Cut himself off from everyone when I was inside. His mum and dad both died not knowing where he was; he didn't have any other family.'

'And you've checked he's still alive?' asked Kate.

Robert shrugged. 'When I was acquitted in '97, I tried to find him. Nothing. There's nothing online. Nothing on social media.'

'Do you think he changed his name, like Forrest?' asked Tristan.

'If he did, he didn't tell anyone.'

'The three of you were close, yes?'

'We was good mates.'

Kate took out a copy of the *Big Issue* article, with Robert, Forrest, and Roland standing in front of the big spray-painted mural. He took it from her.

'This is a blast from the past.' He sighed and rubbed his face. 'Jeez. Little did I know.'

'What do you mean?'

'This was taken a few months before Janey Macklin went missing, and it all fell apart.'

14

'Can you tell us what happened on the night Janey Macklin went missing?'

Robert put the photo down on the little pile of photocopies on the table, sat back, made a steeple with his fingers, and rested them on his chin.

'I was seventeen at the time. I used to see Janey around. Mostly on Friday nights when her old ma, Doreen, used to send her down to Reynolds to buy fags. Janey had dropped her scarf in Reynolds a couple of weeks before, and I found it under the counter. I knew I would see her, so I took it to my van, and forgot about it. The next week, when she came to get fags, I gave her a lift back to The Jug, 'cos it was blizzarding. I had to brake on the ice on the road and she was thrown forward and banged her head. . . I gave her the scarf back, and she used it to dab the blood off her head. It was a small cut. I drove her up to the fish-and-chip shop near here. Carlucci's. It's still there. She was starving and cold. I bought her a cone of chips, and then I dropped her back outside The

Jug. We can't have been gone for more than fifteen or twenty minutes. Seriously. She was frozen and starving, and she forgot her scarf again. That's how I still had it.'

'Do you remember what time you dropped her back at The Jug?' asked Kate.

'It was thirty years ago. Reynolds used to shut at six pm on weeknights, Janey came just before closing, so I suppose I dropped her off outside The Jug after we had chips at around six twenty-five pm.'

'And you saw her go inside the pub?'

'I dropped her at the entrance. I remember looking back in the rearview mirror and seeing her at the pub door.'

'It says in the magazine article that the police found her scarf in your bedroom, two weeks after she went missing,' said Tristan.

'Yeah, like I said. When we got chips, she left it in the van, and then when I dropped her off, she forgot it again. I put it in my backpack intending to give it back to her,' said Robert.

Kate wished they had more details from the police reports from that evening.

'And that was the last you saw of Janey?' she asked.

'*Yes.* I bought her some chips and made sure she got warmed up in my van. That's all. I dropped Janey off. I didn't touch her.'

'Do you think Janey went missing on the road outside the pub?' asked Tristan.

'It was a Friday night. The Jug used to get crowds from around the King's Cross area who would go there for a swift half before getting their trains from the station. The road was busy that evening – lots of cars behind me, I remember. Isn't your new theory that Peter Conway picked her up in or close to the pub?'

Kate looked at Tristan.

'Peter Conway was seen drinking in The Jug with a couple of underage girls in the weeks leading up to Janey going missing,' said Tristan.

'And wasn't that his signature way of doing things, the Nine Elms Cannibal? He abducted young girls. Then dumped their bodies,' said Robert, opening his hands as if to say, *That's your answer.*

'What did you do after you dropped off Janey?' Kate asked.

'I was doing some work for the youth club,' he said, indicating the photo with the mural. 'There were some art projects that I had to collect and put into, er, storage.'

'All this in the evening of 23 December?'

'Yeah. That's why I had use of the van. I used to do stuff for the youth club, maintenance, moving furniture, pool tables, and the art projects. The youth club was art focused.'

'Did anyone help you that evening?'

'No. I was on my own. I wanted to get it done before Christmas so I could have the holidays free. I stayed until just after midnight, and then I went back home. My mum was only able to give me an alibi from midnight.'

'What were Forrest and Roland doing that night?'

'Roland was home with his parents. Forrest was out in London at some club.'

'Do you live alone?' asked Tristan.

'Yeah. Mum died three years ago. I was her carer for the last few years of her life.'

'I'm sorry,' said Kate.

'I recently did the place up. She left it to me in her will, God bless her.'

'Why did the police arrest you?' Tristan asked.

'A woman was at the Golden Fry, the chip shop, a few doors down. She saw Janey getting into my van.'

'Why did you take Janey all the way to the fish shop near your house if the Golden Fry was only a couple of doors down from Reynolds newsagent?' asked Tristan.

Robert hesitated for a moment.

'I had a bit of form with the owner of the Golden Fry. We'd got into an altercation a few months before. The police didn't arrest me until after Christmas. I talked to them voluntarily before that, 'cos I was one of the last people to see Janey. They also talked to Fred – Forrest – and Roland. They both backed me up, about moving the stuff from the youth club in the van.'

'When did the police arrest you?'

He blew out his cheeks and sat back, as if he hadn't had to think about this for some time.

'First week of January, I think. I know the newspapers didn't pick up on Janey's disappearance in the new year. The Lockerbie air crash happened on December 21, and it dominated the news over Christmas. It was only after Janey made the national news that the police brought in a sniffer dog. They searched all along the road up to Reynolds newsagent. The dog traced Janey's scent inside Reynolds and into the backyard to an old pipe. I still don't know, hand on my heart, how Janey's scent ended up in the backyard. She'd dropped her scarf in the shop. I don't know if her scent was transferred onto Jack, maybe his shoes or something. Then a few days later, there was crime reconstruction on TV. That's when the girl from the Golden Fry came forward and called the hotline and named me. The police were under pressure. They came up with the theory I killed Janey, stashed her body in the water pipe behind Reynolds for a few days, and then moved it and dumped it or buried it. They had no proof, no body, but this coupled with the fact I already had a criminal record . . .'

'What did you have a criminal record for?' asked Kate. He waved this away as if it were a silly detail.

'It was the aggro in the Golden Fry. I was with a girl who had also been with Vince, who owned the Fry. I went for him and she was in the way, and I ended up punching her. Hand on my heart, I meant to punch him, but the police were called . . . The girl backed Vince . . . I ended up with domestic violence on my record. Three months, suspended sentence. First offence. That was a few months before. My brief, my solicitor, told me not to worry and that nothing would stand up in court. I got legal aid, but my brief was crap. He was unprepared, and I think my attitude stunk. I was angry when they put me on the stand. The jury found me guilty.'

'And you served eight years?' asked Kate, watching him carefully.

'Yeah. Pretty soon after the verdict was handed down, my mum, God bless her soul, went to work on an appeal. I got a new brief, and she was excellent. She said that there was a chance of getting the verdict overturned 'cos the police never found a body. It took a fucking, sorry, a bloody age, but there was a retrial in late 1996, and I was acquitted in March 1997. And there's still no body.'

There was a long silence. It was cold in the living room. Kate shivered and wanted to put her coat back on.

'What do you think really happened to Janey?' asked Tristan.

'Well. That letter is interesting. Thomas Black saw Peter Conway chatting up young girls in The Jug. Janey and her sister were there every week. She could have been one of his victims.'

'Has Forrest really not been in contact with you about this? You were friends.'

'No. I told you, we're not in contact no more. That was a long time ago. Fred, Forrest, has gone off; he has a new life. He was always ambitious. I don't know. I've learned not to second-guess things in life anymore. What if Janey ran away and got lucky, met some guy, and she's living it up somewhere, lying on a beach? Stranger things have happened.'

'Or we find Janey's body,' said Kate.

Robert smiled.

'And if you do, I might finally be vindicated.'

15

It was dark, and the flat in Percy Circus was freezing when Kate and Tristan arrived back. They'd picked up some groceries and two takeaway pizzas on the way home, and they sat in the kitchen, in their coats, eating, whilst the flat warmed up.

'My God, that was good,' said Tristan, popping the last crust in his mouth and closing the box.

'You've finished? You inhale your food,' said Kate. She was still on her second slice.

'And I'm still hungry.' Tristan got up and unpacked the bag of milk, teabags, bread, and butter they'd bought. He opened the fridge. 'Someone left behind lingonberry jam,' he said, taking out a jar.

'Let me guess, they bought it at IKEA?'

'I could just eat an IKEA hot dog.' He put the stuff away and checked the cupboards. 'They've left us olive oil, out-of-date spices, and a bag of half-eaten penne pasta.'

'I'm not going to eat all of this,' said Kate, pushing her

pizza box towards him. 'Have some. I don't work out like you do.'

Tristan came and sat back down and took a slice. 'You swim every day,' he said, biting into it.

Kate swallowed and took out her phone. 'Which reminds me, I looked up where I can go swimming,' she said, scrolling. 'Pancras Leisure Centre is just on the other side of the train station. They've got a big pool, and a gym.'

'Do you want to walk over there, when I've finished this?'

'Okay.'

'I feel like I should be seeing London, when I'm here. It's so buzzy and alive compared to Ashdean.'

Kate's phone chimed in her hand. 'I just got an email back from Varia Campbell.'

'Telling us to take a hike?'

Superintendent Varia Campbell had been a police officer in the Devon and Cornwall police, and Kate and Tristan had helped her out in the past. She'd moved to London and been promoted to superintendent in the Met Police. Kate had emailed her a couple of days ago, when they first knew they'd be working on the Janey Macklin case.

'No. She's going to see if she can get us access to the Janey Macklin case file. It's in storage at her nick in West End Central.'

'Bloody hell, that's good of her,' said Tristan. 'Where is West End Central Police Station?'

'Charing Cross, but she's asked to meet us in a coffee place nearby . . . Oh. And I've had a *strident* email from Forrest Parker.'

'Maddie must have bent his ear when she got home,' said Tristan, getting up and filling the kettle.

Kate continued to read on her phone.

'Whenever someone uses the phrase *as per*, you know that they're seething inside. He starts the email with, *As per your conversation with Madeleine* . . . He's her fiancé and calls her Madeleine? And we all have to call her "Maddie" and be forced into some kind of fake intimacy.' Tristan laughed. 'Okay, well, he does want to meet. *I would be happy to meet with you at a time convenient to us both, but regrettably, I am out of town until*' – Kate scrolled down – '*January 7*. He's asking us to send him suitable dates.'

Tristan switched on the kettle.

'I just don't buy it that Robert and Forrest are no longer in contact,' he said, coming back to the table and sitting down. 'Maddie was at pains to say it this morning before she stomped out in a huff, and then Robert said the same thing. I'd understand if Forrest had moved far away, but he lives in Barnes in West London, and Maddie said that he's a Superhost for this flat when it's rented out as an Airbnb. It's less than a mile from here to Golden Lane.'

'Yeah, but people can be weird. One of the lecturers who works at Ashdean Uni has a sister who lives in the town, and she hasn't spoken to her for twenty years.'

'Why?'

'The sister slept with her husband.'

'Fair enough. This awful thing happened, and Robert was found guilty for murder, and I understand that Forrest didn't want to have anything to do with him when he went to prison, but Robert was then acquitted. And Forrest's mother lived in the same block as Robert and his mother.'

'Robert said that Forrest's mother died while he was in prison, and he tried to get permission to go to the funeral but it was denied. And what about the flat Forrest – Fred – grew up in? Golden Lane is made up of council flats and ex–council flats slap-bang in the middle of London. Either Forrest inherited a council tenancy when his mum died, or his mother bought the flat through the right-to-buy scheme in the 1980s. Either way, wouldn't a poor actor want to keep hold of a central London base?'

'Or he sold it in the 1990s when his mum died?' said Tristan.

'To go where? This is central London,' said Kate. Tristan looked at her blankly. 'When I lived in London as a copper back in the 1990s, it was a bloody nightmare to find a place to live, even on a decent wage.' She looked in the pockets of her jacket, found one of the little free Tube maps they'd picked up that morning, and unfolded it on the table. 'Look, we're in Zone 1 here in the centre by King's Cross, and so is Golden Lane, and then it goes Zone 2, 3, 4, 5, 6 as you get further out of London. Most people who live in London want to be as near to Zone 1 as possible; it's where everything is. And I'd think even more so for actors; all castings, theatres, TV companies would be in Zone 1 or 2. Why would Forrest graduate from drama school as an actor and then move?'

'To steer clear of Robert?'

'But Robert would have still been in prison. He didn't get released until 1997. Do you think Forrest had such strong morals that he'd give up a central London base because his former friend the murderer lived two floors down? This is London. People don't have the same attitudes like in Ashdean. There isn't a small-town mindset. I lived in my flat in Deptford for four years and I rarely spoke to a neighbour.'

'He could have sold the flat when Robert was acquitted in 1997.'

'Yes, but when Robert was acquitted, he was found innocent. And Robert and Forrest have both said that they severed contact in 1988. Why wouldn't they reconnect? It doesn't add up. And what about the third friend, Roland Hacker, who's cut himself off from everyone and no one knows where he is?'

16

It was coming up to 8.30am the next morning, and Darren Twigg had spent the past fifteen minutes locked in a cubicle in the staff toilets at HMP Wakefield, cradling a flip phone in his hand.

He'd been a dental anaesthesiologist in the prison service for the past four years, and he was a good one, too. He was only twenty-six and knew he was about to cross a line. He'd heard that plenty of the prison guards took bribes from the outside to smuggle stuff in and out for prisoners – drugs, mobile phones, and weapons – but he was medical staff. It felt different.

A posh woman had approached him two weeks ago, offering *three grand* to smuggle a mobile phone to Peter Conway, the Nine Elms Cannibal. It had seemed like a lot of money at the time, but now he had the phone in his hand, he was having second thoughts. He'd made the mistake of googling Peter Conway. He'd found gory crime scene photos on a Reddit forum. It was something about Conway biting his victims and Darren working in dentistry that horrified him. A picture swam back into his mind. A girl's body with bite marks so deep in her back that her spinal cord was exposed.

The posh woman had told him she was a journalist and had lied unconvincingly, saying that the phone wouldn't be used for criminal purposes. What did she think it was going to be used for? Ordering pizza?

The consequences if he were to get caught would be dire. He'd lose his medical licence. No. He wasn't going to get caught. He would do this just once, and he could pay off a chunk of the gambling debts which kept him awake at night.

Medical staff were rarely searched in the prison, but he'd still panicked that morning when he'd arrived at the staff entrance. He'd breezed through, though, which made him feel even guiltier.

Darren put the phone into the pocket of his blue medical scrubs and wiped his sweaty hands on his trousers. He flushed the toilet, left the cubicle, and checked his reflection at the sinks. He was a tall, thin lad with hair dyed blue and lip- and nose-rings. He had seven grand's worth of payday loans at a crazy interest rate. He'd been paid a grand, with the next two owed on completion. It would take the heat off him with the bank. And what had the journalist said? Once a channel was open, things could stay lucrative. He shook the thought away.

Darren's colleague, the dentist Gemma Thurlby, was waiting for him in the surgery room.

'Morning. Happy New Year. Did you have a nice Christmas?' she asked briskly.

'Yeah. Happy New Year. Did you?'

'Wonderful, thank you,' she said without offering more information. The dentist surgery at Monster Mansion was grim, with a stained grey carpet, yellowing paintwork, and water stains blooming up one wall. There were four panic buttons dotted around the room, and also an adaptation to the dentist's chair fixed in the centre of the large room so it looked a little like an executioner's chair, with a loop on each armrest for handcuffing and restraining a prisoner.

Darren stared out the window at the car park, and the tall furnace chimney belched black smoke against the grey sky.

'We still need to prep. He'll be here in fifteen minutes,' said Gemma. Her tone indicated he should already be prepping.

'Yes, of course,' he said. He swallowed. His mouth was dry.

Gemma sat typing at her computer in the corner, and Darren went to work preparing the IV and propofol for sedation. He then laid out five scalpels, scissors, a selection of tooth probes, tartar scrapers, and a small round dental mirror. They gleamed on the silver tray. He added suture material for stitches and sterilised needles.

Darren jumped at the loud buzzing sound. He followed Gemma to the small video screen on the wall. Two tall, broad prison guards stood on either side of an elderly hunched-over man with his hands cuffed in front of him.

'Is everything ready?'

'Yes.'

Gemma pressed the entry button, and the two guards led Peter Conway inside.

The first guard eyed Gemma and Darren. He was small

but very broad and muscular with huge pale-blue eyes, which seemed to burn with anger. Darren had seen him before and had privately nicknamed him 'Psycho Eyes.'

'Morning,' said Gemma briskly.

'Morning,' said Darren.

'Darren, your hair. It's different every time I come 'ere,' said Peter. His voice was croaky and a little hoarse. Darren was surprised Peter remembered his name. His hair had been blond during the last visit, two weeks ago.

'I fancied a change,' he replied. His voice was trembling. Psycho Eyes remained stationed at the door. The second guard was well over six and a half feet tall and equally muscular, with his red hair trimmed into a greasy bowl cut. Darren had named this one 'Ginger Lurch.' Peter seemed so frail and elderly. His grey hair clung to his head in wisps, and Lurch held his arm and supported him as he eased into the dentist's chair. *What bad things could this old guy possibly do with a phone?*

'Looks like that stuff you can put down the lav to keep it extra clean,' said Peter.

'I'm sorry?' said Gemma, pulling on a pair of latex gloves.

'His hair,' said Peter. 'What's it called?'

'BlueLoo,' growled Psycho Eyes. His face remained passive.

'Darren. That's an unfortunate name,' said Peter. 'You never hear of a Prince Darren? A King Darren? Or a superhero called Darren?'

'Right, let's have a look inside your mouth,' said Gemma firmly.

'I'll be here,' said Lurch. 'No funny business, Peter.'

'Don't you worry,' said Peter. 'I'm gonna be knocked out, so I won't have to look at Darren's ugly mug.'

'That's the pot calling the kettle black,' said Lurch with a toothy smile. Peter smiled and then winced. Darren felt anger flash inside him. He wanted to come back at Peter and say, *Careful what you say to the man who's got the pain medication.* But Gemma did things by the book, and she always insisted they treat the rapists, murderers, and paedophiles with courtesy.

Gemma activated the chair as it simultaneously reclined and lifted Peter level with her stomach. Prisoners on the high-security psychiatric wing wore their own clothes, usually tracksuit bottoms and a sweater, and today, Peter wore a blue tracksuit and an old pair of New Balance trainers on his feet. Where his thin wrists were bound tightly in front of him, the veins on the backs of his hands stood out, shiny.

'How have you been over Christmas, Peter?' asked Gemma, in the same breezy, forced tone a hairdresser might ask where you've been on your holidays.

'Apart from having to drink my Christmas dinner through a straw? Fucking marvellous.'

'I'm afraid that when I see you is out of my control.'

'Enough of the chit-chat. Are you gonna pull 'em out?'

'Let's have a look.'

Darren scooted around so he was close to Peter's head, the wheels of his stool rattling on the carpet. Peter's pupils contracted as Gemma pulled the dental operatory light from above, angled it down, and began to examine his mouth. His eyes were brown, and his face was an odd mix of handsome with a good bone structure, even in his emaciated state.

There was something else there, too, swimming below the surface: menace. The smell of pus and infection was overpowering.

Darren felt the flip phone in his right pocket. The empty pocket of Peter's tracksuit bottoms gaped open. Gemma worked methodically, probing inside his mouth.

'Christ!' Peter snapped. Gemma moved her hands back. 'Go easy.'

'I'm being gentle, but I do need to examine you. Four of the teeth are now dead, and the surrounding gum is badly infected. I think it would be best to extract them all.'

Peter contemplated her with his brown eyes, both soft and menacing. 'I hope you're gonna knock me out?'

'Yes. Darren will give you a general anaesthetic.'

'Go on then, Super Darren. Knock me out,' said Peter.

Darren quickly prepped the propofol for the IV and rolled up Peter's sleeve, exposing a pole-thin arm. His hands were trembling, but he hit the bull's-eye the first time with the needle, coaxing the IV into a vein. Peter winced but didn't complain.

'Okay, if you can count back from ten . . . ,' Gemma said. Darren hooked the IV bag up onto a stand, and when he turned around again, Peter was unconscious.

The officers seemed to relax a little. Darren covered Peter with a cape and a dental bib, and using these as a cover, he took the small flip phone from his pocket and quickly pushed it into the open pocket of Peter's tracksuit bottoms.

When Darren moved around to the other side of the chair to switch on the suction, he saw Psycho staring at him.

17

Peter Conway woke up in his cell a couple of hours later with a mouth full of what felt like cotton wool and a terrible dull ache in his jaw. There was drool all down the front of his sweater. He heaved himself into a sitting position and rested his head against the wall.

There was a tap on his door, and the hatch opened. Lurch – he was called Lurch by most people – was on the other side.

'How are we doin', Pete?' he asked.

'Whadyioufsthink?' he tried to answer. He worked the two strips of cotton wool out from under his gums and spat them into his hand. They were soaked with blood.

'You've got painkillers there. I left them on your table with your profesis. Dentist says she gev you dissolvable stitches. You've 'ad five teeth out.' Peter nodded, gratefully. 'You were lucky to be unconscious. I watched 'ellraiser last night, and that dentist working on you was way more gory.'

Peter chuckled and then winced, and put up his hand to say thanks. Lurch closed the hatch. Peter got up off the bed and tottered unsteadily over to use the commode. It was only when he pulled down his tracksuit bottoms and sat down that a flip phone fell out of his pocket and clattered onto the stone floor.

————

Darren left HMP Wakefield just after lunch. He had to get to Kingfisher Young Offenders Prison by 2pm. He was still shaken. Maybe Psycho Eyes hadn't seen him put the phone in Peter's pocket. He might have dodgy eyesight or just have been zoned out. He looked like that a lot.

Darren got into his car and was just putting on his seat belt when Psycho Eyes got into the passenger seat and closed the door.

'Drive. Drop me at the bus stop.'

Darren's heart was pounding. They were silent until they passed through the prison security barrier.

'Have you done it before?' asked Psycho. Darren swallowed, and he felt a flash of white-hot panic. 'Don't say "done what?" You know what I'm talking about. I saw you plant the phone in Peter Conway's pocket.'

They pulled up at a traffic crossing as the lights turned red. A stream of pedestrians, all pissed off and grey faced, passed the car. A big drop of rain exploded on the windscreen, followed by another and then another.

'It was the first time.'

'Who did you do it for? Family? A friend? A crazy fan? You know, Peter Conway had a fan a few years back. The copycat murderer who broke him out.'

'A woman. She said she's a journalist.'

'A journalist from where?'

'London.'

'What does she want?'

'She wants an interview with Peter Conway. She wants to record a phone call with him. A private phone call.'

'And used for what?'

'I dunno. An article.'

'Did she pay you?'

Darren nodded.

'How much?'

'A grand.'

'You get good at reading liars in this job. How much, really?'

'Three.'

Psycho whistled. '*Three grand.* Is that the going rate for a little chat with the Nine Elms Cannibal?'

Darren shook his head. He thought he was going to be sick. 'I'm in debt,' he said, and regretted it the moment it was out of his mouth.

'We all are, mate. Does this journalist want you to do any other courier work for her?'

'I don't know.'

'I'm not judging. Lots of the screws do a bit of courier work on the side. With the wages they pay, I'm surprised it's not all of us.'

The lights turned green, and Darren had to put on the windscreen wipers. The sky was suddenly very grey, and the road ahead was shrouded in the gloom of the cloud cover.

'You work at Kingfisher, Waltham, Paxley, as well as Monster Mansion?'

Psycho was referring to the three young offenders institutions where Darren assisted the dentist.

'Listen. That was just a one-time thing, smuggling in the phone. And I said to her, I won't do it if there are drugs involved. I hate drugs,' said Darren, the panic rising in his chest.

'That's very moral of you,' said Psycho. 'Give me her phone number.'

'What? No.'

'*No?* I don't think you have the luxury of telling me no.'

'I'm sorry. I just think that—'

'Shut up. You are going to give me her number. And then you're going to text her and introduce me as her new courier. *Capiche?* You might lose out on another fee, but you'll keep your job. Us guards live in a more rough-and-tumble world. A bit of courier work might lead to a suspension. If I lose my job, I can work in security. But you. No one likes a crooked quack . . . What are you?'

'I'm a dental anaesthesiologist.'

Psycho held out his hand. 'Unlock your phone. Show me her number.'

Darren bit his lip. He wasn't going to cry. He took one hand off the wheel and unlocked his phone, scrolling through.

'Here,' he said. Psycho brought the phone close to his face and, using his stubby thumbs, tapped in a message and pressed send. Then Psycho's phone pinged in his pocket, as he sent the contact to himself. He slid the phone into

Darren's top pocket and then patted his leg. 'You can drop me here.'

He pulled the car over at the bus stop. Psycho got out and slammed the door and joined the queue of people on the pavement. He winked, and only the bus honking behind Darren broke him out of his fear.

————

Peter sat back on the bed and turned the phone over in his hands. He hadn't had much experience with mobile phones beyond seeing them on TV. When he escaped prison a few years back, the method of communication then had been decidedly analogue, with notes written on paper.

How had it ended up in his pocket? He'd been knocked out by the anaesthetic. And there certainly hadn't been a phone in his pocket when he arrived at the dentist's.

It was maybe a guard, but why would a guard put it there without telling him? Or asking for payment? That stick-up-her-arse dentist looked like she was by the book . . . That scally lad with the blue hair.

Peter mused on this for a moment.

The phone wasn't one of the ultramodern touch screen ones. When he flipped it open, he saw it had large buttons, the type for old biddies. Taped to the back were two black squares. He peered at them closer. One was a battery, the other a magnet? He held the phone near to the hot-water pipe running down the wall beside the bed. It leapt out of his hand and adhered to the metal.

Ching.

The magnet was strong. Peter pulled the phone off. If he switched it on, would it make a noise?

He heard footsteps in the corridor. They stopped outside his door, then moved on. Peter knew you could take the back off the older mobile phone models. It was fiddly, but thankfully, he had long nails and managed to unclip the thin plastic backing. A small, neatly folded piece of paper was tucked inside, between the battery and the cover.

He put the phone down on the bed and unfolded the tiny note. The text had been printed off by a computer.

> BATTERY AND BACKUP BATTERY FULLY
> CHARGED. LOADED WITH £100 PREPAID
> CREDIT.
> THE PHONE IS ON MUTE/VIBRATE FOR WHEN
> YOU SWITCH ON + WHEN IT RINGS.
> PRESS 1 FOR SPEED DIAL TO SPEAK TO ME.
> I'M A JOURNALIST, WITH A PROPOSAL. CALL
> ANYTIME, DAY OR NIGHT. LINE IS SECURE.

He wondered what kind of proposal a journalist could have for him. He was banged up for a whole life sentence, so there was no chance of parole. If they wanted to pay him for a story, he couldn't spend the money. And if he was honest, the thought of leaving his prison cell . . . It scared him. A few years back, when he'd escaped, he had been a lot younger. And he'd been committed to one last roll of the dice. But now, he was old beyond his years, and toothless.

Still. This was entertaining. It wasn't every day in prison that a mobile phone fell into his lap. Or out of his pocket. He put the note back inside the phone, and the back cover with the magnet clicked back in place easily.

Peter quickly looked around his cell. There wasn't time to wonder who was writing to him. Didn't that old fucker

Thomas Black say that someone would be in touch? He didn't expect this, though. Peter held the phone a few inches from the pipe, and the magnet pulled it onto the metal again with a satisfying *ching*.

The phone was grey, and the hot-water pipe was white. The pipe snaked its way from above the door, along the ceiling above his bed, and then down the opposite wall into the floor. On his desk were his books, writing paper, and the felt-tip pens they allowed him. His hands were now so shaky that his solicitor had managed to get him approved to use correction fluid, for when he wrote his letters, he made so many mistakes. After the tooth extraction, Peter was desperate to sleep and still very drowsy from the anaesthetic, but he knew he had to hide this phone – and hide it well – before he went back to the land of Nod.

Working as quickly and neatly as possible, Peter opened the correction fluid and, with the small brush, painted the front curved grey shell of the phone white. The sides were black, and it took two coats of correction fluid to cover it all, but when he was finished, half the phone and the sides were white. He placed it down on a blank sheet of paper. Luckily, the correction fluid dried fast, but the room was beginning to stink of whatever chemical was in the white stuff, and if someone stopped outside the door, they might think he was trying to get high, so he opened the window despite the cold air.

Fifteen minutes passed, and Peter had to stay by the window to keep awake. Finally, with the phone dry, he stood on his bed and stuck it on top of the pipe where it ran along the wall above his bed.

Ching.

It almost matched in colour, but you could still see it. Peter moved it along where the ceiling met the wall and the pipe curved around and down.

Ching.

The pipe cast a little shadow on the wall, but in that sweet spot, the phone was invisible, even if you looked pretty hard.

Peter finally lay down on the bed and slept. Dreaming of who might answer the phone.

18

_____

Late the next morning, Kate and Tristan met Varia Campbell at the Caffè Nero on the Strand. She was waiting for them at a table in the corner.

'My God, Kate, and Tristan. I never expected to see you up in London,' she said, beaming.

'Thank you for meeting us,' said Kate.

'Not at all. You intrigued me – a cold case involving Peter Conway!' She gave Kate a hug. 'And look at you,' said Varia, turning to Tristan and grabbing him in a hug. 'All the boy has been rubbed off, and now you're a man.'

'You look amazing – I mean, great,' said Tristan.

Varia laughed. 'I think London suits me far better than the West Country. Although I do miss the sea.' When Varia had been a police officer in Exeter, her hair had been a sleek, shiny helmet, and she'd dressed like a bank clerk. Now she wore her hair in long dreadlocks tied back, and a long black dress with huge pockets. Tristan thought how comfortable and confident she looked compared to the nervous, on-edge police officer she'd been eight years ago. They sat down at the small table.

'I'm sorry I haven't got a lot of time,' said Varia. She picked up a big white carrier bag from the floor and put it on the table. It was filled with a stack of folders. 'I had to go deep into evidence stores for this one. As far as I can see, it hasn't been touched since Robert Driscoll was sent down in 1989.'

'This is the original Janey Macklin case file?' asked Tristan, peering into the bag and seeing the yellowing paper.

'It is. I had the whole thing copied, but my bird-brained assistant gave me the wrong one, so guard this with your life. There's also a VHS inside of the *Crimewatch* TV reconstruction. And I brought this,' she said, picking up another carrier bag.

'A VHS machine,' said Tristan.

'I figured you might not have one, and you're away from home. All the leads and the remote are in there. We still use them, when we have to pull surveillance videos or evidence that hasn't yet been digitised. This is a spare one I've had in my office drawer for ages.'

'Thanks, Varia,' said Kate.

'You're welcome. But I have to say, if you solve this case or come close to a breakthrough, I'll be sharing in the glory.'

'Of course. How long can we have this all for?' asked Kate.

'I'm on annual leave for the next two weeks. I'll need to meet you when I'm back and for all that to return to me, pristine and accounted for, in the bag,' she said, tapping the case files. 'What's your feeling about this one? You think Peter Conway did it?'

'That would be the logical option,' said Kate. 'But if he managed to get rid of Janey Macklin's remains and they haven't been found in thirty years, it's going to be hard to prove.'

'Yes. The CPS will only be interested in revisiting this if you find her body. Robert Driscoll's acquittal led to the resignation of the two police officers who worked on the case.'

'Where are they now?'

'DCI Peter Berger, who led the case, died six years ago. Alcohol abuse. And DI Nathan Barrett is in a nursing home up north, and he suffers from dementia. There might be some names of the other officers who worked on the case in the files. I only had the chance to skim through.' Varia placed both hands on the table in a gesture of finality. 'I'd love to stay and talk to you more, but I have to get back. And this meeting never happened. Okay?'

'Are you going away anywhere nice on leave?' asked Kate as they all got up.

'Yes. St Lucia with my husband.'

'Wow. Enjoy the sunshine,' said Tristan.

She smiled and put her hand on his arm. 'I'll be in touch.'

They watched her go and then looked around at the crowded coffee shop. The front doors were open, and a cold breeze was blowing inside. Tristan hitched up the bag and peered at the contents.

'Come on,' he said. 'Let's find somewhere quiet.'

———

They moved to a Starbucks on New Oxford Street with a huge upstairs section, which was half-empty. They got settled at a couple of chairs in a quieter corner near the back, ordered coffee, and then settled down with the plastic bag of case files.

Inside were four folders bursting with papers and photos. They took two each and started to read.

'I've found a report on the Met Police canine sniffer dog they sent in to try and locate Janey,' said Tristan. 'She was called Molly, an ironical name for a dog who looks for drugs. It was on 28 December 1988. Police were given two items of Janey's clothing from Doreen Macklin, a T-shirt and a pair of leggings. The dog was taken first to Robert Driscoll's van, and she detected Janey's scent in the front passenger seat and also detected Janey's scent in the back of the van against the right-side panel,' said Tristan. 'The search team then moved to Reynolds newsagent, which had only been closed on Christmas Day; it had been open all over Christmas.'

'Newsagents only close on Christmas Day. That's the only day of the year they don't print newspapers,' said Kate.

'Yes, and the police were concerned that there would have been too much footfall since Janey was seen there on December the twenty-third and the dog wouldn't get anything. However, the dog detected her scent on the floor of the newsagent, close to the entrance, next to the racks of magazines and behind the till, where there was a door leading out to the yard. Molly then detected Janey's scent in the small hallway leading to the back door. They let Molly into the garden, and she was there for a couple of minutes before she found Janey's scent on the metal lid covering a drainage pipe.'

'Was Jack Reynolds there when they did the search?' asked Kate.

'It doesn't say. Wouldn't the police clear the premises for when they do a dog search?'

'Normally, yes.'

'It says that the drainage pipe wasn't used anymore. It had been there when the houses had a septic tank in the 1950s, but now the whole street was on the sewage system. The tank had been removed, but the pipe was still there. They lifted the lid, and Molly found Janey's scent on the inside of the lid, and all along the pipe for four metres. Forensics then went into the pipe . . . They took blood samples from inside the clay pipe and another sample which was found on the butt of a cigarette, but they weren't large enough to yield an accurate DNA sample to match Janey's blood.'

Kate and Tristan flicked through the photos in the case file. The back garden of Reynolds had been a tiny, overgrown square surrounded by high brick walls. A picture showed three police officers standing next to the metal lid on a small length of concrete path with Molly the sniffer dog, a German shepherd, with her nose down and her back arched up.

The final two photos were of the dark-grey pipe inside, and the space was filled with soil, some broken glass, and a couple of cigarette ends. Molly was inside the pipe.

'That pipe is quite big,' said Tristan. 'Molly was a German shepherd and could fit inside standing up.'

'I wonder if the pipe was some kind of hiding place for

teenage kids? It could have been a place where someone flicked their cigarette ends.'

'No, look at the cover on top of the pipe,' said Tristan, indicating the big metal cover standing up against the wall. 'It must be a couple of metres wide and heavy.'

After a moment, he asked, 'Can the results of canine sniffer dogs be used in UK court trials?'

'Not if key evidence is based solely on a sniffer dog detecting something. Then a judge would explain that canine sniffer dogs aren't 100 percent reliable and can be influenced by outside factors.'

'How long are DNA samples kept by the police?'

'If it's a serious crime, a violent attack, murder, or sexual assault, and the case remains unsolved, then it should be indefinitely,' said Kate.

'Robert Driscoll was sentenced for Janey Macklin's murder, then acquitted, but her body has never been found. Would the case now be classed as a murder or a missing person?'

'Varia said the case file hasn't been touched since 1989, so I doubt the CPS has even reviewed it. There's been so many breakthroughs in DNA profiling since 1988. If the blood samples are still on file, we could have it retested. It could tell us if Janey's body was stashed in that pipe.'

19

Peter woke in his cell later that afternoon. His mouth throbbed, and his sweater was covered in drool again. He pulled himself up and went to the mirror, flicking on the small overhead light. His tiny cell lit up behind him, framing his swollen face. He'd never been vain, but it had been easy in his youth to look good. And he'd always been an attractive man. Losing that and seeing the gaunt, swollen, hunched-over little creature staring back at him was difficult to handle.

He rinsed his face with cold water and slowly opened and closed his mouth. Despite the dull, throbbing pain, he felt better. He leaned into the mirror and saw the neat row of black stitches in his gum. He went to switch off the light and noticed the little bottle of correction fluid sitting in the middle of the desk, and then it all came back to him. He heaved himself up onto his bed, retrieved the phone from the pipe, and switched it on.

The screen lit up, and a moment later, he saw he had full bars. Back in his day, a full bar had been a busy pub.

'Pee-cher pie-char piched a peach of pichled peppersch,' he said. He repeated the same sentence a couple of times, trying to work the feeling and dexterity back into his tongue. The numbness and swelling were affecting his voice, but he was keen to know who had taken the risk and trouble to plant a contraband phone in his pocket.

He pressed the speed dial number on the one key, and it rang for a long time before a woman answered.

'Hello?' she said shakily. He could hear people talking in the background.

'Hello, this is Peter Conway,' he replied. There was a long pause. 'Please excuse my voice. I've just had dental surgery. Although you probably know that,' Peter added, speaking slowly and carefully to minimise his slurring and lisping.

'Thank you for calling me,' said the woman. 'I can do most of the talking.'

'Please do.'

'I won't tell you my name. It's easier to keep these things anonymous.'

'I'm listening.'

'What would it be worth for you to talk to me, on the record, about things in the past?'

He gave a wheezing laugh. 'You've gone to all this trouble to ask me that?'

'Yes. There is only so much you can say through an official phone line.'

'What if I knew where a body was buried?' said Peter. Although it came out sounding like, '*Whath ith I neuth wheth a bodith whath berith?*'

'Sorry. I didn't catch that?'

There was a bang on the hatch of Peter's cell door. He ended the call, closed the phone, and pushed it under his pillow. The hatch opened.

'How you doing?' asked Lurch.

'Been better.'

'You hungry? I brought you some lunch.'

'Famished.'

Peter ate what he could of his lunch, but it was agony to chew and swallow. He waited for the tray to be taken away before he called back the number. The woman now seemed on edge and whiny. There was nothing he despised more than weakness. She wanted to record an interview with him and talk about Janey Macklin, and, specifically, if he had any involvement with her disappearance. He could still feel the after-effects of the anaesthetic, and told her he needed time to think. Would it be in his interests to go along with her, or could he gain more leverage by shopping the bitch to the prison governor?

In the meantime, he had his own phone. Who else could he call?

20

Back at the flat in Percy Circus, Tristan had to lift the flatscreen television off the wall so Kate could plug in the SCART lead for the video recorder. It took a few attempts to get the TV hooked back up, and then Kate inserted the videocassette.

The TV screen went fuzzy, and then a countdown timer appeared on screen with the type 'BBC CRIMEWATCH RECONSTRUCTION 234 05.01.1989.' A moment later, a view of Midland Road at night appeared. It was dark, and the road and surrounding buildings seemed to glisten black on the damp January night. The camera swung around to show The Jug pub. The windows were steamed up, and Christmas lights shone through the condensation.

The sound boomed out. *'On the evening of December the twenty-third, fifteen-year-old Janey Macklin and her younger sister, Maxine, met their mother at The Jug public house in Midland Road near King's Cross St Pancras station,'* said the posh male voice-over. Kate turned down the volume. On the screen a teenage girl with rabbity teeth and short brown hair walked up to the pub, holding the hand of a younger girl in a long brown duffel coat. They opened the door and went inside.

'Janey's mother had just finished her shift as a cleaner at The Jug, and she'd stayed for a Christmas drink.'

Kate noted how rough The Jug circa 1988 looked inside, with tatty red chairs and chipped furniture. Cigarette smoke hung in the air, and Janey and Maxine were shown playing on a *Space Invaders* video game, whilst the actress playing their mother, who looked worse for wear with bedraggled curly black hair, and wearing denim dungarees, was running a bright-yellow duster over the end of the wooden bar top.

'Janey grew bored of waiting for her mother, and decided to visit the local newsagent to buy some sweets.'

The actress playing Janey re-emerged from the pub, hurried across the street, and started walking away. Kate glanced at the school photo in the folder beside her laptop and thought how the actress they'd chosen was the spitting image of Janey, with her big eyes and freckled cheeks.

'Janey left The Jug at around five forty-five pm, and she walked past this fish-and-chip shop, the Golden Fry, where several people were dining inside.'

'Dining,' repeated Tristan.

'This was 1989. Everyone who appeared on the BBC spoke with very posh voices,' said Kate.

'Janey then reached Reynolds newsagent on the corner of Midland Road and Gosport Street. The proprietor was just about to close, so Janey bought her sweets and left shortly afterwards.'

Kate paused the video on the image of Janey stepping out of Reynolds with a small paper bag of what looked like penny sweets.

'Robert Driscoll told us that Janey's mum sent her to buy cigarettes from Reynolds.'

'And Stan told us that Janey and Maxine would meet Doreen after she finished work,' said Tristan. 'They airbrushed the family to make them look more wholesome. Look at Doreen dusting the top of the bar.'

'I wonder if the police wanted viewers to sympathise with the family, so more people would be inclined to come forward if they saw something,' said Kate. She pointed at the screen to the young actor they'd hired who looked like Robert Driscoll, who was packing up the racks of newspapers outside Reynolds.

Kate unpaused the video. The posh male voice-over continued: *'Janey stopped to talk to a young man who worked at the newsagent and then headed back to meet her mother at The Jug. This was a short walk on the street, and there were lots of pedestrians and cars passing.'*

The video showed Janey walking along the road back, past the Golden Fry, and into the dimly lit part of the street.

'Police are appealing to anyone who was on Pancras Road between five forty-five pm and six thirty pm on December the twenty-third. You may have been having fish and chips in the Golden Fry, or you may have paid a visit to The Jug public house, or you were just in the area at this time. If you may have seen anything, however small, please call our hotline number.'

'They featured Robert but didn't mention his name, and they didn't show Jack Reynolds,' said Tristan.

The number flashed up on the bottom of the screen, and then they showed Victoria House.

'Janey was a popular young girl and lived locally; she attended weekly classes at the Glenda La Froy dance school, and lived here on the Victoria House estate just a few minutes' walk from Pancras Road.'

Kate paused the video again. 'This appeal was broadcast on January 5, 1989. That's thirteen days after Janey went missing. And the police at this stage still weren't aware that Robert gave Janey a lift in his van?'

'Robert said the police spoke to him and Forrest and Roland a couple of days after Janey went missing. Did he tell them that he gave Janey a lift, or that Janey just came to Reynolds to buy sweets and cigarettes? And after the police appeal was broadcast, that's when the woman from the Golden Fry came forward and tells the police she saw Janey getting into Driscoll's van.'

'Yes. They arrested Robert Driscoll and charged him two weeks after she went missing. So that's a day or two after this appeal was broadcast.'

'This appeal doesn't mention anything about the police using the sniffer dog and finding Janey's scent inside Reynolds and in the pipe in the backyard. That was five days after she went missing,' said Tristan.

'The police might have been holding that information back,' said Kate. She pointed at the TV. 'Look at this video taken outside Victoria House. The paving slabs in the courtyard have all been pulled up, and the statue in the middle is missing.'

They were silent for a moment, staring at the frozen image.

'We need to establish a timeline for all of this,' said Kate. 'And read all of the statements given to the police.'

Kate ran the video back to the beginning, and they watched again as Janey and Maxine walked into The Jug.

'Do you think they hired extras? All those people look authentic,' said Tristan. Kate stared at the screen as Janey and Maxine picked their way through the drunk-looking men and women chatting and laughing through a haze of cigarette smoke. 'And we have to keep in mind Peter Conway might have been in the pub that night, or Thomas Black.'

'I don't want to think about that,' said Kate. If either one of those men abducted Janey, it would have been a long, slow, and painful death.'

21

Kate and Tristan spent the next few hours going through the case files, and then at midnight, Tristan said he was going to bed. Kate was wide awake, so she stayed up a little while longer. Around 1am, she went to the kitchen to make herself another cup of tea, when her phone rang. It was Jake.

'Mum, sorry to call you late. Did I wake you up?' he said, sounding agitated.

'I'm still up. Are you okay, love?'

'I don't know. I just had a phone call from Peter.'

'Peter?' repeated Kate. Her mind was still on the case, and for a moment, she didn't know who he was talking about.

'Peter Conway.'

'Oh.' Kate hesitated. To ask how he was seemed disingenuous.

'He's in a bad way. He had to have five teeth extracted, and he's got a serious infection,' said Jake. Kate could hear the conflict in his voice.

'You're allowed to feel sympathy for him.'

'I do, sort of, but it's not that, Mum. I don't think he called me from a prison phone.'

'What do you mean?'

'When I usually get a call from him, there's this recorded message which says something like, *A prisoner from HMP Wakefield wishes to connect with you. Will you take the call?* And you press one, and then there's another message that says that calls are monitored and recorded. There was none of this – he was just there when I answered, and the number on my caller ID began with zero seven, which is a mobile number. It's usually the Wakefield prison switchboard number where they route the calls that shows up.'

Kate sat down on one of the kitchen chairs, and it creaked and echoed in the flat. 'Did he say anything threatening or weird?'

'He told me . . . that he loved me, and he wished that he'd had the chance to be a real father.'

'That does sound out of character. Can you give the number he called you on?'

'Sure.'

Kate grabbed a pen and scribbled it down on the back of a takeaway menu.

'Do you think he's escaped again?'

'No,' said Kate. 'I'd have been warned, and you too. We're on the list of people who get contacted.'

Despite this, she got up and went to the front door, checking it was locked and bolted.

'What are you doing?' asked Jake. She could hear the concern in his voice.

'I'm just checking the doors are all locked and there's no

one here,' she said. The living room felt chilly, and she peered through the gap in the curtains. Percy Circus was empty. The orange street lights were burning bright and snow was falling heavily, covering the road and cars in a blanket of orange-tinged white.

'Mum, I don't think he's escaped.'

Kate went to Tristan's door. She could hear him snoring softly. She put her hand up to knock, and then stopped. Peter Conway was far away.

'I remember when he escaped last time. And I met him for the first time. He checked my teeth. His sick joke . . . His hands were dirty, and I remember the nasty taste in my mouth of his fingers. Like metal. Metallic.'

Kate came back and sat on the sofa. The TV was on with the sound down low, showing a wildlife documentary in the South Pole. 'Metallic? That was probably from the helicopter rail.'

'It's kind of badass that they landed a helicopter in the prison yard and broke him out,' said Jake.

'I've never thought of it as "badass." It always scares me that he nearly got away, taking you with him.'

'I wouldn't have gone.'

Kate had always hoped this was true, but it was strange the hold people could exert on others. If Peter and his mother had taken Jake to Spain and managed to stay there, would Jake have eventually been willed or brainwashed to accept his new life?

'He seemed different on the phone just now. Like old age has taken away all the evil.'

Kate wanted to refrain from debating this with Jake. Peter

Conway was evil. Always had been, and always would be. 'I'm going to call Wakefield prison. It sounds like Peter got hold of a mobile phone,' she said.

They were silent for a moment, and Kate watched the camera as it flew through a tunnel in the polar ice. 'Is it warm there in Manhattan Beach?'

'Yeah. I'm in a T-shirt and shorts. I'm sitting opposite that taco place we used to go to with the fish tacos.'

'I loved it there. The sunshine and the salt spray off the sea, and the feeling that anything is possible.'

'What's it like there?'

'Cold. Dark. And it feels a bit weird not being at home.'

'You know, you're always welcome here. And Olivia's parents would love to meet you.'

Kate made a suitably enthusiastic noise at the mention of Olivia's parents. When she did have the chance to go to Los Angeles, she wanted to spend all her time with Jake.

'I'm going to work out dates . . . soon,' she said.

'You'll let me know about this thing with Peter's phone? I thought I should tell you.'

'Yes. Love you,' said Kate.

'Love you, too, Mum.'

Kate came off the phone, and the silence descended. The wind whistled around the building, and she heard someone in the flat upstairs running water. The case files were on the table in the living room, and she opened the first page and stared at Janey Macklin's school photo. The young girl's hopeful smile against the blue background. Kate went back to the kitchen to fetch her tea, and she stared at the mobile phone number she'd written on the takeaway menu.

'Fuck it,' she said. She went back to the living room and dialled the number. It rang for a long time, and she thought it would go to voicemail, and then she heard a rustle as it was answered.

A voice, thick and almost unrecognisable, said, 'Hello. Who is this?'

'Is that you, Peter?'

'Yes.'

'It's Kate . . . Kate Marshall.'

There was a long silence, and Peter took a deep, wheezing breath and sounded like he was sitting up. 'Kate. Hello. How are you?'

The last part came out as *'Howach youo?'*

It was the most bizarre question. As if they were just picking up where they had left off. But where *had* they left off?

'I'm really very good,' she said, hearing the defiance in her voice. Why did she feel the need to tell him how great things were? 'How's life treating you, at Her Majesty's pleasure?'

'Dreathful.'

'Peter, why am I able to phone you direct?'

His breathing was heavy. He chuckled. 'A phone, quite literally, fell into my lap . . . It appeared in my pocket when I went to visit the dentist.'

'Who gave it to you?'

'I dunno. Some . . .' He coughed. 'Some bitch wants my voice. Wants a piece of me.'

'Who?' she said, shuddering at the way he said *bitch*. Even in his slurring voice, it made her shiver. 'Is there a journalist or someone on the outside who wants something from you?'

'Hang on. Is this really you, Kate? *My Catherine?* I was just talking to Jake.'

Kate winced at being called *My Catherine*. There was so much she wanted to say. So much anger, hate, and fear balled up in her chest, ready to burst out. He gave a hacking cough on the end of the line, and his breathing was laboured.

'I don't know who gave me the phone. Some journalist left a note inside asking me to call her. No name.'

'How do you know it was a *her*? Did you call her?'

Peter exhaled. His breath sounded wet. 'Er, no. I didn't. The writing on the note looked . . . *girly*. I wanted to speak to Jake, which I did. I love my son. Even though you don't think so.'

'I don't think that,' said Kate. She gripped the phone. The photo of Janey Macklin smiled up at her. Forever fifteen. If Peter was feeling emotional and maudlin, now was a good time to ask him.

'Peter. Do you remember when you were training at Hendon and living in London in 1988?'

'Ah. That was a long time ago.'

'Did you . . .' Kate swallowed. 'Did you . . .' She didn't know how to word it. She didn't want him to get angry and shut down. 'Did you meet a young girl in King's Cross? Her name was Janey Macklin. It would have been a couple of days before Christmas in 1988. You would still have been at Hendon.'

There was a long silence, and she heard him breathing

heavily. She'd said it all too fast. Kate repeated it all again, slowly.

'Janey . . . She was young?'

'Yes. Janey Macklin was her name. She used to go to The Jug pub on Pancras Road. She had short dark hair, and a heart-shaped face. The story of her going missing was in the papers.'

'The papers?'

'Yes. A young man called Robert Driscoll went down for murder, but the police never found a body. Do you know anything about it? Did you do something to her?'

'Sothith. I. I'm *thorry*.'

Kate gripped the phone harder, her heart racing in her chest. 'Sorry about what? Do you know what happened to Janey?'

'I think I do.'

'You do? What do you know?'

'Sothith Catherine.'

There was a beep, and then the line went dead. Kate stared at her phone for a long frustrating moment and then tried calling again, but she got a recorded message saying that the number was unavailable.

22

Peter Conway had been in terrible pain the night after his surgery. General anaesthetic always made him woozy, but this was like the world's worst hangover, with a crashing, white-hot pain through his jaw, ears, and neck muscles. Lurch had been concerned enough about him to call in the prison doctor, who begrudgingly prescribed antibiotics and codeine.

He'd spent the rest of the day in his cell, in bed, unable to sleep or think straight. It was later that evening when he remembered the phone and suddenly felt the impulse to talk to Jake. Peter's paternal instincts seemed to ebb and flow. For many years, he felt a sense of ownership and indifference towards Jake, but over the past few conversations, he'd heard Jake talk about his life in Los Angeles and all his plans. For the first time in Peter's life, he'd been able to see past the anger that controlled him and see his son as a person. And a part of him he could feel proud of.

The second call, from Kate, had been quite the shocker,

and by this time, he was burning up, and feeling delirious, so he wasn't quite sure if it had really been her on the phone. Or had he imagined it? She'd talked about Jake, who he knew was his son, and there was another name, a girl called Janey Macklin . . . He'd heard that name recently. Did he have a daughter? No. He would remember that.

And then he saw the phone in his hand and heard footsteps in the hall outside. He sat up, and with his head spinning, he heaved himself up to a crouching position, then stood on the bed and reattached the phone to the pipe. When he turned and attempted to crouch down, it was as if a fizzing surged up from the ground and filled his body like white noise, and then the blood rushed away from his head.

Peter felt the room tilt. He tried to grab on to the water pipe, but he fell forward off the bed. He landed on his right foot, his ankle gave way under him and propelled him forward as his head slammed into the edge of the porcelain sink.

———

Lurch had checked on Peter Conway every thirty minutes since the doctor left. Dr Benson was old school, a tough old goat, close to retirement. Benson also had a bit of form with Conway, who'd bitten him a few years back. Lurch understood how manipulative prisoners could be, but as a seasoned watcher, he could see that something was seriously wrong.

Lurch was on his way to check on Peter at 1.30am when he heard a loud crash inside his cell. He opened the hatch with his nightstick at the ready, and the first thing he saw was blood spattered all up the wall and the mirror above the sink. He opened the door and found Peter on the floor in a pool of blood. He was still breathing, but there was a deep dent on the right side of his head, and he was bleeding badly. Lurch sounded the alarm.

———

Psycho Eyes was in the break room when he heard the bell ringing. When he reached Peter Conway's cell, two paramedics were carrying him out on a stretcher. His head was covered in huge squares of white gauze bandages, and amongst the mess of blood, he wore an oxygen mask.

'We think he fell getting out of bed,' said Lurch, hurrying out with the paramedics. 'Can you do a sweep, get this place cleaned up?'

Psycho nodded. He waited until he heard their feet receding in the corridor and closed the cell door. He pulled on a pair of latex gloves from inside his pocket.

It was like a bloodbath around the sink, and when he moved closer to the mirror, he saw something stuck to the glass. He took out his torch and shone it on the lump of gore. Was it brain? No. It was a chunk of gum tissue with black surgical stitches. *Ouch.*

Taking care not to stand in the blood, Psycho searched the cell. It was the procedure to search for drugs or weapons which could be used for self-harm when a patient had an accident, but he was looking for a mobile phone.

He almost gave up. Only when he put his head flush with

the wall above the bed and shone his torch up and under the water pipe did he see the white square attached to the metal.

Sneaky.

He stood on the bed and pulled the mobile phone off the pipe and inspected the correction fluid paint job. Then he heard footsteps again in the corridor and jumped down, pocketing the phone.

'Anything?' asked Lurch, coming back into the cell.

'Nothing,' said Psycho. 'What's happened?'

'It's serious. They were going to take him to the hospital wing, but then he started fitting. He's been taken to Pinderfields Hospital.'

'You look worried, Lurch. You know what he is. Don't forget that.'

'Fuck off. And don't call me Lurch.'

23

Tristan got up early the next morning, when it was still dark, and walked through the snow to the gym at St Pancras leisure centre. He had a good workout, then picked up coffee and croissants on his way back. The sun was just peeking above the rooftops and illuminating a sliver of the road outside the flat and the frozen treetops. When he arrived back, Kate was sitting in the kitchen.

'Morning. You okay?'

'No. Not really.'

Tristan was immediately concerned. Kate looked rattled, with a white, drawn face and big bags under her eyes. For a horrible moment he thought she might have fallen off the wagon. He went to the cupboard and opened it, pretending to search for a plate, when he was looking to see if the bottle of schnapps was still in the cupboard. It was, and it was still half-full.

Tristan felt relieved and took out two plates. 'Did you eat?'

'I'm not very hungry . . . but I'll take one of those coffees.'

'What's wrong?' he said, handing her one of the cups.

She told him that Peter Conway had called Jake using a private phone number.

'Bloody hell. How did he get a phone?' asked Tristan, feeling shock, but also relief that this wasn't anything to do with Kate's sobriety. 'Is Jake okay?'

'He's fine. Apparently he called Jake to tell him that he loved him, and that he wished he'd been a better father to him.' Tristan didn't know how to respond to this, so he just raised an eyebrow.

'And then I called Peter. On that number. . . He sounded surprised to hear my voice, and maudlin. His voice was all slurred from the medication. He had five teeth extracted. Peter said that a mobile phone fell into his lap, quite literally, when he was at the dentist's.'

'The prison dentist?'

'Yeah. There was a note inside from a journalist asking her to call him.'

'The note was signed?'

'No. Peter said the note was anonymous, and when I asked him if he called the number, he said no. Then later he said, "Some bitch wants my voice. Wants a piece of me."'

'Wants him to go on record, or do an interview?'

'Why else would someone smuggle a phone to him? Unless it was drug related.'

'Or someone wants to break him out again?'

'I don't think it's that. God, I hope not . . .' Kate took a sip of her coffee, and Tristan could understand why she hadn't slept. The thought of Peter Conway escaping. Again. Kate went on, 'After I called him, I rang the governor at Wakefield prison. Well, I left a message with the prison governor, alerting them to the fact Peter Conway has a phone.' She drank more of her coffee. 'I asked Peter about Janey Macklin.'

'And?' asked Tristan hopefully.

Kate shook her head. 'I don't know if he was genuinely out of it on the phone, or if he was giving me the runaround, but he was vague and didn't deny it, but that's when he ended the call. I tried to call back, but the phone was switched off.'

'If he was training to be a police officer back then, then he must have heard about the case. It was high profile enough to warrant a *Crimewatch* reconstruction on TV.'

'And back then there were only four TV channels. No internet. He must have been aware of it . . . Just before you got back, I had a phone call from the governor at Wakefield. He told me that Peter collapsed in his cell in the early hours of the morning and he's been taken to hospital and he's in intensive care. Blood poisoning and septic shock. He said Peter's cell was searched, but they didn't find anything.'

'Shit. Mobile phones are pretty valuable in prison. Both to prisoners and the guards.'

Kate nodded. 'I know. I tried the number again this morning. It's switched off.'

'Someone else could have the phone?'

'Yes, it could have been traded with another prisoner or a guard.'

Tristan hesitated, not knowing how to phrase his next question. 'I know intensive care means it's serious, but how serious is it for Peter?'

'Could he die? Yes. It's not looking good.'

'Will Jake want to see him?'

Kate stared at the table. Thinking. 'I don't know. I think, yes.'

'Is he conscious?'

'I don't know.'

'If Jake goes to see him, would you be willing to go, too? If only for the case. You could ask him about Janey.' Kate crossed her arms. Tristan could see she didn't look happy at the idea. 'I know this is a big ask. But you have the kind of access to him no one else can get.'

24

On Sunday morning, Psycho Eyes was on duty in the small exercise yard reserved for vulnerable inmates, and he watched through the small glass window as Thomas Black was wheeled into the yard.

It had taken two years for Black to go from a large, athletic man who'd had to be restrained by three or four big guards on several occasions to this sad little sack of skin in a wheelchair. Psycho had seen him a week ago, before the New Year, and today, Black looked even smaller, bundled up in a huge fleece coat. His skinny legs dangling over the edge of the wheelchair were clad in leggings, and his feet were topped with giant tartan slippers.

When Black was alone, Psycho pulled on his coat and left the guard station.

'Morning,' he said to Black.

'Is it?' croaked Black in return. He brought up a withered hand and removed his enormous black sunglasses. He blinked in the pale winter light. His eyes seemed to protrude from his sunken face, and they reminded Psycho of the giant gobstopper sweets he used to buy with his pocket money when he was a boy. A bird chirruped and landed on the thin net covering the enclosed courtyard. 'Fuck off!' yelled Black, and the bird flew away. 'One of them shit on me yesterday,' he added to Psycho.

'Did the bird have a good aim?'

Black looked at him and made a hissing sound, baring his teeth, which seemed to protrude from his mouth as prominently as his eyes did from his face.

'Shat right on the top of me 'ead.' Black smacked his lips and closed his eyes against the light. 'What do you want?' he added, opening his left eye.

'You heard about Peter Conway?'

'He's a multiple murderer? That's old news.'

'No. Took a nasty tumble. He's got blood poisoning from a gum infection, and he's in intensive care.'

'Poor bastard. Really?' replied Thomas.

'You've been talking to Conway a bit lately?' said Psycho.

'Not really. Just two old fucks passing the time of day.'

'Know anything about Conway having a phone?'

'Nope.'

'A journalist wants to talk to him.'

'Bollocks.'

'It's not.'

'Then why are you asking me?' said Black.

Psycho moved closer. ''Cos I've got the phone,' he murmured. 'It was smuggled into Conway's last dentist appointment.'

Black rolled his eyes. 'Talk normally. Do you know how suspicious you look?'

Psycho turned his back on the guard's window, which was empty, but there was a security camera inside.

'I've spoken to the journalist. She's investigating the disappearance of a girl called Janey Macklin outside The Jug public house in King's Cross.' Black's face remained impassive. 'You had a pen pal, Judith Leary, and you wrote in a letter to her that you saw Peter Conway around the same time in the same pub, with young girls, buying them drinks.'

'Go on.'

'Go on? That's it.'

'That's not it . . .' He squinted up. 'Do you think you have eyes that make you look like a psycho?'

'There are worse things people can say about you.'

'I've always thought your eyes are a bit vague. Perhaps indicating a slight retardation.'

'Listen, you old fuck. Do you want to make some money? Do you want enhanced privileges? A little dicky bird tells me you want to have your chemo in another hospital.'

'Yes. I'd pay handsomely for a window. That's all I want. A window with a view. And a hospital room better equipped for my needs. But you can't make that happen. I don't want to talk to the monkey; I want to talk to the organ grinder.'

'This journalist is willing to pay a lot of money to get an interview with you on the phone. You'd have to sign away the rights to them using the recording.'

'How do they know I have anything worth selling?' snarled Thomas.

'Have you? Do you know where Janey Macklin's body is?'

'Possibly. If this journalist can get me what I want.'

'The governor is easily persuaded. He's not the cleanest,' said Psycho.

Thomas put his shades back on and sighed. 'Good to know.'

'I have the phone in my pocket. Fully charged. I found it in Conway's cell. They spoke to him twice. The journalist is on speed dial. You just need to press one.'

'And she's expecting my call?'

'No. I wanted to ask you first. I wouldn't presume to make an arrangement without your consent.'

'Consent,' repeated Black with a hiss.

'Why is that funny?'

'Do I look like I'm *consenting* to anything in my life?' he said, spreading his arms to indicate the chair and where they were. Psycho crouched down and peered underneath his wheelchair, where his catheter bag hung, along with an IV line with his meds. 'What the fuck are you doing? Get out of it!' he shouted. It was the first time Psycho had heard distress in Black's voice.

Psycho reached up and pushed the mobile phone into the folds of his jacket, and his hand brushed against Black's. It felt dry, warm, and scaly, like a snake.

Psycho recoiled and stood up. 'Are they searching you?'

'Not if they can help it. The last time was a newbie, and as he was poking about under my chair, one of my bags overflowed.' Black gave that same evil hissing laugh again.

'Enjoy the sunshine,' said Psycho, and he returned to his

post in the booth behind the window. He'd done his part, and it took a long time for him to shake off the nausea from being close to Black.

25

On Monday morning Kate and Tristan went to meet Forrest. Maddie had been due to attend the meeting but left a voicemail an hour before, saying she'd unexpectedly been called into the office.

'Please be respectful of Forrest. He's also your client,' she'd added, with obvious pain in her voice, before signing off. Kate and Tristan were a little intrigued by this. At no point had they thought Forrest was the client.

'Can you believe these houses fetch a million each?' said Tristan as they walked up Westmoor Avenue in Barnes, West London, where Maddie lived with Forrest.

'I can, unfortunately,' said Kate. They'd passed an estate agent on their walk from the train station. It was a charming suburban street of terraced houses, but none looked worth the £1 million price tag.

'I have sleepless nights about my mortgage, and it's tiny in comparison.'

Kate had been through so much in her life, she never

thought or worried about her mortgage. She was just wondering if this was a good or bad thing when they reached Number 17, where Forrest lived.

It had a tiny concrete front yard strip with a storage unit adorned with padlocks. The blinds were down on all the windows, but Forrest opened the door before they could ring the bell.

'Morning, Kate and Tristan!' he said with a broad smile, announcing their names as if he were a radio DJ. He was rail thin and dressed for a trip on a sailing boat: white shorts, a stripy blue-and-white T-shirt, and blue moccasins with white braiding. Kate mused that people who dressed like this rarely had their own boat or even an invitation to go on one. His strawberry-blond hair was long and brushed back off his forehead, and he had very fair eyelashes and eyebrows, so fair that they were almost as white as an albino's, but his skin, in contrast, was a little leathery and florid. He held out his hand to shake theirs. 'Come in, come in out of the cold. I've just made a cafetière of coffee. Would you care for a cup?' He spoke carefully, the way people did when they'd spent a lot of time trying to eradicate a regional accent.

He left them in a large living room, heaving with bookcases and Chesterfield furniture in green leather studded with buttons. A desk in the corner had a matching legal lamp with a green glass shade. On the wall above were some framed photos of Forrest as a young actor. Three of the photos looked like they were from the same theatre production, of Forrest with short black hair, wearing a baggy shirt and gesticulating towards some smoke; in another, he smiled animatedly at an older actress Kate recognised. In the third, he was carrying a spear and wearing a red velvet doublet with beautiful beading as he stood sentry at a door. Kate estimated he had been in his early twenties.

'Ah, you've found my ego wall,' said Forrest, pushing open the door with his right moccasin and carrying a tray with a steaming cafetière of coffee, china cups, and some biscuits. He put it down on the coffee table between the two sofas and came to join them.

'How long were you an actor?' asked Tristan.

'Still am!' he said with mock indignation. 'That was me in *Henry V* at the National Theatre. I did a season there; when was it? Must be twenty-four years ago now.'

'The National Theatre on the South Bank?' asked Tristan.

'There's only one! Fabulous, it was. One of the best seasons.'

'The building is interesting.'

'Yes, it hums and resonates. All those famous actors who have graced the stages.'

'I meant more the brutalist architecture,' said Tristan. 'Like the Golden Lane Estate where you grew up.'

The smile slid off Forrest's face. 'That's a bit too much concrete for my liking. Like being buried.'

'Golden Lane or the National Theatre?' asked Kate.

Forrest hitched up his smile again. 'It's such a long time ago. I also did some telly. *Midsomer Murders*; I played a postman in *Bergerac*, one of my first tellies. You might not know *Bergerac*, the cop show set on Jersey?' he added to Tristan.

'My mum loved it,' said Tristan.

'That makes us feel old,' said Forrest to Kate. For some

reason, Kate didn't like the way he included her, but she smiled and nodded in agreement. She turned her attention to the bookcases. They were filled chiefly with hardback fiction titles in a variety of genres. 'The books pretty much all belong to Mads.' Kate wondered if Forrest was really this laid-back or if he really didn't think this meeting would be a big deal. It put Kate on her guard, and she could see Tristan felt the same way. 'Maddie's been in publishing for the past twenty years, and she's acquired quite the collection of first editions.'

'Maddie left a message to say she couldn't be here,' Tristan said when they all sat down.

'Yes, Fidelis is having client problems. Maddie's been brought in to soothe things, as per always. Otherwise, she'd be here. Fidelis isn't blessed with tact. You didn't hear that from me.' He tapped his nose and winked. He checked his watch. 'That should be nicely brewed.' He pushed down the coffee plunger. 'How's the flat?'

'It's very nice,' said Kate.

'Anything you need, just ask. I have one hundred percent positive feedback as the Superhost on Old Percy. That's what I call the flat.'

'Thank you,' said Kate as he handed her a coffee.

'We heard it was your idea to hire us and research the Janey Macklin case,' said Tristan, taking his cup.

'No! No. It was Maddie's idea. Most of Fidelis's great ideas come from Mads. I had this connection to the Janey Macklin case, writing for *Real Crime*.'

'How did you come to do that?' asked Kate.

'I dabble in a little journalism when I'm resting. *Real Crime* takes in open submissions for articles.'

'You obtained copies of the Thomas Black letters from your friend Judith, where Janey Macklin is named, and your childhood best friend was convicted and then released from prison over Janey Macklin's disappearance. That's more of a connection to the case.'

Forrest hesitated and took out his mobile phone. 'I forgot to say that Mads would like me to record this meeting. For her records.'

He set it recording and put it on the table, looking somewhat awkward. Tristan took out his mobile phone.

'Could we do the same?' he said, placing it on the table next to the tray of coffee.

Forrest eyed it and then pulled a face, a sort of awkward grin. 'Ah. Eek. I'm not sure that's allowed,' he said.

'Allowed?'

'Mads mentioned that you haven't yet signed an NDA. Which you really need to do. Until then, all personal recordings with me and the facts of this case are off-limits.'

Tristan glanced at Kate. As yet, they hadn't been sent an NDA.

'I think Maddie or Fidelis would need to bring this up with us,' said Kate. The atmosphere in the room became frosty.

'This is from Maddie,' said Forrest.

'We need to be able to take notes or a record of our investigations.'

'I don't think you're investigating me,' he said, his demeanour changing. His lip curled, and he seemed combative. 'I'm giving you my time. Helping you.'

'Yes, of course. And we greatly appreciate you giving us

your time. Your help in connection to this case will be so valuable,' said Kate, deciding to kill him with kindness. 'And, of course, everything we find, record, or write down remains the property of the client, of which you are also.' This wasn't technically true, but she could see that Forrest needed to hear it.

He eyed Tristan's phone. 'Okay. Well, as long as we have that established.'

'Thank you. How would you describe Judith Leary's relationship with Thomas Black?'

'Ah. Judith. She would get attached to people. She visited prisons with a theatre group, back in the early nineties, and she formed a friendship with him. Through letters, and she visited him a few times in prison,' said Forrest.

'Was The Jug your local pub?' asked Tristan.

'It wasn't local to where I lived, but yes, I would go there.' He leaned down under the coffee table and picked up a newspaper. 'Have you seen this?'

It was a copy of the *Mirror* newspaper. Kate could see he had the corner of a page turned down in preparation. He opened it to the fourth page, and held it out. The headline across the top read:

NINE ELMS CANNIBAL HAS JUST DAYS TO LIVE

In the article there was a cluster of heavily blurred photos, taken through the window of a room on the ground floor of the hospital, of Peter Conway lying in a bed surrounded by machines, a nurse with a pixelated face leaning over him. And another of the same nurse with a doctor consulting a chart. In the centre was a close-up photo. This time, it was very clear of Peter Conway's face staring up at the camera from behind an oxygen mask. His eyes were open.

'Terrible, isn't it? The way the press intrudes,' said Forrest, pursing his lips and shaking his head.

'I've seen it,' said Kate. This wasn't true, but she didn't want to show she was on the back foot. Tristan glanced at her, and she could see he hadn't seen this, either. In the close-up photo, it looked like the photographer had managed to get into the intensive care unit and stick a camera inches from his face. The governor of HMP Wakefield was keeping in touch with Kate and Jake via their solicitor to say that Peter's condition was stable but unresponsive. The 'days to live' headline hadn't been mentioned, but Jake was going to book a flight back to the UK.

'I know all about the Nine Elms Cannibal case. Who doesn't?' said Forrest, looking Kate up and down. 'And I read *No Son of Mine*, the book by Conway's mother. I also have my own Peter Conway story.' He eyed the two phones recording. 'Do you want to hear it?'

26

'It was a Friday night. We were up at The Jug. Myself, Roland Hacker, and Robert Driscoll,' said Forrest. He spoke quietly, and the atmosphere in the room suddenly turned cold.

'Can you remember the date?' asked Kate.

'No. It was a few weeks before Christmas, the Christmas Janey Macklin went missing in 1988. It was early November; it might have been Guy Fawkes night. It's late, and packed with people, and I went to the loo. The toilets there were bloody horrible in this freezing bit out the back, like a prewar fabricated lean-to. It stank even in the cold. I went to the cubicle in the middle of three. There was a tiny hole in the wall between my cubicle and the one on the end. Someone had made it with a screwdriver so they could spy on the next occupant.'

'Like some kind of gay cruising?' asked Tristan.

'I suppose so, yeah. I was chewing gum, and I took it out of my mouth and stuck it in the hole. Anyway. I was there, and I heard this whimpering noise. And a young girl's voice, saying, "That's enough. It hurts." But her voice was muffled, and she sounded like she was panicking. I don't know why, but I took the piece of chewing-gum out of the hole . . . and looked through.' Forrest hesitated and wiped his brow.

'What did you see?' asked Kate.

'Peter Conway. He was sitting fully clothed on the toilet, and a young girl had her back to him standing up. She was very skinny. She was wearing red, shiny, tight leggings, and her T-shirt was bunched up around her neck. She wasn't wearing a bra. Her hair was long and a bit wavy and messy . . . He was running his lips over her back and biting her. He had one of his hands down the front of her leggings . . . and with the other hand, he was . . .' Forrest looked like he was still in shock from the experience.

'He was what?' asked Kate.

'Masturbating.'

Kate shuddered. 'Did he bite her hard enough to draw blood?'

'Yes. She was squealing.'

'How long did you watch?'

'I don't know. Not long. He seemed to give the girl one last bite, really hard, and hold on with his teeth. She was trying to pull away, and she cried out proper loud. Her blood was on her back and running down his chin. He held on to her like a dog with a chew toy, and her skin was stretching . . . still between his teeth. And then he ejaculated. And he let go of her.'

Kate felt Tristan glance over at her, but she kept her eyes on Forrest.

'Do you think it was consenting if they were in a toilet cubicle in the men's toilets?' asked Tristan.

'I don't know if *consenting* is the right word. She didn't look old enough to give consent. There was this moment where they, he, finished. Conway was cleaning himself up, and the girl was sort of turning around in the small space and mopping the wound with tissue. He gave her some money, what looked like a few notes rolled up. One was a twenty-pound note. A lot of money back then.'

'How old was she, do you think?' asked Tristan.

'Young. Fourteen, fifteen.'

'And it was definitely Peter Conway?' Kate asked.

Forrest was quiet for a long moment.

'The young girl left the cubicle first. I was still looking through the hole, and suddenly, the man crouched down, facing me, looking right at me . . .' Forrest's voice was shaking. 'The lights were very bright in those toilets. I remember his face. The brown eyes. He stared at me, and I'll never forget what he said.

'"Enjoy the show, did you?" And I was so stupid and young, and I said, "Yeah."' Forrest put his head in his hands. 'This poor young girl was being bitten, and I said I'd enjoyed the show.'

'How old were you?'

'Seventeen. I said it because I was scared to say anything else. He laughed and then left the cubicle. Washed his hands and left the toilets. I waited a few minutes, until I thought the coast was clear.'

'Did you tell anyone else about this?'

'No. I mean, it was King's Cross back in the 1980s. There

were tons of weirdos around. Prostitutes on every corner, or sex workers, as we now say. I saw him in The Jug a couple more times over the next few weeks, drinking on his own. Thank God he never knew what I looked like, so he didn't pay me much attention. It's just that Janey and her sister, Maxine, used to be at the pub, often on a Friday night when her mum finished cleaning.'

'Did you ever see Peter approaching Janey or Maxine? Or any other young girls?'

'There was this one time. It was a Friday night, quite early. Janey and Maxine used to play this *Space Invaders* game that was built into a glass table. The tabletop was the screen. It wasn't like a touch screen – there was a TV monitor under the glass. I once saw Peter Conway at the bar waiting to get a drink, and he went over to the girls as they played, and he watched. They didn't pay him much attention. At the time, it was all part of the rough and tumble of life back then. Poor people in poor circumstances. It was only when the whole Nine Elms Cannibal thing came out a few years later that I knew it was him I'd seen.'

'Was Peter Conway ever wearing a policeman's uniform when he drank in The Jug?' asked Kate, thinking back to the contents of Thomas Black's letter.

'No! Anyone would have been mad to wear a copper's uniform in that pub. This was in the late eighties. Lots of unrest. People hated the police.'

Kate nodded. 'And the night that Janey went missing. Where were you?'

'I was out at a club. Yes. That's what I told the police. I

spoke to the police voluntarily back then, because I was friends with Robert Driscoll. In his sphere.'

'Close friends.'

'Yes.'

'Which club?'

Forrest laughed. 'It's getting on for thirty years.'

'And yet you remember so much else in detail.'

'I was at the Astoria nightclub in Soho. It's no longer there, sadly. It was knocked down a few years ago.'

'Where did you first meet Robert Driscoll?'

'Um. That's a good question . . . I'm not sure.'

'Robert told us you met at the Old Street Youth Club.'

'Yes, of course. Yes. We met there, probably when we were fourteen.'

'Maddie didn't mention the *Big Issue* article?' asked Tristan, taking it out of his bag. He placed it on the table.

Forrest stared at it, clearly trying to work out what the right answer was. 'She did not.'

'We've spoken to Robert.'

'Sorry. Yes, she did. She did tell me about the article. She wasn't happy at being accosted.'

'We didn't accost her,' said Kate. 'We haven't been able to get in contact with Roland Hacker. Do you know where he is?'

'I really don't. A few months after Robert went down, Roland went off travelling.'

'Where?'

'Australia, Japan, India. I think he was away for a few years. He did all sorts of odd jobs. It hit him hard, what happened to Robert.'

'How did it hit you?' asked Tristan. Forrest seemed surprised at the question.

'Badly, of course.'

'But when Robert was put in prison, you went off and made something of your life. You changed your name. Changed how you spoke.'

'I changed my name because Fred Parker was taken with Equity, the actors' union. I then made it official legally. But the first impetus in doing that was my work . . .' He frowned and sat back. 'And also it was a huge kick up the arse what happened to Rob, Robert. His life was taken away, and I knew I wanted to live mine, so I made it happen. I also had elocution lessons, as most actors do.'

'Do you think Robert did it?' asked Tristan.

'No. I don't. And a court of law have also made that decision.'

'So why aren't you and Robert back friends?' asked Kate. 'He's innocent.'

Forrest was looking pained at all the questions being fired at him. 'People move on. He was gone for eight years. By the time he came out, I had a different life.'

'Did Roland keep in contact with you before he went travelling?'

'At first, I had a few letters from him. Then he wrote to say he was coming home.'

'When was this?' asked Tristan.

Forrest ran his hands through his hair. 'Maybe four years after it all, so 1993, maybe '94. He said he wanted to come back and get a job and settle down.'

'Did you ever hear from him again?'

'No. But I know he came back. I saw him one day, on a Tube train. It was just before the election in 1997. He was wearing a suit. He'd chopped off all his hair, and he looked miserable. He didn't see me. It wasn't my usual Tube train; well, I was going for a casting in Watford. Not the kind of place I usually went for castings. I should have gone over to him and said hello, but it was a bit of my past I didn't want to reopen. I had a new life, far away from Victoria House and Golden Lane.'

27

Kate and Tristan left Forrest's house and walked back to the train station in silence for a few minutes.

'What did you think of all that?' asked Kate.

'I want to listen to it again,' said Tristan, holding up his phone.

'I know.'

'Is it convenient?'

'How?'

'He *happened* to spy on Peter Conway biting a young girl in the toilets at The Jug.'

'So much stuff in the Peter Conway police case file has been made public over the years . . . When he was arrested and interviewed, he boasted about picking up young girls, young sex workers, in bars and around train stations in London and taking them into the toilets or finding an underpass, and he liked to bite them. And we have those letters from Thomas Black to Judith Leary where he talks about seeing Peter in The Jug a few weeks before Janey went missing.'

'Forrest could be making it up to lead us more to Peter Conway being the culprit.'

'Yes, but what's that saying? *The simplest explanation is usually correct*? Peter Conway was an active serial killer between 1990 and 1995. He left Hendon in early 1989 and went to Manchester for a couple of years, where he killed Caitlyn Murray, who was sixteen. He came back to London in 1991. Shelley Norris was the second victim we know of; she was seventeen and dumped in a junkyard on Nine Elms Lane. Dawn Brockhurst, his third victim, was fifteen. Carla Martin was seventeen; Catherine Cahill was sixteen. They all looked younger than legal age. If Peter was seen in the area, isn't the logical conclusion that he abducted and killed Janey Macklin but managed to hide her body somewhere on the wasteland that was King's Cross?'

They reached the Barnes Bridge train station entrance, which was accessed by steps up to an old viaduct. They began to climb. It was cold and windy, and when they reached the platform, it was empty. The electronic board said the next train to Waterloo was in four minutes.

They sat under an awning, where a discarded copy of the *Mirror* was on the other end of the bench. Kate picked it up and turned to the article about Peter Conway: **NINE ELMS CANNIBAL HAS JUST DAYS TO LIVE**. The close-up photo of Peter Conway's face stared out at her.

'Bloody hell. I don't know if I'll ever escape this,' she said. The photo was the first time she'd seen him in close-up for years. He was so old, and yet it was like the young Peter

Conway was staring out at her from inside a mask of prosthetic old make-up. A three-inch scar above his left eye was visible, even amongst the wrinkles. It was a clear curving line. Kate closed her eyes, and the memory of the night she gave him that scar returned to her. The night she cracked the case and worked out that he was the Nine Elms Cannibal.

———

'Kate!' She heard Tristan say her name, and saw that their train was now waiting on the platform, with its doors open, and he was standing next to the door. 'This is our train.' They boarded just as the doors closed. Only a few seats were taken, and they sat far down the carriage. 'Are you okay?'

'It's just the inevitability of it all. I'm going to have to visit him. Peter Conway. Jake wants to fly back to see him. None of what Forrest told us is a surprise. It's just tough when it's the father of your child. I have to separate Jake from Peter. And I've managed. I don't think he's like his father in any way. But now this case comes along. And then Peter is dying. It feels like there's no boundaries, and it's all bleeding together into one.'

'I can't begin to imagine how this feels. Can I ask you something?' Tristan looked uncomfortable, like he wanted to be anywhere but here, sitting next to her on the train.

'Did he ever bite me?'

'I'm sorry. That's really . . .'

'No. This is what we're investigating. You have to ask. No. The Nine Elms Cannibal never bit me. He was never violent. He was my boss, and I was a naive twenty-five-year-old who mistook an affair with her boss for finding her soulmate, and then, of course, it was all a lot worse than an affair at work.' Kate took a deep breath. Tristan pulled out a packet of tissues.

'I don't need one. Thank you. I've shed so many tears over the years for this. I decided a long time ago I wouldn't give any more.'

Tristan put the packet of tissues back in his pocket. The train whizzed through the London suburbs, ducking in and out of bridges and across viaducts.

'If it is Peter Conway who killed Janey Macklin, we're running out of time.'

'We're running out of time to talk to him. We're not running out of time to find her body . . . if there's a body to find.'

———

Kate and Tristan bought sandwiches at Waterloo and ate them back at the flat in Percy Circus with big cups of hot, sweet tea.

'This place doesn't want to warm up,' said Tristan, cranking up the thermostat on the wall in the living room. He tried the door on the locked cupboard. 'Some extra blankets would be good right now.'

Kate sat on the sofa, still wearing her coat, her hands cupped around her mug of tea. She felt a little better after some food.

'It's so quiet here, for central London. Do you think the flats above are empty?'

'This whole circle seems dead. Oh, there's a postman, poor bastard in this cold,' said Tristan as a small man wearing thick mittens, a woolly hat, and a winter coat and carrying a heavy postbag lumbered past the window with his head down. 'It's forecast to snow again later.'

'I want to find Roland Hacker. It's important that we talk to him,' said Kate.

Tristan pulled his coat and hat on and came to sit on the sofa. The sun broke out from behind the clouds and shone weakly through the window, casting the room in a silvery light that only helped show up the dust and damp patches on the walls.

'I checked with the credit scoring agencies and the DBS database. Social media. There's nothing.'

Kate stared out the window. The grey sky was heavy, like the clouds were ready to dump snow on the capital.

'Did you leave the case files on the floor?' she asked, noticing the two files piled one on top of the other next to the leg of the coffee table.

'No. You were still looking through them all when I went to bed last night,' said Tristan.

'I was reading Roland's statement to the police. He was at home with his parents on the night Janey went missing. He said they had a Christmas tradition of all wrapping presents together on December 23.'

'Is that a tradition? We all have to wrap presents,' said Tristan.

'No. It's just the way he phrased it, sounded so cosy and homely. Like they were a tight-knit unit, him and his mother and father. It just doesn't make sense that he left home and then cut off all contact with them.'

Kate went to pick up the files off the floor, but her phone rang. She didn't recognise the number. She answered and listened for a moment.

'Really? Thank you, Betty. We'll be over shortly.'

'What?' asked Tristan when she hung up.

'That was Betty Cohen, Doreen Macklin's next-door neighbour. Doreen returned home last night, and Maxine is with her. Apparently Doreen's been in America visiting, and they've both come back to pack up Doreen. She's moving.'

It started to snow when Kate and Tristan approached Victoria House. The afternoon was fading, and a few lights glowed in the windows on the top floor of the flats.

The concrete paving stones in the courtyard were shiny, and the gritty little snowflakes rattled as they blew around their feet. The *F* from the graffiti on the statue had been scrubbed away, but whoever did it had given up, so it now read 'UCK OSTERITY.'

The lift seemed colder than it was outside, and when they walked along the outside corridor to Doreen's flat at the end, Betty opened her front door and pounced on them.

'Hello, loves,' she said, folding her arms over her cardigan. She glanced side to side and then spoke sotto voce. 'Doreen arrived back at two in the morning, making no end of a racket. She's been in California with Maxine. It's lovely to see Maxine. Looks very well.' The next door opened, and a slight woman with a stylish short brown bob stepped out. She wore tight blue jeans and a beautiful royal-blue sweatshirt with white piping on the sleeves. She had a cigarette on the go and brought it to her lips, puffing at it with a wrinkly mouth.

'Is this them?' she asked, her eyes flashing angrily.

'Yeah, Doreen. These are the detectives I was telling you about,' said Betty, suddenly all smiles.

'Look, I don't mean no offence, but I don't want to dredge up the past. I'm in a good place. I'm moving away from here.'

Kate was surprised Doreen looked so elegant. In her mind, she'd seen someone else entirely, and she felt a bit guilty for her prejudice.

'Hello, Doreen. I'm Tristan Harper. I work with my colleague here, Kate Marshall,' he said, holding out his hand. Doreen seemed to clock how handsome and tall he was.

'Hello,' she said, smiling. Her teeth were crooked, but Kate wondered if she'd just had them whitened. Kate leaned over and shook hands. She didn't get quite as broad a smile as Doreen had bestowed on Tristan.

'We'd like to talk to you about your daughter Janey's disappearance.'

At the mention of Janey, Doreen seemed to deflate. Her poise vanished, and she looked her age. 'Who's hired you?'

'Sorry. I couldn't remember the name of your agency,' said Betty.

'It was on the card we gave you. We're working for a creative agency who wants to make a true crime project about Janey's disappearance. And, of course, we'd like to solve the case.'

'That would mean finding her, wouldn't it? It's been thirty years. She's dead,' said Doreen. The finality in her voice and the sad lost look on her face broke Kate's heart.

Speaking to Janey's mother suddenly brought the case more into focus on the victims' feelings. They were all silent on the landing as snowflakes whirled around them.

'Could we just talk to you?' said Tristan. 'Ask some questions, and make sure we have the facts straight? We really won't take up a lot of your time.'

Doreen sighed.

'Okay. Just the two of you . . . I'll catch up with you later, Betty.'

Betty's face gave a flash of annoyance that she wouldn't be included. She nodded and then went back into her flat.

Tristan and Kate followed Doreen out of the Arctic cold and into the warm.

28

'I bet she's already on the other side of the wall with a glass against her ear,' said Doreen as she shut the door against the snow. 'You can hang your coats up here.' She indicated a row of hooks on the wall.

The flat stank of stale cigarettes. It had the same layout as Betty and Stan's. The front door led past a small kitchen, where every counter-top space was filled with shopping bags, and into a big living room. A thin woman, whom Kate recognised as Maxine, sat on the sofa watching *Countdown* on TV. The ceiling was stained yellow with nicotine, and the patch was particularly dark above the sofa where Maxine was sitting.

Doreen grabbed the remote and pressed mute. 'Maxine, these detectives want to talk to us about your sister.'

'Who hired you?' asked Maxine. 'Do you have any leads? Any new information?' She spoke with an American accent, which still had a hint of British in her vowels, but she was very polished with a smart purple trouser suit in loose fabric and lots of silver jewellery. Her long hair was sleek and straightened.

Tristan explained who'd hired them. 'We believe that Janey could have been the victim of a . . . a known serial murderer,' he said. Kate could see how uncomfortable it made him to say this to them.

'A serial murderer?' repeated Doreen. She sank onto a small leather pouffe by a bookshelf where the shelves were covered in dead spider plants, and she lit up a cigarette.

'I need to open the window,' said Maxine, waving her arm and getting up. She went to the window overlooking the balcony and slid up the whole pane of glass, which looked like it lifted on a counterweight. A cold blast of air rushed into the smoky flat, and a few snowflakes skittered across the carpet.

'Not that much! You're letting in a bloody freezing gale!' said Doreen, jumping up and pushing the window back down.

'You have no air in here, and you smoke so much.'

'Well, sorry, I ain't got air-conditioning like you have at home!' Doreen adjusted the window so there was the tiniest sliver to let the air in.

'I'm sorry if that was blunt to just come out with it,' said Tristan.

'No. I'm sorry. I think we're both jet lagged,' said Maxine, coming to sit back down. Kate noticed a photo on the table beside her, taken of Janey and Maxine dressed in leotards and tutus at a dance recital.

Doreen went back to the little pouffe and perched. She closed her eyes for a second, shaking her head.

Maxine followed Kate's gaze to the photo. 'Janey was always a better dancer than me.'

'Was this a dance school?' asked Kate.

'Yes. The Glenda La Froy Dance School for Girls,' said Maxine, imitating a matronly voice. 'Miss La Froy was a battle-axe.'

'She was also a professional ballet dancer, and The Corporation paid for your tuition,' said Doreen, waggling her finger at Maxine. 'Don't say I never let you girls do anything.'

Maxine rolled her eyes and crossed her arms. Kate and Tristan were silent.

'The weather was like this, the night Janey went missing' said Doreen, gesturing to the window with her lit cigarette. 'I used to drink too much. And after I finished my cleaning work at The Jug, I'd have a few jars. More than a few, some nights. The girls would meet me there after school or after their dance classes. Ain't that right, Maxine?'

Maxine nodded. They all watched Doreen's face, etched with pain.

'You did your best. Times were tough with money.' Maxine seemed eager not to blame her mother.

'Money.' Doreen laughed bitterly. 'I've spent my life worrying about it. Not having it. Did old nosy parker next door tell you I won the lottery?'

'Yes,' said Tristan.

'A hundred and fifty grand, I won on a scratch card,' she said, tapping her cigarette into an ashtray on the shelf. 'I've cleared me debts. Mortgage. I can sell this place, and I'll be quite well off with my pension, too. And you know what? I don't feel any different. I spent so many years thinking money would solve my problems.'

Doreen got up and went to the window. She looked out over the London skyline.

'For a while after she went missing, I could sense she was still alive . . . and then, one day, I got this terrible pain in my chest, and I knew she was gone. She's dead. Maxine has asked me to go to America to live, but I don't know if I can, knowing Janey might still be out there.' She turned back to Kate and Tristan. 'Who was this multiple murderer? That's fancy talk for *serial killer*?' she said wearily.

'His name is Peter Conway,' said Kate. She withdrew a printout from a folder in her bag. It was Peter Conway's police warrant card from 1989. 'This was taken a few months after Janey went missing.'

Doreen came to look at the photo.

'He was a copper?' she asked, shocked.

'He was training in Hendon when Janey went missing, and shortly afterwards, he became a police officer. Do you recognise him? Did you ever see him at The Jug?'

'I dunno, there were a lot of fellas and a lot of late nights in The Jug back then. What do you think, Maxine?'

Tristan got up and handed the picture to Maxine. She picked up her glasses from the table and slipped them on. Her eyes went wide.

'Yes. I do remember him,' she said, handing back the photo.

'You do?' asked Doreen, her cigarette frozen in midair.

'Did you see him in The Jug?' asked Kate.

Maxine nodded. 'Me and Janey used to like to play this

Space Invaders game in The Jug. It was set into a table so we could sit with our Coke and crisps and play. Janey loved it, but we didn't often have the money to play. It took five-pence coins.'

It sounded odd to hear Maxine say this in an American accent.

'She wanted money for that game the night she went missing. I said no to her,' said Doreen, breaking down in tears.

Maxine got up and went to her, crouching down beside her mother and holding her hand. 'Mum, it's okay.'

'It's not, Maxine. It fucking well ain't,' she snapped, shrugging her off. Maxine stood up and crossed her arms. Almost standing sentry over her mother.

'It used to be a thing when you wanted to play *Space Invaders*, and someone else was playing, you'd put down your five pence on the edge of the table. Like with billiards – I mean snooker. This one time, an older boy was playing the game, and Janey put down her money. He played through and then used her coin for the next game. Janey stood up to him, but he got threatening with her. At this point, that man came over and told the boy off. He slapped the kid around the head. The kid must have been sixteen or so. Told him to stop picking on young girls. I remember seeing how hard he hit him. It was a big ringing slap, and this kid's drool splattered on the carpet. You know, with the force of it. He gave Janey a few five-pence pieces, grabbed the kid by his neck, and dragged him off.'

'Did anyone do anything?' asked Tristan.

'It was The Jug. It was rough; argy-bargy like that

happened all the time,' said Doreen. 'But there was like, a code, not to get rough with any young girls or kids.'

'Did young girls and kids go there?'

'Sometimes.'

'Were there any kids there on their own?'

'It was a different time. People weren't as . . .'

'We had a lot more freedom as kids back then,' said Maxine kindly.

'Yeah. I was just with Maxine in California, and her kids, my grandchildren . . .' Doreen smiled. 'They're grown up now, but they didn't play out on the street by themselves when they were younger.'

'San Luis Obispo is very safe, but no, they didn't. And I've always been scared to let them out of my sight.'

There was an awkward moment between Maxine and Doreen.

'Okay, so if we can go back, Maxine. The man you think was Peter Conway stuck up for you and Maxine with this kid on the *Space Invaders* game. What happened next?' asked Kate.

'After he helped us?' said Maxine.

'Yes.'

'I don't know. Maybe he went to the bar to order a drink. We just wanted to play *Space Invaders*.'

'What date was this?' asked Tristan.

'I'm sorry. I can't remember exactly.'

'Was it near to the time Janey went missing?'

Maxine had to think. 'It was . . . maybe a month or so before she went missing. It would have been a Friday. That was the day we used to go there.'

'Did you see him again?'

Maxine nodded. 'I think so, not to talk to, but I might have seen him again from a distance.'

Kate thought about their meeting with Forrest and how he'd seen Peter in The Jug. 'Did you ever see Robert Driscoll and his friends in The Jug?'

'Yes,' said Doreen. 'Often. Though if you ask me, I don't think Robert Driscoll had it in him.'

'What do you mean?' said Kate.

'Well, to abduct Janey. And hide her, for thirty years. I always thought he was a bit of a pansy.'

'Mum,' said Maxine with a warning tone in her voice.

'Well, that's what we used to say! He worked at Reynolds newsagent. He was always a bit sickly. Jack, who owned Reynolds, used to think he was robbing gay mags on the sly. Him and that Fred, we all thought they were, you know, carrying on.'

'Are you saying you thought Robert Driscoll and Fred Parker were gay?'

'That was the rumour,' said Doreen.

'Mum, I think if you look back on that now with today's perspective, they were just a bit different. Not into football. They liked to do those art projects at the youth club.'

'And they used to drink Babycham,' said Doreen. 'Up The Jug. Robert and Fred used to order bloody Babycham. They was asking for a good kicking. And Fred used to work in the pub downstairs here. He was the manager for a few months, around the time Janey went missing. Although it wasn't a lot to manage. Sometimes I used to go down for a jar or two. You kids weren't mad on it, were you?'

'There weren't any good games. I remember it was quite a stuffy old place. They used to serve awful food,' said Maxine.

'It still hasn't changed, Maxine. Everything done in the microwave. A lot of the old boys who lived alone would go down there for a pie and a pint.'

'Did Jack Reynolds go there a lot?'

'He was always there, for his dinner most nights. His wife died back in 1986, and there was no one to cook his dinner.' Doreen tapped her cigarette. 'I know the police searched Reynolds with sniffer dogs and they picked up Janey's scent. But that was 'cos of the scarf she dropped there. Isn't that right, Maxine?'

Maxine nodded.

Kate and Tristan had agreed not to mention that the police were testing the blood sample found in the pipe in the yard behind Reynolds. 'Yes,' said Doreen. 'But I don't think Jack had anything to do with it. Jack was a sad, broken old man in the years after his wife died. He couldn't have fought his way out of a wet paper bag.'

'When did Forrest, Fred, leave working at the pub downstairs?' asked Kate.

'I dunno.'

'I think it was a few weeks after Janey went missing,' said Maxine. 'I think Roland got drunk and got into a fight with Fred. A load of glasses got broken, and the management heard about it and he got the boot.'

'Roland could get a bit lairy when he was drunk.'

'How do you mean?' asked Tristan.

'Roland liked a drink. He could get out of hand, mouthy.

Sometimes, he got himself in fights. Robert and Fred would always run in the other direction when he did.'

'Do you have any idea where Roland is now?'

'Now? God no. I knew his mum and dad, Shelia and Paul, a bit before they died. Just to say hello. When Robert went to prison, Fred went to drama school, and Roland drifted. He was on the dole and drinking. He was barred from the social club downstairs, and The Jug. I think a few other boozers. He decided to jack it all in and travel for a few years, which he did, and then he came back and cut off Shelia, Paul, and everyone around him. They never heard from him again. Nor did anyone else. Then Shelia and Paul got ill, and they both died within a few months of each other. Heartbroken. That must have been 1995 or '96.'

'Did they try and find him?' asked Tristan.

''Course they did. But he was an adult. There was rumours he went up north, or he never came back.'

'We spoke to Fred earlier today. He says he saw Roland on the Tube in 1997. Near Watford. He said Roland was wearing a suit.'

Doreen shrugged and took out another cigarette. 'Maybe he did, then. Janey going missing affected a lot of people around here, not only us. We were part of a community . . .' She lit up, stared out the window, and then sighed. frowned. 'I'm very tired. I think I need to go and lie down.'

'Can I just ask one more question? Robert was arrested for Janey's disappearance. Fred changed his name to Forrest and moved on with his life. Did Roland ever have any kind of interaction or friendship with Janey?' asked Kate.

'No. Janey was fifteen. She fancied a couple of lads at

school, but nothing serious. We were quite naïve, when I think back,' said Maxine. She looked to Doreen.

'Yeah. I don't remember having to worry about any shenanigans. And Roland? No. He was older, and he wasn't a creep around young girls. He preferred his drink.'

'I think my mother needs some rest,' said Maxine. 'You can leave your card, and if we think of anything else, we'll let you know.'

Kate thought how broken and bereft Doreen looked. In an hour of talking about Janey, she'd aged twenty years.

29

The wind was now blowing a freezing gale and snow onto the corridor outside the flats. Kate and Tristan went to the lift and pressed the call button. The cold was a shock compared to the warmth inside Doreen's flat, and it made Kate's eyes water.

As they waited for the lift, they looked down to the courtyard below. The snow was deep, a blanket of white tracked with a single line of footsteps running past the statue. The views out over London were beautiful, even where the light pollution seemed to catch in the low bank of clouds with an orange-grey glow.

'I'm surprised Doreen has lasted so long living here. So many memories,' said Kate.

'She probably didn't have a choice,' said Tristan. 'She was trapped by her circumstances, until now. Maybe winning the lottery was karma, for all her suffering.'

'I don't believe in karma. If it were real, Peter Conway

would have been dead long ago.' The lift finally arrived, and they hurried inside out of the wind.

When Kate and Tristan stepped out of Victoria House, the clouds parted, and the moon was just rising, pale and large on the horizon, and it bathed the snowy landscape in an almost magical glow.

'Are you hungry?' asked Tristan.

'I don't know. Do you want to go to the pub?'

'No. I meant go for a drink or a coffee. We can talk about what happened today. And I don't fancy going back to the flat. It's so cold and echoey.'

'I know. It feels so empty, and yet there are so many noises. I haven't seen a neighbour, but I keep hearing footsteps and creaks in the night.'

'You've lived in a house on your own for too long.'

'I still hear creaks at home, but I'm used to them. They're *my* creaks.'

The most direct journey back took them through Pancras Road. It was busy and bright, with the offices and shops under the arches all open with lights on in the windows. The Starbucks, formerly Reynolds newsagent, was crowded with people, and a group of teenage girls talked and laughed in seats in front of the window. As they drew closer to The Jug, it seemed surreal to be in this beautiful, bright, snow-covered landscape when, thirty years ago, this had been a dangerous, lonely road. Tristan stopped outside. They peered through a large picture window, which had been recently added. It wasn't in the old pictures of the building from 1988.

'What do you think? It's as good a place as any to have a drink?'

'Okay. Let's check it out.'

The inside had been recently refurbished, and it was very busy. Kate wondered if it had always looked like a modern warehouse space, or if they'd knocked out all the interior walls and the original ceiling. A few booths ran along the windows. The wall behind the bar was lined with hundreds of spirits in bottles, all lit up, and on the corner of the bar was a large silver ice bucket filled with champagne bottles.

A waitress whizzed past them with a couple of long rustic wooden boards containing a baked brie with bread and olives and a selection of oysters on ice, with a shucking knife.

'It's table service,' she said to Kate and Tristan, having to manoeuvre herself around them. They grabbed the last available booth by the window. Kate ordered a ginger tea with honey and lemon, and Tristan ordered a craft beer and some crisps. A group of office workers arrived, and the two women with the group of men were dressed beautifully in expensive trouser suits. Kate felt scruffy compared to them, in her jeans and jumper with her two-year-old winter coat. It was a silly thought to have, considering what they'd just been talking about, and Kate shook it away.

'I wonder where the *Space Invaders* game was?' she said.

'So now Maxine has put Peter Conway here in the pub around the time Janey vanished. She's the fourth person, after Thomas Black, Robert Driscoll, and Forrest,' said Tristan.

'I think I believe her the most out of all of them. She has no reason to lie about seeing him.'

'Maxine would have been in America when you had Peter Conway arrested in 1995. Betty said she went to America for that summer camp when she was eighteen or nineteen. We need to check that again, but if she was twelve in 1988, she would have been nineteen in 1995.'

Their drinks arrived with the same harassed-looking waitress. She plonked them down and hurried off. Kate lifted the lid off her teapot and stirred her tea. Her phone rang, and she saw it was a FaceTime call from Varia Campbell. Kate answered it, and they saw Varia sitting in the busy lobby of a resort-style hotel with a stunning view out over the blue sea sparkling under the sun. She was wearing a T-shirt and sunglasses on her head. People in shorts and T-shirts were milling around behind her.

'It's both of you, good,' she said, leaning closer to the camera.

'Where are you?' asked Kate.

'Four Seasons St Lucia.'

'It looks gorgeous,' said Tristan.

'It is. My husband's banned me from working, but I just had to call you both quickly. Listen. Forensics just came back on the blood found in the pipe behind Reynolds newsagent. The DNA from that tiny sample of blood found in the pipe matches Janey's blood. Her red scarf is still in the evidence store, and they match. We don't have an official DNA sample for Janey in the database. I want to get a DNA sample from the mother, just to rule everything out, but it's pretty much confirmed.'

'It means that Janey was in that pipe or close enough for her blood to splash onto the inside of the pipe,' said Kate.

'If we can put Janey's body in that pipe four days after she went missing, this changes a lot,' said Tristan.

'And it gives more weight to the evidence from Molly,' said Kate.

'Molly?' asked Varia.

'The sniffer dog, Molly. She traced Janey's scent from inside Reynolds, down the passage, and out of the back door into the yard and the pipe.'

'It means that Janey could have been killed in or around Reynolds newsagent and her body was stashed in the pipe for a few days before being moved,' said Tristan.

'Listen. I can't talk for long,' said Varia, looking over her shoulder. 'I need those Janey Macklin files back a-sap. The CPS wants to review everything, with a view to reopening the case.'

'When do you need the files?' asked Kate.

'If you can give me your address, one of my officers, someone I can trust to keep quiet about you two having the case file, can come over tonight.'

'Can it be first thing tomorrow morning?' asked Kate. 'Just so we can review everything.'

Varia rolled her eyes. 'Okay. First thing tomorrow. Text me the address.' She looked up, and they heard a man's voice in the background. Her hand came close to the camera, and the screen went black. They heard a muffled voice. 'This is work . . . No. It's important. Look, I won't be a minute.' Varia took her hand away from the camera. 'Look. I have to go. Couples massage.'

'You lucky thing,' said Tristan.

'Yeah. I should feel lucky, but trust a juicy case to come up right now. I blame you two.' Varia peered at something off-camera. It looked like she was waiting until her husband was out of earshot. 'I'll have my phone on vibrate. Call or text me if anything important comes up. And text me your address. I'll get one of my colleagues to come over first thing tomorrow morning to collect the case files.'

She ended the call. Kate and Tristan were silent for a moment. The significance of their location wasn't lost on them.

'Where does this leave us now with Peter Conway, if Janey's blood puts her in that pipe behind Reynolds?' asked Tristan.

'I don't know,' said Kate. 'Four people say they saw Peter in The Jug. What about near Reynolds newsagent?'

'Yes. Peter Conway could have visited Reynolds, got to know Jack Reynolds.'

'But Jack Reynolds is long dead. What time is it?'

'Coming up to seven pm,' said Tristan, checking his watch.

'We need to find a printer or a scanner. I want to make copies of the case file before it's picked up tomorrow.'

'I've got an app on my phone – it scans with the camera, really good quality,' said Tristan.

'Seriously?'

'Yeah.'

'Okay. Well, let's get cracking. We need to copy all the case files tonight.'

30

Kate and Tristan arrived back at the Percy Circus flat and began to copy the Janey Macklin case files. They pushed the sofa and coffee table against the TV, clearing space in the middle of the living room floor.

They worked in a production line. Kate unfastened the case files and laid the individual papers and photographs in a row so Tristan could move along and take a photo of the front and then the back of each sheet. Kate could then gather up the ones he'd photographed and lay down new pages. There were four folders with around a hundred pages in each.

They were so absorbed in what they were doing, and Percy Circus seemed so quiet, that they forgot to close the curtains in the front room. After a few minutes of scanning the documents, Tristan noticed something from the corner of his eye.

He stopped and looked up. A man with a camera was taking photos through the window.

'Kate. Look out!' he said, jumping up and closing the curtains.

'What?' said Kate, sorting a fresh sheaf of the case file.

'Journalist, I think. A guy with a long-lens camera.'

'Shit,' said Kate. They heard a rustle outside. She put her finger to her lips. There was silence, and then they both jumped as the door buzzer rang out stridently. Kate looked at the pages from the case files, still lined up across the floor. 'If he's got a telephoto lens and he's been snapping us from outside, then he could have clear photos of these documents.' The buzzer rang again longer. Kate jumped again. 'Shit. Peter Conway's back in the news, on his deathbed. He's the monster. I'm going to be trotted out again as the bride of Frankenstein.'

'Frankenstein was actually the doctor who created the monster. People often make that mistake . . .' Tristan saw Kate's face and how annoyed she was. 'Sorry.'

The buzzer rang again for a third time. Kate looked around at the case files. 'I don't want to risk any of this getting into the press. If the media get hold of any of this, they'll have a field day.'

'Do you want me to go and talk to him?' asked Tristan.

'No. I'll talk to him. I'm who they want. In the meantime, clear all of these away. But keep track of what we've copied. Actually, see if you can replace them with boring paperwork. We could pretend we're doing this for a tax audit or something.'

'What are you going to say to him?' asked Tristan, moving to clear up the case file pages.

'I don't know.'

Kate left the room and went to the door as the buzzer rang for the fourth time. She slipped on her coat and opened their front door. She hesitated for a moment inside the communal entrance, took a deep breath, and then opened the main door. It was freezing outside, and a young man with a moustache and woolly hat, wearing a thick bomber jacket, jeans, and heavy boots, had his camera ready. He fired off a few shots, and Kate was dazzled by the flash.

'Steady on,' she said, avoiding her instinct to raise her hand. The press loved that kind of photo. They made you look defensive and out of control. 'I'll talk to you, and you can have some photos. What's your name?'

'Marcus Gale. I'm freelance.' He held up his camera again and fired it off in her face.

'Jeez, Marcus. Give a girl some warning,' she said.

He smiled. 'Is that your boyfriend inside? *Toy boy?*'

'He's my colleague. I'm a private detective.'

'Yeah. I know. Aren't you based down south, though? What are you detecting?'

'A missing person case. That's all I can say.'

Marcus peered past her inside the door. The circle and the trees were covered in a layer of thick white. The snowflakes falling were lit up in the beam of the orange street lights. His phone rang, and he pulled it out and answered. 'Yeah. I'm talking to her now. She answered the door.'

Charming, thought Kate. *How did he know I was here?* She had to think on her feet. What could she give this little shit in exchange for the photos he'd taken?

'You know that Peter Conway is in hospital, on life

support?' asked Marcus, with the phone tucked under his chin.

'I do.'

'You going to see him?'

'No plans.'

'You hear that? Okay. Good.'

Marcus ended the call.

'I'll answer some questions if you have them,' said Kate.

'I'm not a journalist. I sell photos.'

'You can have more photos. Inside.' *What the hell am I doing?* thought Kate as she heard the words coming out of her mouth.

Marcus rummaged in his bag and pulled out a copy of *No Son of Mine*. It was the hardback edition.

'I have this copy with the signatures of Enid Conway and Peter Conway,' he said. Kate had worked on a case to find a missing journalist called Joanna Duncan a couple of years back. A friend of Joanna's had been down on her luck, and Kate had taken pity and signed her copy of *No Son of Mine*, which also had both Enid's and Peter's signatures. Kate had expected her to sell it for a couple of thousand, so it had been a shock to hear the young woman had sold it at an auction for £15,000. It was dubbed 'The Triple Crown Signed Edition.'

'If I sign that for you, will you delete the photos you took through the window?' asked Kate. Marcus considered this. 'When Conway dies, and it's looking likely, think how much it will increase in value.'

'Do you know when he's going to die?' asked Marcus. He was being serious.

'Not exactly, but he's in a bad way.'

'Can I get a photo of you signing it?'

'Okay.'

'And a picture of you looking detective-ish could be good to have.'

Kate felt grubby negotiating like this. It seemed that the photographer wasn't aware of the Janey Macklin case, or it wasn't important to him.

'Delete the photos now, in front of me, and we have a deal.'

Marcus held up the small screen on the back of his camera and went through a cluster of photos showing Kate and Tristan with the case files. He went through, deleting them one by one.

'Okay, come in.'

Kate saw that Tristan had found some old utility bills and papers lying around, and he'd lined them up on the floor, replacing the case files. Marcus was inside the flat for only five minutes, but Kate still felt violated.

'Thanks,' he said, his eyes lighting up when Kate handed him the signed copy of *No Son of Mine*. 'See you around.' He picked up his camera bag and left. Tristan closed the door and looked over at the end of the DVD shelf where Kate had just posed for pictures. The movies *Halloween*, *IT*, *The Texas Chainsaw Massacre*, *The Silence of the Lambs*, and *Misery* had been turned facing out.

'You okay?'

'No. I think I'm going to regret those pictures,' said Kate. 'But he deleted the ones of us with the case files.' There was a long beat. She knew what Tristan wanted to say, that the journalist would have probably just deleted the pictures in exchange for her signature in the book. 'We should get the rest of this case file copied,' she said.

Kate knelt down and started to gather up the papers Tristan had laid out, and they recommenced scanning the rest of the Janey Macklin case files. They worked in silence for the next half an hour, and then Tristan stopped over a set of photos of Pancras Road, taken in early January 1989.

'We've missed a page,' he said.

'Where?' asked Kate, looking up from unclipping the papers in the fourth cardboard file.

'I'm sure there was the police interview with Roland Hacker here, and look, it jumps from page 237 to 239,' he said, checking the sheets of paper laid out in a row on the herringbone wood floor.

'Hang on, let me check I didn't miss anything,' said Kate. She went back through the third file, which was nearly all done. 'There's not a page 238 in here.' They searched through the papers on the coffee table, but it was all the junk mail Tristan had found in the drawer under the TV.

'Did you take any of the pages out of the case files?' asked Tristan.

'No.'

He looked around. 'That's really weird. Can you check the fourth file, in case I'm mistaken and there's the Roland Hacker police interview there.'

'It's late. Shall we just carry on and I can tell you if we find it?' said Kate. She was feeling tired and fractious.

'I just remember the interview being in the file the page before these photos of Pancras Road. They're the only photos taken in the sunshine, and they stood out to me in the case file.'

'Tristan, let's carry on. Please. It's late.'

They went back to work. Tristan photographed the last five pages of the third file, and then they went through all of the fourth file. There was still no page with the interview between Roland Hacker and the police.

'What did the page say?' asked Kate, perching on the end of the sofa. 'It was just him confirming that he was at his parents' flat on the night Janey Macklin went missing?'

'Yeah. You asked me if I moved the files onto the floor. Earlier today, before we got the phone call about Doreen and Maxine being back.'

'Yeah. They were both piled up next to the table leg. When I went to bed, after you, I left them on the coffee table here.'

Tristan looked around the room. 'You mentioned a couple of times hearing noises.'

'Yeah. I meant the kind of creaks and noises from other people in this building.'

'I haven't seen or heard anyone upstairs, or next to us.'

'Do you think someone broke in? And took a page out of the case file?'

'I don't know, but it's gone. And it was there. I didn't imagine seeing it. His name was printed across the top, Roland Giles Quintus Hacker. We both commented on the middle names, didn't we?'

'Yes.'

'We still have Robert Driscoll's police interviews. We just copied them, and Fred Parker's, Forrest . . .' Tristan stopped and clicked his fingers. 'Hang on. Roland Giles Quintus Hacker. What's Fred's middle name?'

'It's on his interview record,' said Kate. She went back to the folders and looked through. 'Paul. Fred Paul Parker.'

'But he's now Forrest Paul Parker. That's how he's listed on the 192.com records for the house in Barnes?'

'Yes. Shit. You think if Roland changed his name, even if he changed first and last, he might have kept the middle names?' asked Kate, suddenly seeing his point. 'Do you have a middle name?'

'Yeah. It's Kevin. I don't use it; it's just on my birth certificate. What's yours?'

'Glenda. Kevin and Glenda.'

'We could be in a 1970s sitcom.'

'Most of us either don't use middle names or we have them for sentimental reasons. There's no reason that many people would know Roland's middle names.'

Tristan grabbed his laptop and sat down while opening it. He pulled up the website for 192.com and logged in. Kate came around and sat next to him as he typed in the name 'Roland Giles Quintus Hacker' and the location as 'Watford.'

'Forrest mentioned seeing him near Watford on the Tube,' he added. He pressed enter and a list of names came up. 'The website gives you the hits closest to the search material, which it did when I checked before, but I didn't include his middle names.' He scrolled down the list. 'There's a Jon Giles Quintus Chase is coming up at an address in Moor Park.'

'Moor Park – that's on the Metropolitan Line, near Watford,' said Kate, feeling excited despite her exhaustion. 'Could it be someone else?'

'It would have to be a lot of coincidences colliding,' said Tristan. 'This could be Roland.'

31

Kate made them cups of tea, and they sat in the living room, tired but buzzing from the potential link they'd found to Roland.

'It has to be him. The middle names. The address he's registered at is near Watford,' said Tristan.

'We also need to be aware that someone could have broken in here and taken the page from the case file, where Roland's middle names are listed.'

'I don't think anyone broke in. They probably had a key. If this place is used as a rental, then any number of people could have keys. Or it was Forrest and Maddie.'

'I think Roland knows something,' said Kate. 'And whoever it is doesn't want us to find him.'

'Isn't it a bit stupid to take the one page out of the police case file?'

'Yes.' Kate shuddered. It was now coming up to 1am. She got up and went to the kitchen. Tristan followed. The overhead strip light inside was harsh, and it shone a square out through the door into the tiny courtyard. 'Have we been locking this with the key and the deadbolt?'

'I think so, but I can't be sure,' said Tristan. 'Someone could climb out of one of those windows on the back of the building opposite.' Tristan peered through the glass pane in the back door. Kate leant over and checked the lock and then shot the deadbolt across.

'There's also a deadbolt on the front door. If someone has broken in, or used a key, it would have to be through the back door, or when we were out and the deadbolt on the front door wasn't in use,' said Kate. 'Have you been outside in that courtyard?'

'Yes, a couple of days ago. Just to get fresh air. You said you heard noises?'

'Yeah. But it could have been you. Someone upstairs – even if you think no one is here, there are three flats above us,' Tristan said. Kate switched off the kitchen light, and they both stood in the dark for a moment, staring out at the snow which continued to fall. It clung on in chunks to a single old dining chair which had been placed outside the back door. Her phone rang.

'Shit! That made me jump.'

'This is Jake calling,' said Kate, seeing his name on the screen.

'I'll leave you be. Say hi to Jake. I'm going to brush my teeth. I need to go to bed,' said Tristan.

———

When Kate had finished speaking to Jake, she hung around in the living room waiting for Tristan to emerge from the bathroom. He'd taken a shower, and when he opened the door, steam billowed out from behind him, and he was wearing just a towel.

'Oh. Sorry. I just had to talk to you before you went to bed.'

'Is Jake okay?'

'Yes. He's fine. Jake's just bought a flight to London. He's going to land in Heathrow at ten thirty tomorrow morning. He wants me to go up north with him and see Peter Conway in hospital.'

'Okay. You said you thought he'd want to.'

Kate nodded. 'I kind of feel odd about it, and it's now almost half one. I'm exhausted. At least we're in London and I don't have to leave too early.'

'I can check out the address for this Jon Chase guy, see if it's Roland.'

Kate nodded. 'Yes. And I can still ask Peter Conway about Janey, and Maxine. And what Forrest told us. If I can get Peter to confirm he saw them in the Jug.'

'Do you think he'll remember? It's thirty years ago, and he's in intensive care.'

'I don't know. Deathbeds have a strange loosening effect on the tongue. And if I have to see him, I'd rather ask the question and see if it can help our investigation.'

'What should we do about the missing page from the case file?' said Tristan. 'Someone from Varia's team is coming first thing tomorrow to pick it up.'

'Maybe don't tell whoever it is who picks it up. We need

to tell Varia. And let's make sure the deadbolts are on tonight on both doors.' Kate checked her watch. 'I need to find a hire car for tomorrow, and pack a bag.'

'You should get some sleep, too,' said Tristan.

'I feel like sleep is going to elude me.'

32

Tristan woke at 7.30 and heard Kate moving around in the flat, making herself a cup of tea in the kitchen, and then he heard the taps in the bathroom.

He stayed in bed to give her time to get ready. They'd gone to bed just before 2 after booking Kate a hire car, and they had spent some time preparing the photos she wanted to show Peter Conway of Janey Macklin, the young Maxine Macklin, Forrest Parker, Robert Driscoll, and Roland Hacker. They also spent some time trawling the internet to find a photo of The Jug as it was back in the 1980s but couldn't find anything. Then Tristan saw a photo in the case file that they hadn't noticed before, taken from the *Crimewatch* reconstruction. They didn't have access to a printer, so Kate had packed Tristan's iPad.

At 8, Tristan did some push-ups on his bedroom floor, then went to shower. The bathroom was Arctic, and the chair in the courtyard behind the flats was now just a big bulge under a deep layer of snow.

The doorbell buzzed just before nine, just as Tristan finished his breakfast. When he opened the door, standing outside was a tall, handsome police officer in his early thirties.

'Hi. I'm DI Sean Bentley,' he said, flashing his warrant card. 'I'm looking for Tristan Harper and Kate Marshall?'

Kate appeared at the door behind Tristan, holding the carrier bag with the case files. 'That's us.'

'Can I come in for a moment?' he said, stepping into the communal hallway and closing the main door.

'Of course,' said Tristan.

He wiped his feet and came into the living room. His black coat was dotted with snow. 'Are you aware there's press outside?'

'There was a photographer last night,' said Kate. Tristan could hear the nerves in her voice.

'Well, you've five guys out there milling around with telephoto lenses. I didn't want to be seen taking police case files from you in clear daylight,' said Sean, smiling.

'It would add to the intrigue,' said Tristan. 'Do you work with Varia Campbell?'

'I'm on her murder investigation team. She's my boss. Thanks for this.'

'Are you going to be working on the Janey Macklin case?'

'Looks like it's being reopened today. Varia's cutting her holiday short.'

'You are aware we're investigating the case, as well,' said Kate, handing him the bag containing the case files. He took it and nodded amiably. A couple of private detectives sniffing around didn't seem to faze him.

'I can't promise that we're going to keep you updated, but let me give you my card,' he added, rummaging in the pocket of his coat and handing one to Kate and one to Tristan.

When he left, Kate went to the blinds and peered out. The snow was melting into a brown slush, and the photographers were lined up on the other side of the road in front of the tiny park. Tristan came to join her at the window.

'I don't want to see Peter Conway. I want to stay here, and work on the case,' said Kate, surprising herself with the emotion in her voice.

'I'm sorry you keep having to deal with this,' said Tristan. Kate took a deep breath, turned from the window and gathered together her bag and coat. 'I don't think you should get the underground down to Heathrow. Those creeps will be able to follow you. One of them has a motorbike.'

'Yeah, you're right. I'll get an Uber.'

When Kate checked the app, the closest car was just a minute away. Tristan got ready to leave with her, and when the car appeared, it drove around the circle and past the photographers.

'I'll lock up. You run for it. Say hi to Jake. And good luck with Peter Conway. Keep in contact. Call me if you need anything.'

'Thanks. And if you manage to talk to Roland Hacker, record what you can.'

'Of course.'

Kate opened the front door, and they went into the hallway. She took a deep breath and opened the main building door. The photographers had correctly guessed the car might be for her, and they were already swarming around it. Kate managed to get in the front passenger seat. The driver was an elderly Indian man with a neatly trimmed grey beard.

'Are you famous?' he asked as she closed the door and put on her seat belt.

'No. More like infamous.'

He accelerated away, and the photographers grew smaller in the mirror of her door. There was a gap in the traffic when they reached the main road, so the driver was able to get them moving, and they lost the photographers. It seemed to take an age to travel to Heathrow by car, and despite the worry and tension she felt, she dozed as the car rumbled through the streets of London.

Jake was already waiting for her at a Starbucks in arrivals. He looked tanned and so healthy, with a glow about him in the cold airport terminal. Kate held back for a second to catch her breath after running up three escalators, and she watched her son. He was drinking a takeaway coffee, and he had his earphones in, watching a video on his phone. He was dressed expensively – or it looked expensive to Kate – in a thick fake-fur coat, skinny jeans, and trainers.

As she watched her son sipping his coffee and adjusting a silver band on his wrist, she knew she had to hold on to this image over the next few hours and days. Jake was nothing like his father. Her son was normal and happy, independent and successful. He'd survived everything that had been thrown at him in his short life, and prospered. Kate was disappointed to see he had a small silver case on wheels, which indicated this was a short visit. He turned and saw her.

'Mum!' he said, pulling the earphones out of his ears. He got up and gave her a hug. He smelt of aftershave and a little sweat. He was all grown up. A man.

'It's so good to see you, love,' she said, holding on to him for just a moment longer than he did her. 'How was your flight?'

'I slept the whole way. Olivia got me a last-minute upgrade to business with one of those lie-flat beds. She has so many air miles.'

'I thought you looked rested. I didn't sleep much.'

'I got you a coffee,' he said, holding up a second cup. 'Do you want to drink it here?'

Kate looked around at the terminal. It was quite empty, with just a few people. She spotted a man sitting on a row of benches with his mobile. He was holding it up at an odd angle, slightly higher than would be comfortable, and kept glancing at them.

'Thanks. Does he look like he's filming us?' said Kate, turning away and inclining her head in his direction.

'I don't know. Don't think so.'

Kate could hear how paranoid she sounded. 'Last night there was a journalist lurking outside the flat we're staying at in London, and this morning *five* photographers.'

Jake moved around and stepped in front of Kate to shield her from the man with the phone. 'I've been checking the news. There's also photographers outside the hospital where Peter's in intensive care,' he said. Kate took a sip of the coffee. It was good and hot. 'How's the case going?'

Kate needed to explain to Jake that as well as them being

there for Peter on his deathbed, she would have to try and question him about Janey Macklin.

'Let's go and get the hire car. It's a four-hour drive.'

Jake nodded and grabbed his suitcase. As they moved away, Kate looked back, but the man didn't follow. He was absorbed in his phone.

33

It took Tristan forty minutes to get from King's Cross to Watford Tube station. It felt odd to be alone in London. It was so vast. So overwhelming. It made him feel like his life was so small and insignificant. He'd always admired how Kate carried the burden of her past. She never shied away from it, and strived hard to overcome an impossible situation. She always said that her greatest triumph, cracking the case and discovering that Peter Conway was the Nine Elms Cannibal, was also her greatest failure. Tristan knew she was praying for Peter Conway to die, but he was Jake's father. He had no idea how she reconciled this every day.

It hadn't snowed as much, so the roads were clear. Jon Chase was registered as living at Baywater House. It was a good twenty-minute walk from the Tube station, and very quickly, the busy crowds who'd left the train at the same stop thinned out as Tristan found himself in suburban streets and then in an area of council estates and high-rise blocks of flats. Baywater House looked like the roughest and most run-down of the lot, sitting in a square of brown scrub-land with a burnt-out car. A basketball court at one end still had a hoop, but there was so much dog shit and broken glass that a game hadn't been played in a long time. Several groups of young men stood around in the harsh light smoking cigarettes, and they looked up at Tristan when he walked past. He'd opted to wear a smart suit and had a leather briefcase with him, hoping he looked like an insurance salesman. As soon as Tristan walked through the open entrance into the block of flats, a short young guy with badly bleached blond hair came up to him.

'Got a cigarette?' he demanded. A younger guy and a young girl emerged from a doorway to join them. They both looked grubby and had the sunken cheeks and dead eyes of drug addicts.

'No,' said Tristan, moving past them to the stairs. He didn't bother with the lift, knowing it was probably out of order.

'A quid, then? You can spare a quid,' whined the girl.

Jon Chase's flat was on the fourteenth floor, and Tristan figured that if the three kids were begging from passers-by, they wouldn't want to follow him up so many stairs. He was right, and after two flights of pestering, they lost interest and fell back.

Tristan and his sister, Sarah, had grown up in a grubby tower block, but it had been a palace compared to this. The concrete stairway was filthy, and the smell of neglect, urine, and desperation choked him. As he climbed higher, he saw glimpses through the open squares in the landing of each floor of the city, prosperous and twinkling far off on the horizon. On the tenth floor, someone long ago had lit a fire on the landing, and a vast patch of soot was smeared in black up the wall. He saw a small pool of ash with weeds growing from a burnt beer can.

When Tristan reached the fourteenth floor, he stopped on the final landing. It had no roof, and as he caught his breath, the air was icy in his lungs. He started along the landing and passed a door where loud music played and a dog barked, and there was the far-off hissing roar of the city. Jon Chase lived at the end, and his front door bore many scars, dents, and scrapes, and a round impression slightly smaller than a dinner plate, and Tristan wondered if it was the dent from a battering ram. He stopped outside and listened. Was the television on? It sounded like music was coming from inside. He knocked. Waited a minute and then knocked again harder. On the third attempt, he hammered on the wood.

Tristan knelt down to peer through the letterbox, but it wouldn't open. It felt like something was behind it blocking it up. Tristan took out his phone and dialled the landline number for Jon Chase listed on 192.com. It started to ring, and a moment later, he heard the phone ringing inside the flat.

There was an odd smell outside the door. Like food gone bad. His hair stood up on the back of his neck. There was something frightening and desolate about this place. The phone was still ringing inside the flat. Roland, or Jon, could be at work. It was perfectly possible on a Tuesday morning. Tristan peered through the grimy window. The blinds were down, but he could see through a small gap at the bottom. A tap was dripping into a sink filled with filthy crockery.

Tristan had his skeleton keys in his bag. He tried calling Kate, to ask what she thought he should do, but her number went to voicemail. He moved back to the door and knelt down. The keyhole was waist high and very old. It wasn't a Yale lock – it looked like it took a big hulking old key.

He placed his backpack on the ground and took out an oblong leather wallet, slightly larger than a long legal envelope. He unzipped it, and inside were a selection of lock picks and skeleton and bump keys. Tristan had been to several courses over the past few years, training in surveillance techniques, evidence gathering, and, his favourite, picking locks. He hadn't had much chance to pick locks in the real world, and this was a perfect opportunity.

Tristan looked around. The corridor was empty. Was he jumping to conclusions? What if Jon or Roland was sleeping off a heavy night, or just sleeping? But there was a really bad smell emanating from inside. He looked up at the battle-scarred door, and decided to try one of the bump keys. He inserted it and turned slowly. No. It was wrong. He withdrew it, and selected a rake key with a serrated edge. The air was so cold, and his hands were numb. He slipped it into the keyhole, and the rake key turned with a click. Tristan turned the handle, and the door opened with a creak. A blast of warm, rancid air gusted out, and he stepped inside.

Tristan put his hand over his mouth and nose. It was very warm, and at first, he thought the terrible smell was coming from rotting food in the kitchen. Then he moved through to the living room. It was decorated simply, with plain furniture, and piled with books and magazines and boxes stacked against one wall. There was a single chair in the middle of the room, facing the television, which was switched on.

Sitting in the chair was the dead body of a man wearing a pale T-shirt and underpants. His mouth and eyes were wide open in a look of terror. Long matted hair clung to the head, and the pale T-shirt he wore was torn and, along with his bare legs, splattered with blood. A table lay on its side, and books and papers were strewn amongst broken glass. An arc of dry blood spatter covered the wall above the TV. With his heart thumping, Tristan moved through and checked the other rooms. The flat also had a small bathroom, where a makeshift clothesline hung above the bath. The bedroom was reasonably tidy compared to the rest, the bed was neatly made, and a stack of books waited on the bedside table.

Tristan was shaking and could feel the adrenaline rushing through his body. He went back into the living room. The shelf unit filled with books also contained some ornaments, a feathery piece of dried coral, and some carved wooden balls in a bowl. There were two framed photos, one of a dark-haired man standing beside a waterfall with two young women. And there was a framed photo of Roland, Forrest, and Robert taken inside what looked like a hall. They stood in front of six large cast iron concrete squares, each a metre square or so in size, which were painted with abstract images of people, walking past a river, standing on a mountain, and herding sheep. It looked like the pieces all made up an image when put together. The three lads were smiling and all wearing gloves used for lifting. Tristan quickly took photos of everything, taking care not to touch anything.

He came back into the hall and saw a pile of unopened

mail on a table. There were sheafs of bank statements, and he took a pair of latex gloves from the skeleton key wallet and slipped them on. He looked through the bank statements, which were all in the name of Jon Chase. It looked like he had been collecting state unemployment benefits every month. Tristan's hands shook as he took a photo on his phone of the bank statement, which contained a transaction dated November 2017 – a bank transfer credit of £300 from Forrest Parker.

34

Kate had put her handbag with her mobile in the boot of the hire car, so she didn't hear Tristan's call.

The journey up to Wakefield took four hours, and it seemed to go so quickly. Too quickly. Jake had been in contact with the governor at Wakefield prison, who had arranged for them to meet one of the prison guards in the reception of Pinderfields Hospital.

'Are you okay, Mum?' asked Jake when they were in the visitors' car park and Kate switched off the engine.

'Yes. No.'

'I don't feel okay, either.'

There was a knock at the window, and a small, squat woman with cropped black hair, wearing a skirt and jacket, peered in through the window.

Kate and Jake got out of the car, grabbing their jackets from the back seat. It was very cold and damp with a light drizzle in the air. They all shook hands, and the woman, Angie, explained she was the press officer from HMP

Wakefield. It was quite a long walk through the car park and then along a path to the main hospital building.

'There are some photographers outside. They seem to have got wind of the fact you're coming to visit. But just keep your heads down and don't say anything. I'll then take you up to Peter's ward.'

Some didn't seem to justify the phalanx of photographers and TV news reporters running the length of the main entrance and the pavements outside. When they saw Kate and Jake, a shout went up, and they were mobbed. Kate reached out for Jake, but the back of his coat vanished into a sea of heads and arms carrying cameras. A strobe of bright flashes went off in her face. They were shouting questions, screaming and yelling. Kate could make out a few voices in the cacophony: 'Are you sad he's dying?'

'What's it like to fuck a serial killer and have his baby?' was another question. Kate could see that Jake had made it almost to the door. That same feeling from years ago flooded through her. The feeling of being hunted, and of being examined when your skin feels so sensitive. They had her surrounded, and no one was moving. The rain and the hot, stinking breath of a reporter were on her face. And then the cameras seemed to part. Jake appeared, towering over them.

'Move. Now,' he said, shoving two of them out of the way. He grabbed her arm, and Kate felt herself being steered through the throng and into the warmth and bright lights of the hospital reception.

It was busy, and everyone turned when they swept through – judgemental and curious faces, and quite a few scowls – as if by just visiting, they were somehow endorsing Peter Conway's crimes.

'Shame on you!' shouted an elderly lady. 'He should die alone, the evil bastard!'

'He shouldn't be here!' shouted a man. 'Leave the sick alone.'

They went up in a large, empty lift, which a police officer had held for them. Angie was smart enough not to try and make conversation. They emerged onto a quiet side ward, where another police officer waited behind a makeshift table.

He stood up. He was very tall and athletic, in his mid-thirties, Kate guessed, and he had a baton and a gun on his belt. Through the glass door, they could see another police officer waiting, and it opened and a female officer greeted them.

'This is Jake Marshall and his mother, Kate Marshall. He's here as Peter Conway's next of kin, his son,' said Angie. This piece of information seemed to land with a thud on the table.

'Afternoon. I just need to do a quick search,' said the officer, speaking to Jake. 'Stand legs apart and put your arms up.' Jake removed his coat and let the police officer pat him down and use a metal-detecting wand. The female officer indicated for Kate to come closer. Kate took off her coat, and the woman patted her down and then ran the wand over her. When she went to pick up her coat off the table, Kate saw there was raw egg splattered down the back.

'Who was throwing eggs?'

'There were a couple of protesters, amongst the press,'

said Angie, ducking out of the way of the metal detector wand, adding, 'I'm not coming in.'

Kate stared at the raw yolk on the back of her coat. She looked at the two police officers. 'What's with the blasé attitude? Throwing eggs at people is assault. Where are the police downstairs?'

'People have the right to protest about things they don't agree with.'

'*Don't agree with*,' repeated Kate. 'You know nothing.'

The two police officers exchanged a glance.

'We're here to ensure Peter Conway doesn't escape,' said the male officer. 'We've not been warned about any protests.'

'You think he's going to escape whilst he's on life support and close to death?' said Kate, feeling the anger rising in her chest. 'And yet me and my son are egged and jeered and threatened by the mob outside.'

There was silence.

'We need you to sign in here, and we'll need ID, passport or photo card driving licence,' said the male officer.

'Mum. It's okay,' said Jake.

'*No*. It's not. I've spent the last twenty years having to deal with this shit. Do these idiots outside "protesting" know that it's because of *me* that Peter Conway was caught? Did you know I solved the case?' The male police officer looked like a rabbit caught in the headlights, and the other two women just stared. 'Well, now you do. I probably saved the lives of a good few young women. Did you know he tried to kill me?' Kate pulled up her sweatshirt, no longer caring what people thought. 'Look at this scar. He did this. I had to fight for my life, and I still managed to call 999, and that's the reason he's been locked up for the past twenty-three years.' Kate was now shaking. Tears were in her eyes, but she wiped them away furiously. 'And here you are shrugging and telling me that it's a legal right for those idiots outside to throw eggs at me and my son!'

'We can have someone review the CCTV from the main entrance,' said the male officer.

'I can get that actioned,' said the woman. 'And if we can identify the person who threw them, we'll pursue an arrest.'

'Thank you,' said Kate, wiping her eyes. She felt embarrassed at her outburst.

'Mum. You okay?' asked Jake, squeezing her hand. 'You don't have to come in with me.'

'Oh. I didn't come this far not to go in,' said Kate. Jake took out his passport, and then Kate realised that she didn't have her bag.

'I've left my handbag in the boot of our hire car.' The male officer was checking Jake's passport, and he handed it back.

'We do need ID.'

'You want me to go back out through all that downstairs?'

'This is my mum,' said Jake. 'Look at my left eye; it's orange and blue. We both have this rare condition called sectoral heterochromia, where the eyes have more than one colour. Look, her eye is the same. I know it's not ID, but she's my mum.'

'I can go to your car and get your bag,' said Angie. There was a careful tone in her voice, like she was placating a madwoman. Angie looked to the police officer.

'Okay, you can go in, but I need that ID a-sap.'

'Thank you,' said Kate, handing Angie the keys. 'It's a

black bag in the boot. There's also an iPad in its case – can you bring that, too?'

Kate and Jake signed in, and the female officer took them through the doors. A small end ward with three private rooms had been commandeered for Peter Conway. Two of the rooms were empty, and Kate could hear the sound of a heart monitor coming from the doors on the left. A nurse was waiting for them.

'Come through. He's just in here,' she said.

35

It took half an hour for the police to arrive, the longest thirty minutes of Tristan's life. He waited outside the front door, pacing up and down to keep warm. As the minutes ticked by, he felt the presence of the dead body inside. The blank-eyed corpse sitting there in the chair, staring at the TV. It struck him how lonely and isolated it was on the top floor of Baywater House. The cold, howling wind seemed to block out all thought, and when Tristan kept peering over the edge of the wall down to the car park below, he couldn't understand why it was so empty and desolate. How did hundreds of people live in this building, and there was no one around?

He saw the three kids wandering around, kicking their heels, but when the first police car arrived, they vanished.

The first police officer to emerge from the lift at the end of the corridor was a tiny, fierce-looking woman with short red hair scraped back off her face. Her large pale ears stood out prominently, and she wore a stab vest with her uniform, which was huge and bulky on her petite frame.

'Did you place the 999 call?' she asked, looking him up and down.

'Yes. The body's inside. I think he's been dead awhile.'

'And who are you?'

'Tristan Harper. Who are you?' he replied, his fear making his tone more challenging than he meant it to be.

The officer grabbed the radio on her lapel and kept her eye on him. 'Yeah, come up. It's the fourteenth floor, end of the corridor. A guy's saying he found the body, but can you get him to the support van for questioning.'

'Questioning? You mean, a statement. I just found the body,' said Tristan.

'And why are you here today?'

He rummaged in his pocket and took out Sean Bailey's card and his agency business card. 'I'm . . . I know this officer. I'm a private detective, and I think this body is in connection with the case I'm working on.'

Two police officers in uniform came out of the lift and jogged towards them in the corridor.

'I'm Constable Megan Levitt,' she said, indicating her warrant card, housed in a plastic pocket in her stab vest. 'I need you to take him down to the van,' she added to her colleagues. One of the officers, a tall, burly lad who looked to be no more than a teenager, put out his hand to grab Tristan's arm.

'I'm coming to talk to you voluntarily, which I'm happy to do.' Megan nodded to the officer, who indicated that Tristan should follow. 'The body is in the living room,' Tristan added, but they ignored him and went into the flat.

———

Tristan was placed in a small grubby police van parked in the empty baseball court. He watched as a forensics van arrived an hour later. Another hour passed slowly. The wind rocked the van, and it was so quiet. As if the sight of the police made the few people who'd been milling around go to ground.

Tristan tried to call Kate several times, but couldn't reach her. He noticed a water cooler in the corner of the van, and he got up to get himself a drink. It was then he tried the door-handle and realised they had locked him inside.

Constable Megan Levitt appeared a few minutes later, carrying a piece of paper. A cold breeze gusted into the stuffy van when she opened the door.

'Why did you lock me in?' demanded Tristan, fuming. 'I'm going to talk to you voluntarily.'

Megan sat on the bench opposite, the tiny plastic table between them.

'How did you get inside the flat?' she snapped.

'I used a key, and I entered because it smelt bad. Like a decaying body,' said Tristan.

'The owner gave you a key?'

'No . . . It was a skeleton key.'

'So you broke in?'

'I just said. It smelt bad, like a decaying body.'

'And you know the smell of a decaying body?'

'Yes. I've had experience of that through my work.'

Tristan took out one of his business cards and slid it across the table.

'Your occupation is private detective?' asked Megan, consulting the piece of paper.

'Yes.'

'And your name is Tristan Harper?'

'Yes.'

'You have a criminal record,' said Megan, turning the sheet over and twisting it around. It was the mug shot taken of him when he was fifteen. He had a sullen look on his face and long greasy hair.

'Yes. A stupid moment of madness when I was a teenager. I broke the windows in my local youth club . . . I think the body up there belongs to a man called Jon Chase, whose real name is Roland Giles Quintus Hacker.'

Megan eyed him. Tristan went on, 'I'm investigating a cold case, the disappearance of a young girl called Janey Macklin in December 1988. Jon Chase – or Roland Hacker, as he was known – was one of the close friends of Robert Driscoll, who was accused and then acquitted of Janey Macklin's murder in 1988. I came here today to try and find Roland Hacker to talk to him . . . Me and my colleague were given access to the cold case files by Superintendent Varia Campbell.'

'Superintendent Campbell is away on leave.'

'You're not listening to me,' said Tristan. 'Were your forensics officers able to tell you anything?'

'The victim was stabbed sixteen times in the chest, arms and neck,' said Megan. 'But you would know that. There's no weapon. You confirm that the front door was locked when you arrived?'

'Yes. Do you know when he was killed?'

'No, but rigor mortis has only just set in, so it was in the last twenty-four to forty-eight hours. There's no key in the door on the inside. Did you remove it?' asked Megan.

'No. I didn't. Whoever killed him locked up and took the key when they left.'

'Oh, you think so, do you? Let's leave the theories up to me. I need a formal statement from you, and I need you to surrender any skeleton keys you have.'

'I'm carrying bump keys,' said Tristan. 'They are completely legal to own.'

'Are you a Locksmith?'

'No, but I was trained by one. I'd also like to put on the record that my intent was not to break in for criminal purposes. I am a private detective, and I had cause to open the door.'

'You should have called the police first.'

'If you contact DI Sean Bailey and the office of Superintendent Varia Williams, they will confirm who I am and that I've been investigating this case,' said Tristan, now feeling annoyed with Megan, the jobsworth. He took out his phone and tried to call Kate again, but the call went to voicemail.

36

Peter Conway lay in a small room with the blinds tightly closed. A single lamp cast a soft glow over the walls. His thin arms were hooked up to wires, and his face was swollen and misshapen. He wasn't wearing an oxygen mask, and his mouth was flopped open, and he was breathing loudly. There was a curved line of black stitches high on his right temple.

'You can sit either side of the bed,' said the nurse. Kate took the chair nearest to the door, and Jake moved around to the other side of the bed.

'What's happened, exactly?' he asked.

'He had five teeth removed, which were badly infected. He'd been taking antibiotics, to minimise the risk of having the teeth extracted, but after the procedure, he contracted a bacterial infection, which has led to sepsis or blood poisoning. It's affected his liver and kidneys. He also has pneumonia. He had a nasty fall in his cell a few days ago, which we've stitched up, but it's all contributing to a weakened immune system.'

'Is he asleep or unconscious?' asked Kate.

'He's been in and out. I've been holding his hand.' Kate looked at the nurse and then back at Peter. 'He's my patient. I don't judge what he's done before he ended up here,' she added, reading Kate's mind. She went to a machine connected to the IV in his arm, and she pressed a button. 'He's getting morphine for the pain, and we're managing it well now. I don't think it will be long. I'm just outside if you need me. He might want some ice. Just put a tiny piece in his mouth.'

She closed the door. Jake hesitated and then reached out and took Peter's hand. Kate sat back. This was a little too close for her.

'Peter. It's Jake and Kate,' he said. Peter opened his eyes. This was the closest Kate had been to him since he'd attacked her.

'Jake,' he said. 'Kate.' His voice was slurred. He smiled.

'How are you?'

Peter took a deep breath.

'Not long now,' he said. His tongue poked out of his mouth, thin and dry, like a piece of grey meat. Jake saw a cup of ice on the nightstand beside the bed. He picked up a tiny piece and put it on Peter's tongue.

Kate shuddered, and she got up and left. She paced up and down outside the room for a few moments. She thought of all his victims. None of them had any comfort or reassurance before they died. They were all killed in the most horrific way, and died experiencing pain and terror. It didn't feel right that they were sitting around as he was given pain medication to make him comfortable, and Jake was holding his bloody hand and giving him chips of ice for his dry mouth. Kate saw the nurse was watching her.

'Tough time?'

'Yes.' Kate didn't want to have to explain anything to anyone else.

The male police officer appeared with her bag. 'Angie just left this for you,' he said. Tristan's iPad stuck out of the top.

'Thank you.'

She was reminded why she was here, took the iPad out, and opened the cover. She found the pictures of Janey and Maxine, steeled herself.

Peter was talking to Jake when she went back into the room.

'I always wanted to go to Los Angeles . . . ,' he was saying, speaking slowly but clearly. He seemed to be alert and awake. 'Catherine,' he added when he saw her come back in. 'I always called her Catherine . . . when we worked together.'

'Yes, it's Catherine,' said Kate. She saw a catheter pipe snaking its way out from under the blankets to a clear bag hanging under the bed. She imagined seizing the pipe and yanking it out of his urethra. Might that make him understand just a tiny fraction of the pain he had caused? Kate sat back in her chair next to the bed. 'Do you know I work as a private detective?'

Peter frowned. ''Course I do. I'm not forgetful. I mean, I remember . . . Jake was just telling me that he lives in America and he's working as a writer.'

'I work for an agent who represents writers,' said Jake.

Peter frowned and coughed. He brought his hand up to his mouth, and the IV in his right arm lifted with it. He looked at it for a moment. 'What's the difference?'

'We do just as much work but only make fifteen percent.'

Peter smiled and chuckled. The sound, like a cross between a baby and an evil goblin, made Kate shudder.

'Can I ask you to look at a photo?' said Kate.

'Is it of Jake when he was little?' asked Peter, and his face lit up. 'I never got to see many pictures of you when you were growing up. Did I?'

'No. This is a photo of a young girl called Janey Macklin,' said Kate, and she opened the iPad and held up the school photo of Janey.

Peter peered at the screen. 'Who is it?'

'She lived in King's Cross. Her mother used to take her to The Jug pub, on Pancras Road,' said Kate. She scrolled through the iPad to the next photo, which was of Janey and Maxine together wearing their dance leotards.

'Two of them,' said Peter, rolling his tongue around his mouth. 'The Jug pub . . . Oh, yes.'

He was silent, and Kate watched his face as he studied the photo.

'Do you recognise them?'

'Liked to play together. Games together. I spoke to them, did I?'

Kate saw Jake holding Peter's hand.

'This girl, Janey Macklin, she went missing in 1988 just before Christmas,' said Kate. 'You would have been training to be a police officer in Hendon at the time . . . What do you mean "games together"? They played on the *Space Invaders* machine in the corner of the pub. The type you put money into. Five-pence pieces . . .' Kate knew her questions were too leading, but she was desperate now to make him answer, to find out information before he fell asleep or unconscious.

'They used to go there with their mother, bit of an old . . . *slag*,' said Peter. He looked over at Jake and repeated the word *slag* with a nasty smile.

Kate scrolled through to the photos of Robert, Roland, and Forrest.

'Do you recognise any of these young men? They would have been around at the same time, in The Jug.'

Peter's eyes widened, and he blinked and looked away from the glow of the screen.

Kate scrolled back to the school photo of Janey, and she held it up again. 'Peter. I really need you to look at this, and tell me what you know about this girl?'

'Too many colours. The world is too bright these days,' he slurred. He squinted at the screen. 'Oh.'

'What?'

'That's the one. The one from our plan. The body buried in the graveyard.'

Kate sat up and leaned closer. 'What body?'

Peter turned to Jake. 'You're my boy?'

'Yeah,' said Jake.

'Peter! What body buried in the graveyard? Please, it's important . . . And whose plan?'

Peter gripped Jake's hand harder. 'I love you, boy. Not sure there's . . . been much love in my heart, but . . . I do . . .' Peter closed his eyes.

Kate scrolled back to the picture of Janey and Maxine.

'Peter. Peter! *Peter!*' she said, raising her voice. She leant out to shake him, but Jake put his hand on her shoulder.

'Mum. Don't shout.'

Kate sat back. Peter breathed in and out. Kate held the iPad up to his face, hoping if he opened his eyes he might say more. The blue background from Janey Macklin's school photo reflected on his wrinkled and hollow face with its half-circle of black stitches on the temple. Peter took a deep breath, and there was a long moment before he exhaled. Kate closed the iPad and felt an overwhelming frustration.

'Mum. Is he . . . ?'

Peter didn't inhale, and they watched and waited for a long moment, and then he wheezed and sucked in air, his chest rising.

'Should I get the nurse?'

'No. You hold his hand,' said Kate. 'I'll go.'

When Kate came back into the room a few seconds later, Jake looked up at them. 'He's not breathing.' The nurse went to check on him. 'Aren't you going to do anything?'

'We've been doing all we can, Jake,' said the nurse.

Peter inhaled, then gave a shuddering exhale, but this time the pause went on and on.

Peter Conway had been pale and drawn, but it was only as the life drained away from him that Kate saw the colour leave his face.

'He's dying,' said Jake, choking back tears. Kate moved around to him and put her arms around his shoulders. 'His hand, it's . . . getting cold.'

The last of the colour and the life of the Nine Elms

Cannibal drained away, and they were left with what looked like a waxwork. An odd emptiness descended over the room. It was as if, even on his deathbed, Peter Conway had generated a towering presence, but now he was gone.

Taking his secrets with him.

37

Tristan finally left the crime scene at Baywater House just after 5pm. Constable Megan Levitt had spoken to DI Sean Bentley, and seemed rather annoyed that Tristan was telling the truth. After he'd signed an official statement, he was free to go, but he was left to walk back to the station by himself. He took the Tube to King's Cross St Pancras station, feeling demoralised. Kate was still not answering her phone, and he wondered what was happening with Peter Conway. The snow was melting, and the pavements and roads were covered in a grimy grey slush. The temperature seemed to drop rapidly, and during the short walk from the station, the brown slush on the roads was turning to ice. When he arrived back at the flat, the photographers were gone, and the circle was quiet.

He let himself into the flat and switched on the heating, standing in the harsh light of the living room. Tristan felt far from home, and he was still in shock from finding the body. He needed a friendly face to talk to, and would have given anything to put on some jeans and a sweater and go down to

The Boar's Head for a pint with his friend Ade. Even seeing his sister and Gary would be nice right now, he thought.

Tristan took a shower, dressed in sweats, and came through to the kitchen. He found the bottle of schnapps and poured a glass, dropping in a cube of ice. He sat on the sofa with the TV off, staring into the middle distance. He was experiencing delayed shock. If someone had killed Roland, it had to be linked to the case. He didn't have much of any value in the flat, and there was no evidence of drugs, which could rule out a burglary. He took a long drink of the schnapps – it wasn't too bad with ice – and it warmed him up and soothed his nerves. His phone rang, and he saw it was Kate.

'Finally. You've picked up your phone,' he said. It came out angrier than he intended.

'Peter Conway died this afternoon,' she said without preamble.

Tristan sat up and felt the room spinning. The alcohol had hit him hard on an empty stomach. 'Bloody hell. Are you okay?'

'Yeah. It was very peaceful, which is more than he deserved. That's why I've been out of contact.'

'Sorry, I didn't mean to snap at you . . . I feel like I should give you my condolences.'

'It's okay. It's a weird one. I thought I'd feel a release when he died, but I just feel a bit empty.'

'What about Jake?'

'I don't think he knows how to feel.'

'Where are you now?'

'We're still here at the hospital. There's tons of press

outside, and they want to get us out through the back entrance before the news is released to the media. Wakefield prison is quickly drafting a short press release, which they want us to see before the news is sent out.'

'Why are they quickly drafting it?'

Kate gave a dry laugh. 'They want to make the evening news, and the morning's papers. That's why they want to get us out now.'

'The photographers are gone from outside the flat.'

'They'll be back.'

'Did you ask Peter about Janey?'

'Yes. I showed him photos. He recalled seeing Janey and Maxine, and he said something that could be everything or nothing. He said, *That's the one. The one from our plan. The body buried in the graveyard.*'

'Bloody hell. What does that mean?'

'I don't know. The inconsiderate bastard then died.'

'Talk about a cliffhanger,' said Tristan.

Kate snorted. 'I shouldn't laugh.'

'I won't tell anyone.'

'How did it go with Roland? I've got so many missed calls from you, but I thought I'd just call.'

Tristan told her about finding the body, and dealing with the police afterwards.

'Oh my word. Are you okay?'

'I will be. Still a bit in shock, really. I'm drinking that old bottle of schnapps someone left behind. They're going to check dental records to ID the body, after I told them about him being Roland Hacker, or Jon Chase, as he's now known. I found a bank statement in the flat, dated almost a year ago.

It showed a payment of £300 from Forrest into Jon Chase's bank account. I took photos of it, and the crime scene.'

'Tristan. That's incredible. If Roland was killed, then . . .'

'Did he know something? Where does this leave us now with Peter Conway? Did he seem out of it on all the meds?'

'Yes. But with him, I'd think that the meds would make his tongue looser, not the other way around.'

He heard Kate sigh.

'I'm sorry I wasn't there when you needed me,' said Kate.

'It's okay. You have a good excuse. Are you staying up there when you get out of the hospital?' asked Tristan.

'I don't want to stay here tonight, and I don't think Jake does, either. When we're finished here, we're going to drive back to London. We'll be back very late, and I have a key. Do you realise we've got our first feedback meeting on Thursday morning with Fidelis and Maddie at Stafford-Clarke?'

'We've got plenty to tell them. A lot of it they probably don't want to hear, or Maddie won't want to hear about Forrest.'

'Yes.'

They were both silent on the phone.

Tristan took another drink of his schnapps. 'Text me when you're close – I might still be up.'

'Don't wait up for us. Get some sleep. You sound exhausted. We can pick up on everything in detail tomorrow morning.'

'Okay. Drive safe.'

When he came off the phone, he poured himself another schnapps and drank it in the dark. He kept seeing the wide-eyed, blood-soaked stare of Roland sitting dead in his underwear in a lonely top-floor flat, so he forced himself to get up, and he went through to the bedroom to put his phone on its charger. When he sat on the end of the bed, a crashing tiredness came over him, and he lay back, pulling the corner of the rug over him. He fell asleep instantly.

————

When Tristan woke up a few hours later, disorientated, it was dark and his head was spinning. He lay for a moment trying to work out where he was, until he saw the dim light shining through the window that looked out at the tiny courtyard behind the flat. His bedroom door was ajar, and he heard a rustling noise out in the living room. The noise came again, papers turning in the silence, soft footsteps on the wooden floor. Tristan sat up. He saw through the gap in the door where a figure stood by the bookshelves in front of the living room window. He stared for a moment, thinking it was Jake or Kate, but as he watched, the figure moved in the shadows, reaching up to the shelves where the DVDs were kept.

Tristan got up from the bed and moved closer, quiet in his bare feet. He stood in the doorway to the living room, and watched as the figure left what they were doing at the bookshelf and moved across the room. The light was dim, but it looked like the cupboard door next to the kitchen, which had always been locked, now stood open. The figure moved to the door and then vanished inside.

What the hell? thought Tristan. He moved into the living room and felt a freezing draft coming from the open door. When he reached the door, a soft glow emanated from inside, and as he drew closer, the cupboard seemed to be very deep, and the light was coming from low down. *Is that a staircase?* thought Tristan.

Suddenly he heard footsteps, and the figure reappeared from inside and came rushing at him. Before Tristan could react, he'd been tackled and knocked down. He landed with a heavy thud on the wooden floor. The figure straddled him and, with lightning speed, had their hands around his throat. Tristan could tell from the size and the strength and the smell of perspiration that this was a man.

Tristan had been using one of the small dumbbell weights he'd brought with him as a doorstop for the kitchen, and as he reached around, he felt his hand close over it. He wasn't able to bring it up with a great deal of force, but he was able to hit the man in the chest and knock him off. He fell back with a yell.

Tristan sat up, coughing, and tried to lift the weight so he could heft it as a weapon, but he fell back and the weight hit him in the face, knocking him unconscious.

38

It was 4.30am when Kate and Jake turned into Percy Circus in their hire car. There was a black taxi ahead of them, and it stopped outside the flat. Tristan got out and paid the driver. He was wearing an old white tracksuit, and Kate could see there was blood on the front of the hoodie and he had a bandage on the left side of his head. He was carrying a small paper bag. Kate pulled into the spot recently vacated by the taxi. Tristan came to the car door.

'What's going on?' Kate asked when they got out.

'Someone broke in,' said Tristan.

'Were you attacked?'

'Sort of. I'm fine. Hey, Jake. Sorry about . . . you know,' said Tristan.

'Thanks,' said Jake. Tristan gave him a hug.

'Hang on, what do you mean you were "sort of" attacked?' asked Kate, peering at the bandage on his forehead.

'Can we go in? I'm freezing.'

Jake took his suitcase from the back of the car, and they followed Tristan. He opened the main front door, and when they were in the small hallway, Kate saw the front door to the flat was covered in a silver fingerprint powder, speckled around the door handle and keyhole.

'I called the police and a paramedic came. They took me to Accident and Emergency,' said Tristan. He opened the front door and switched on the light. Fingerprint powder was dotted around the walls, on the locked cupboard, and on the DVD shelf. Kate saw a five-kilogram dumbbell lying beside a dent in the wooden floor. 'I used that in self-defence, but I ended up dropping it on my head,' said Tristan. 'When I came round a couple of minutes later, the intruder was gone.'

'What did they say at the hospital?' asked Kate, looking around the room and feeling dismayed.

'I had a scan and tests. I'm okay, but I have three stitches and some antibiotics and painkillers,' said Tristan, holding up the paper bag.

'Okay.'

'I don't know how they – he – got in. After I spoke to you on the phone, I went to my room and fell asleep. When I woke up, the lights were off, and there was a man here in the living room looking around the shelf there. That cupboard door was open, and he went inside. I went to the door, and that's when he attacked me and knocked me to the ground.'

'Did you see his face?' asked Kate.

'No. It was dark, and he might have been wearing a balaclava. He was strong when he tackled me to the floor. Maybe a little shorter than me, but I'm pretty tall.'

'What did the police say?'

'They asked if anything had been stolen, which there wasn't. My laptop and wallet were on the table, and this guy didn't take them. By the time the police got here, he was gone. They think the intruder picked the lock, or had a key. There was no sign of forced entry. I'm sorry. I didn't put the deadbolt on when I came back.'

'Don't apologise.'

'The forensics officer arrived when they took me to A&E,' said Tristan, indicating the fingerprint dust all over the walls.

Kate went to the cupboard door and tried the handle. 'Are you sure this was open?'

He nodded. Kate could see Tristan and Jake were exhausted, and she'd never felt so tired in her life. The thought of having to find somewhere else to stay was too much. 'Let's check the doors, make sure they're locked with the deadbolts on. The windows all have bars. Let's try and get some sleep. It will be light in a few hours. Okay?' Tristan nodded and went off to the bathroom. Jake went to the sofa and pulled off two huge cushions. 'Will you take those cushions and sleep on the floor in Tristan's room? I just want to make sure he's okay.'

————

Kate woke late when the door buzzer sounded. She checked her watch and saw it was 2pm. She pulled on her jeans as the door buzzed again. Tristan's door was shut, and Jake must have moved in the night, he was now snoring under a blanket on the sofa.

Maddie was standing on the doorstep when Kate opened

the main door. She had a carrier bag hooked over her arm. Three photographers stood by the railing circling the small park, and they fired off their cameras at the sight of Kate, bleary eyed and dishevelled.

'Kate. Hi. I had a call from the police about a break-in,' said Maddie, her face etched with concern. She turned around to look at the photographers. 'May I come in?'

'Yes,' said Kate, her voice still thick with sleep. Maddie came through to the hallway and closed the door. She was wearing a big brown duffel coat with a green snood. Her glasses started to steam up. 'My son, Jake, is asleep on the sofa. We just got back late from Wakefield.'

'I know about Peter Conway's death. I've seen the papers,' said Maddie, shaking her head.

'It's in more than one?' asked Kate, realising the stupidity of the question as soon as she said it.

'All the front pages, I'm afraid. Where does it leave us with the Janey Macklin case?'

'I don't know.'

Maddie shook her head again. 'Is it frightfully strange for Jake?' she asked, as she craned her neck ever so slightly, to try and see round the living room door.

'Yes. Having these photographers following us isn't fun.'

'I suppose we'll never know about all the things he did – Peter. Anyway, I didn't come to talk shop. We can do that when you come in tomorrow morning for our weekly update. I just wanted to check that Tristan's okay. The police said the intruder attacked him?'

'Yes. But he's okay. He had to have three stitches in his forehead.'

'Oh, God,' said Maddie, putting a hand up to her mouth. Kate noted she was wearing green mittens which matched her snood. 'Poor chap.'

'The police think that whoever did it picked the lock or had a key, to get through this outer door and the flat's front door,' said Kate.

Maddie stared at the fingerprint dust on the door. 'Picked a lock?'

'Or had a key.'

'Well, I'm the only one with a key. We also have a key that Forrest uses when he lets in guests, and then two other keys, which you and Tristan have.'

'Where was Forrest last night?' asked Kate.

Maddie put her glasses back on, and she pulled a dismayed face. 'Are you serious? He was with me last night,' she said, breaking into a laugh of disbelief.

'Sorry. It's been a long, weird couple of days.'

'Of course. That's fine. But the door is okay? There's no damage to the lock?' she said, turning to check it.

'No.'

'This is usually such a safe place. There hasn't been a break-in here for as long as I can remember. Well, I just wanted to check on you, and I've brought this,' she said, holding up the carrier bag. 'It's my peach cobbler. The peaches are from my parents' house in Kent. I didn't know what to do, so I thought, bring dessert!' She laughed awkwardly.

'Thank you,' said Kate.

'Right, I'll let you be. And of course, if you need anything, just shout.'

Kate went back inside and heard the photographers yelling questions, and Maddie trilling, 'No comment, sorry!' Kate peered out of a crack through the blinds and saw Maddie getting into a car Forrest was driving.

A little while later, Tristan ventured out to buy food and all the newspapers. It was as Kate feared: not only did every tabloid dredge up Peter Conway's crimes, but there were several lurid articles about Kate, and Jake's parentage. More than anything she wished she were back in Ashdean, far away from everything, with her own space to walk on the beach and swim in the sea. Around 4pm, Kate made them all eggs and bacon, which they finished with the peach cobbler with some ice cream.

'I'm going to have a shower,' said Jake, pushing out his chair and getting up. 'Thanks for the food, Mum.'

Jake went out to use the bathroom and closed the door. Kate gathered up the dirty plates and started to stack the dishwasher. Tristan waited a moment and then asked, 'How is he?'

'I don't know. He spent an hour on the phone to Olivia when you went out for the papers, but I don't know what they spoke about. He seems okay. Maybe we need a distraction.'

She went to the DVD shelf and started to look for something to watch. Tristan went to the blinds on the living room window and lifted them a tiny crack. 'Five photographers. They all look frozen,' he said.

The toilet flushed, and a minute later, Jake poked his head out of the bathroom door. 'Is there a spare towel, Mum?'

'There's a dry one on the top of the heated rail,' said Kate, staring at the line of fingerprint dust on the bottom shelf. 'DVD boxes . . . Have you looked in any of these?'

'No. I haven't had time to watch anything,' said Tristan. 'We just arranged a few of them for that photographer.'

'And we've assumed they all contained DVDs?'

'Yeah.'

Tristan came over to the shelf. Kate pulled out one of the DVDs on the first shelf and opened the case. It contained a disc. Tristan pulled out another one, and then they started to work along the shelves, pulling out the boxes, checking behind them and inside. On the second shelf, Kate pulled out a DVD for the film *Gigli*. The box felt heavier. She opened it, and taped inside was a small digital voice recorder, no bigger than a slim cigarette case. The small screen showed the seconds counting and that it was recording.

A look of alarm passed between them. Tristan leaned over to switch it off.

'No. Prints,' said Kate. He went and got his backpack. He put it on the sofa and took out a pair of latex gloves and a clear plastic evidence bag. Using the tip of a biro, Kate switched off the voice recorder. There was a beep, and the counter stopped.

'I've seen these before. It's voice activated, and it holds a couple of thousand hours of audio.'

'It's showing it's been running for fourteen hours,' said Kate.

'Which would be from when that intruder broke in last night,' said Tristan. 'Whoever it was, they were doing something on this shelf when I saw them. I only saw their shadow. How high up was the DVD?'

'It was on this shelf at eye line,' said Kate. She examined the box. 'Look, there's a square of plastic missing on the back.'

Tristan took the DVD box from her. 'It's so there's only the DVD inlay paper covering the microphone,' he said.

'Do you think whoever broke in had a key and expected the flat to be empty?'

'And what if it's not the first time someone has broken in?' said Kate.

39

'We need to call Varia Campbell,' said Kate, holding the bagged-up voice recorder. Tristan still had his backpack and took out the skeleton keys. He went to the locked cupboard door, and tried the handle. He knelt down by the keyhole and peered inside.

'I'd forgotten with everything that happened. When I followed the guy to this cupboard and the door was open, it looked bigger inside than you'd think.'

'What can you see?' asked Kate.

'Nothing. It's dark.' He unzipped the leather wallet with the selection of lock picks and skeleton and bump keys. 'It doesn't look very sophisticated. I think a bump key would get it open without doing any damage,' he said.

Tristan tried one of the bump keys. He turned it slowly. 'No.'

He withdrew it, and Kate put the voice recorder on the table and joined him. She knelt down, activated the torch on her phone, and peered through the keyhole. 'Try a rake key.'

Tristan selected one of the silver keys with a serrated edge. Kate sat back on her heels, and he slipped it into the keyhole. The lock sounded well oiled. The rake key turned with a click, and the door opened with a creak.

A cold blast of air gusted into the living room, carrying a strong smell of perfumed air-freshener. It wasn't a cupboard at all – it was a short passage with a set of stairs leading down.

'Maddie told us this was their cupboard for storing bedding and towels,' said Kate.

There was a light switch inside the door, and Tristan flicked it on. The wooden staircase curled around a corner. The air seemed to crackle with excitement as Kate and Tristan stepped inside.

They went down the narrow staircase and found another light switch. The stairs opened out into a large basement with crumbling plaster walls, lit by a single dingy bulb. Stacked up against one wall were sacks of cement, an old wheelbarrow, spades, and buckets.

Kate angled her phone light up to the ceiling. There was a line of solid gel air-fresheners in their little plastic housings lined up along one ledge on the wall. The floor was uneven and made of bare concrete.

'The smell is a bit much,' said Tristan, putting his arm over his mouth and nose.

'And they're all lemon scented, which makes it worse,' said Kate, putting her arm over her own mouth and nose and feeling the sting of the chemicals in her eyes.

'There's thirty sacks of cement,' said Tristan.

'A wheelbarrow.' Kate knelt next to a plastic storage box

tucked between the wheelbarrow and a couple of buckets and opened the lid. 'This looks like overalls for doing painting and decorating.' She lifted them up and pulled out rolls of bin liners and packets of wet wipes, and then at the bottom, she found a couple of large square packages. 'Tris. Look.'

He came over to where she was crouching down, and she held up one of the plastic-wrapped packages.

'White chlorine-free body bag – adult size,' he said, reading the sticker on the packet. He picked one of them up.

'Adult standard size, ninety by two hundred and forty centimetres. Reinforced polythene, with stitched seams, leak resistant. Includes three paper toe tags and adhesive biohazard pouch. And there are four,' said Kate. She'd now taken everything out of the plastic box. 'There are a load more air-fresheners in their boxes. The same lemon-scented smell.'

Tristan looked around the concrete basement. 'Forrest and Maddie? No. This doesn't make sense.'

'What about all these air-fresheners? There's ten on that ledge?'

Kate swung her phone torch around. She lit up a wet patch running along the wall on the right-hand side, and there was some black mould peppering the damp. There was also a damp patch in the floor, around where the concrete dipped unevenly.

'It could be to deal with any smell it's making in the rest of the flat? Listen. Without the body bags, this is all building stuff,' said Kate.

'They've hired us as private investigators,' said Tristan.

'Like I said. There could be an explanation for all of it. They want to do building work on the place. Maybe they got overalls mixed up with body bags when they ordered online. Can you order a body bag on Amazon?'

Tristan checked on his phone.

'Yes. You can,' he said a moment later. 'Okay, this is the actual description: "Body bag for dead people . . . Waterproof human bag with four reinforced handles." Eighteen ninety-nine plus free delivery.'

Kate leaned over to look at his phone.

'With a four-point-six-star review average. And they come in four colours: white, black, coffee, and beige. Even though this is very strange, we can't jump to conclusions, Tris,' she said. He took photos, and then she started to pack everything back into the box.

Tristan noticed something in the corner. It was the packing from a sandwich, bought from Tesco supermarket, and an empty can of Coke. He picked up the sandwich packet.

'The use-by date on this is three days ago,' he said. 'Was someone spending a lot of time down here, when we were upstairs in the flat?'

40

The next morning, the press photographers were gone from outside the flat. Kate and Tristan took the train over to High Street Kensington for their first weekly meeting with Maddie and Fidelis at the offices of Stafford-Clarke.

The office was much busier than it had been when they met in December, and despite them being bang on time, a receptionist asked them to wait in a small, chilly room just off the entrance which was filled with books and easy chairs.

Tristan popped a couple of painkillers out of a foil packet and took them with a swig of water.

'You okay?' she asked. He'd removed the gauze compress from his forehead and covered the stitches with a small flesh-coloured plaster. He touched it lightly with his fingers to make sure it was sticking.

'It feels better today.'

The front door buzzed, and they heard the click-clack of heels on the wooden floor.

'India, darling! How are you?' said a booming male voice.

'Cold. This weather!' There was a lot of *mwah-mwahing* as they air-kissed. 'I'm sorry the heating's on the blink. Come upstairs. Julian's ready for you, with a gas heater!' Their footsteps retreated upstairs.

'I feel like we're waiting to see the headmistress,' said Tristan.

'She's not going to like what we have to say.'

They heard a door open, and then Fidelis's assistant, Sophie, poked her head around the door. 'Morning. They're ready for you.'

Fidelis was waiting to greet them in her office, which was very cold. She wore another one of her tabard-style dresses, which were very baggy with lots of pockets, and she had on thick woollen stripy socks and slippers. Maddie and Forrest sat on wooden, high-backed chairs next to Fidelis's desk.

'Hello, we didn't know you would all be here,' said Kate as Forrest stood up. Despite the cold, he was wearing jeans and a flannel shirt open at the neck and moccasins with no socks. Maddie, in contrast, had on denim dungarees with a huge, thick fleece jacket and green UGG boots. They all air-kissed, which felt completely at odds with the nature of the meeting they were about to have.

'I do hope you're not too shaken up?' said Fidelis. 'We heard about the break-in.'

'The police sent someone who fingerprinted the whole flat,' said Kate.

'Really? That's optimistic,' said Forrest.

'I would have thought that's good,' said Maddie.

'The police don't seem to bother with so many things these days. Did they find anything?' asked Forrest.

'We'll see.'

'And, of course, hello,' he said, shaking their hands.

'Do sit down,' said Fidelis, indicating the sofa opposite her desk. Kate and Tristan sat down, and it felt a little like they were at a job interview in front of a panel.

'We've heard the sad news about Peter Conway. I'm unsure whether or not to give my condolences,' said Fidelis.

'No need,' said Kate.

'I don't know if you buy into the concept of silver linings, but Peter Conway's death has renewed interest in this case. I've had several inquiries about our potential true crime project. Audible and Apple, to name but two. How long do you think you would need to reach a satisfying conclusion?'

Fidelis raised her eyebrows expectantly.

'There are a few things we need to discuss,' said Kate.

'By all means; this is our first weekly catch-up and your chance to brief us on your progress.'

Kate and Tristan started by revisiting the conversation they'd had with Forrest and his sighting of Peter Conway in The Jug around the time that Janey Macklin went missing. Kate also told them of Peter Conway's last words, when she showed him the photo of Janey Macklin: *That's the one. The one from our plan. The body buried in the graveyard.*

'Which plan did he mean? And do you believe the body is the body of Janey Macklin? Are you thinking that it was Peter Conway who abducted and potentially killed her?' asked Fidelis.

'Yes. But without any more information, it's going to be very difficult to proceed,' said Kate.

Fidelis nodded. 'Well. This DNA sample found in the pipe behind Reynolds newsagent. That's a real breakthrough in terms of where Janey's body lay, even if it was then moved to another location. And it's still early days. That could give us something for the project to start with?'

'We're thinking that first and foremost this is a murder investigation, not a project,' said Kate.

'Of course. I'm thinking with my publishing brain . . . What do you propose next? You mentioned that you have a working relationship with the police officer who is planning to reopen the case. Will you have the opportunity to share information with them? New leads?'

Kate hesitated. 'We do have another thing to talk about. This concerns you, Forrest. There are some things troubling us about your link to Janey Macklin.'

'Like what?' he said. Maddie glanced at him, and Fidelis kept the expectant smile on her face.

'When we spoke to you a few days ago in Barnes, you said that you were no longer in contact with Roland Hacker. Is that correct?'

Forrest hesitated. 'Well . . . what do you mean?'

'On Tuesday morning, we traced Roland Hacker to an address near Watford, in the Baywater House estate where he was living for the past two years. He'd changed his name to Jon Chase,' said Tristan. Maddie looked to Forrest.

'When I said I didn't know his whereabouts, he was no longer Roland Hacker . . .' He laughed awkwardly and looked to Fidelis for help, but she was watching curiously from behind her desk. 'Can I just say. This meeting feels like I'm being investigated, which I'm not,' said Forrest, standing up. 'I'm here as a courtesy to you.'

'Forrest. Please, sit down,' said Fidelis. He did so, obediently. 'Jon Chase isn't necessarily an unusual name. Even with my name, there's another Fidelis who works as a desk editor for HarperCollins.'

'Another Fidelis Stafford?' asked Kate.

'Well, no,' snapped Fidelis, looking embarrassed. 'I'm merely illustrating the point that some people can have the same names.' A vein pulsed in her forehead, and Kate could tell she didn't like being contradicted.

'Roland's full legal name was Roland Giles Quintus Hacker, and Jon Chase shared the same middle names, which, are unusual,' said Kate.

'On Tuesday, I visited the flat belonging to Jon Chase,' said Tristan. 'And that's where I found him dead. He'd been murdered. Stabbed sixteen times with a knife.'

There was a crashing silence, and Maddie turned to Forrest. When their eyes met, she looked away and back to Kate and Tristan.

'A dead body?' repeated Maddie.

'No. *His* dead body. The police used dental records and have proved that Jon Chase was Roland Hacker. A postmortem is being carried out today,' said Tristan.

Kate could see that Forrest was itching to leave, but Maddie was gripping his hand.

'I found this bank statement at Roland's flat, dated November 2017,' said Tristan. He produced another piece of paper with a section highlighted. 'It shows a payment of three hundred pounds being credited from your bank account, Forrest. Can you confirm this is your bank account?' He held it out to Forrest, but Maddie took it. Fidelis was silent.

'Yes, that's Forrest's bank account,' said Maddie in a small voice.

'We've had troubling issues with this case from the beginning,' said Kate. 'We weren't aware when we first took the job that Forrest was a close friend of Robert Driscoll and Roland Hacker. When we interviewed Forrest last week, he went on record to say that he was no longer in contact with Roland.'

'Excuse me, I'm sitting right here,' said Forrest.

'Yes. I think it would be best to let Forrest explain?' asked Fidelis. He was sitting with his shoulders hunched over. His eyes were wide. Maddie let go of his hand and flexed hers, as if he'd been gripping it too tight. They waited, and Forrest blustered for a moment.

'Okay. This is . . . I should say, I didn't mention this because of Roland's, Jon's, mental health issues. Yeah? Which are private. He has suffered for many years with mental illness, and part of that manifested itself as him wanting to be a recluse . . . So yes, we did have sporadic contact, and I helped him out a few times with money.'

Fidelis looked between Maddie and Forrest.

'A few times?' repeated Kate.

'The details are none of your business. I'm sorry. I'm drawing the line here. I just tried to help an old friend, a *mentally ill* old friend, who, I've just heard, has been killed!'

Forrest got up and started to gather up his coat. 'I'm done here.'

Fidelis stood up. 'Forrest, just hold on. I think what Kate and Tristan are asking is that we put our cards on the table and share what we know. And in the spirit of that goodwill, they would of course deal with any information discreetly. Yes?'

'Of course,' said Kate. Forrest stood by his chair, gripping his coat.

'They've signed an NDA, haven't they?' he asked.

Kate looked over at Maddie. A flicker in her eye indicated that someone in the agency had screwed up. Maddie knew there wasn't a signed NDA in place, but she was too afraid to tell Fidelis and Forrest at this late stage. Kate decided to go out on a limb, and lie.

'Yes, of course we have,' she said. Tristan caught on and nodded in agreement. There was a sticky moment where Kate thought Maddie would speak up, but she didn't say anything, and looked down at the carpet.

Fidelis looked relieved.

'I always say that an NDA chases the blues away . . . So you see, Forrest, we're all on the same side here. Anything said in this room is confidential.' She looked at him and raised an eyebrow.

'I just want you to know that I've done nothing wrong. In fact, you must be able to understand this is why I changed my name. This bloody . . . This Janey Macklin case has followed me like an albatross around my neck.'

Maddie had been sitting very still and watching warily the

whole time. She seemed to relax her shoulders a little when he sat down.

'Thank you, Forrest,' said Kate, understanding that he was a childish man prone to tantrums. 'May I ask, just so we can have the facts straight: When did you last have contact with Roland?'

He took a deep breath, and his shoulders seemed to sag. 'A few days before I sent him the money . . . and then, we only spoke on the phone. He called me one night in distress. I wanted to help.'

'What kind of distress was he in?'

'Financial. He'd lost his job in an office doing data entry. He wasn't sleeping. He had arrears in rent. He'd cut himself off from everyone, and his parents had passed away. What money they'd left him was gone.'

'You sent him money. Did you go and see him?' asked Tristan.

'No. I didn't know where he lived!'

'How often did you send him money?' asked Kate.

'I don't think that's relevant,' said Maddie.

'Really? We expect some resistance when we investigate cold cases; what we don't expect is people closely connected to the client to . . .'

'Lie to us,' finished Tristan.

'I was trying to protect my friend. He had nothing to do with all of this. He was a sweet guy with problems,' said Forrest.

'Are you in contact with Robert Driscoll?' asked Kate.

Forrest rolled his eyes. 'I did speak to him a few years ago about Roland. Again, it was on the phone.'

'What about when Robert's mother died three years ago? Did you attend her funeral?'

Maddie shot a look at Forrest.

'Yes, we did. But I didn't hang around to talk to Robert.'

'You both went to the funeral?'

'Robert lived in the Golden Lane flats, and Forrest had a separate relationship with Robert's mother. She was kind to him when he was little,' said Maddie.

'Did you speak to Robert Driscoll at the funeral?' asked Kate.

'Fleetingly.'

Kate sighed. 'You've both lied to us.'

'We did *not lie*!' said Maddie, raising her voice and slapping the back of her right hand against the palm of the left. Her eyes were wild.

'Okay. Let's just take a step back,' said Fidelis, watching the sudden outburst from behind her desk. 'We have an NDA. This is good. We can all speak the truth in a safe space.'

'We don't have an NDA!' shrilled Maddie at Fidelis. 'They haven't signed anything!' There was a long silence.

'What the? Jesus fucking Christ, Fidelis. I've given them an interview on record. They told me there was an NDA!' said Forrest

'Let's just all remember where we are,' said Fidelis with a hint of danger in her voice. Maddie kept her eyes on the carpet.

'I'm sorry,' said Forrest, swallowing hard and seeming to realise how strong his outburst had been. Kate decided to go in for the kill.

'Madeleine. When we first met you at the Percy Circus

flat and you gave us the keys, you told us that the locked cupboard in the living room contained bedding and towels. . .' Maddie looked up at her. 'When the flat was broken into, Tristan disturbed the intruder, who had the door to that cupboard open. Yesterday we unlocked the door and found it leads down to a cellar filled with building materials, cement, spades, and buckets, and there was also a plastic box with several disposable body bags,' said Kate. 'Can you throw any light on this? It does seem rather suspicious when we're investigating a missing person.'

Tristan glanced at Kate. This was going further than they'd agreed.

'You broke into that door?' asked Maddie.

'We opened it. We didn't break the lock. It's an internal door in a property we were renting.'

Fidelis was now looking concerned.

'I told you it was a cupboard because of health and safety,' said Maddie. 'The cellar has an uneven floor, and we're storing building materials down there for when we redo the property. I meant to buy groundsheets for the building and decorating work.' Maddie touched her hand to her stomach. 'I'm actually pregnant . . . and all of this anger is not good for my unborn baby.' Kate and Tristan remained silent. Fidelis looked deeply concerned. 'I've been suffering from memory loss and some fogginess. The body bag product looked very similar on the online product listing of groundsheets. When they were delivered, I didn't open the packaging for a while, and by the time I did and saw the mistake, the date had passed to get a refund.' Maddie's hand on her stomach was shaking. She looked up at Kate and Tristan. 'So you see, there's an explanation for everything. And I'm sorry, Fidelis, about the NDA.' Maddie stood up and turned to Kate and Tristan. 'I think that a line has been crossed here. If you two think throwing out an accusation with that gravity, with no evidence, is good detective work, then I question your skills as private detectives.'

Fidelis stood up.

'Yes. I think you both need to leave.'

41

It was snowing again when Kate and Tristan left the offices of Stafford-Clarke. They walked in silence until they reached an old-style Italian deli on the corner. It was half-empty, and they went inside to warm up and ordered coffee.

'Did we just screw that up?' asked Tristan as they took a table by the fogged-up picture window. A blur or cars and people moved past on the other side. 'We've only been working on the case for just over a week.'

'Perhaps. But I also think that pushing people's buttons tends to get the best results. I should have asked them about the voice recorder we found hidden in the living room. Thrown that in for good measure.'

'When do you think Varia will come back to us with the results of the fingerprints on the voice recorder?' said Tristan.

'I hope soon,' said Kate. 'Was the intruder wearing gloves?'

'I can't remember.'

'Fidelis seemed to think we're all working towards a

creative project, rather than this being a murder investigation. Were you watching her face? Most of what happened seemed to catch her off guard. Particularly the lack of an NDA.'

They sipped their coffee for a moment.

'At what point do we rule out Peter Conway?' asked Tristan.

'We don't, yet. I want to talk to Thomas Black and ask him about Conway's final words. *That's the one. The one from our plan. The body buried in the graveyard.* We also need to keep the heat on Robert and Forrest. They were this tight unit with Roland, and then after Janey Macklin went missing, they all flew apart. I understand why Forrest might want to distance himself from Robert Driscoll, but Robert also lied to us when we went to visit him. He said he's had no contact with Forrest or Roland. Why? What's he got to lose? He's been tried and then acquitted for Janey Macklin's murder. Their denial is in synch.'

'There's no crime if we can't find a body. I doubt the CPS would want to try anyone again unless there is a body.'

'What are our options? Robert Driscoll did it, Forrest did it, or Roland.'

'Peter Conway did it, or Conway helped them to hide the body?' said Kate. Tristan shook his head.

'That's too complicated. If Conway knew about it, then why didn't he spill the beans when he was locked up for all those years? Information like that is gold. And it would have been sport for him, to know where the body was buried. His silence doesn't make sense.'

'Forrest and Maxine remember seeing Peter Conway in

The Jug. And when I spoke to Peter just before he died and showed him the photos of Janey and Maxine, there was a spark of recognition. . . But he was out of it. . .Thomas Black puts him in The Jug in his letters.'

'Maxine is the most believable witness for me. She's the only one who has no reason to lie.'

Kate's phone rang and she pulled it out of her pocket. 'It's Fidelis.'

She answered and put it on speaker-phone.

'Kate. Hello. I just thought I should touch base after our meeting, which I think got a little out of hand,' she said.

'I'm here with Tristan. We've got you on speaker-phone.'

The coffee machine began to hiss in the background, and Tristan leaned closer to hear.

'We've just had a discussion here, and we're feeling that perhaps we should leave things there, for now.'

'I don't understand,' said Kate.

'When we took your agency on, we thought you would be best placed to help uncover the story, the tragic story of Janey Macklin. We're so very grateful for all of your work, but I think it's best if we don't move forward with anything more.'

'You're firing us?' said Tristan.

'Our original contract is for thirty days. I'm happy to pay you your full fee until the end of the thirty days, plus any reasonable expenses. Maddie will give you until six pm to vacate the flat in Percy Circus.' Kate looked at Tristan. He folded his arms and shook his head.

'Are you still there?'

'Yes, we are.'

'This is very generous of us. You've only worked eight

days, and we're going to pay you for thirty, plus expenses. After what seems like an oversight on Maddie's part, we will need you to sign a nondisclosure agreement. Us honouring the contract and paying your expenses is dependent on this. My assistant has just emailed it over to you.'

Their fee for the month would be considerable, and they had already accrued significant expenses for travel.

'Thank you for this information, Fidelis,' said Kate, and she hung up.

Kate and Tristan sat in silence for a moment, and then the number for their food order was called. Tristan went up to collect it. When he came back, Kate was scrolling through a document on her phone, and she looked furious.

'What?'

'It's a Draconian nondisclosure agreement. We have to sign away all of the evidence and information that we've gathered so far. We also have to sign that we won't pursue any kind of investigation into this case, or any other case that would be associated with it. And we're barred from ever talking about it or writing about it. It's a gagging order.'

'What do we do?' asked Tristan. Kate looked at him. 'I don't want to give up.'

'Okay. Well. We've got until six until we have to go and get our things. I can ask Jake to pack for us. What do you think about having another crack at Robert Driscoll?'

42

They found Robert Driscoll sitting in The Jug with a pint of Guinness and a plate of chips, looking out of place amongst the city workers and media types having lunch meetings.

'I thought I might hear from you again,' he said, indicating the two seats opposite him in the booth. Kate noticed that he had a walking stick propped up against the window.

'Can we get you another pint?' asked Tristan when the waitress came to their table.

'I'll have another half, love,' he said, holding up his glass.

'I'm not your love,' said the waitress.

''Course not, sorry.' Kate and Tristan both ordered tea. 'This place has changed since I used to come here,' he said when the waitress left.

'Did you come here often?' asked Kate.

'Is that a chat-up line?' He grinned, baring his tiny teeth. Kate and Tristan remained silent. His smile dropped and he looked uncomfortable. 'Yeah. I came here loads back then.'

'And you never saw Peter Conway drinking here?'

'I don't think so.'

'Forrest told us he saw Peter Conway here, and Maxine, Janey's sister, also says she saw him more than once.' Kate took out her phone and found the picture of Peter taken in 1989. 'Do you recognise this picture?'

Robert squinted at it. 'Yeah, but I never saw him.'

'Did Forrest ever tell you about seeing Peter Conway in the toilets?'

'No.'

'Have you been back here since Janey went missing?' asked Tristan.

'No, but when I heard about Roland being found dead . . . Thought I should have a drink in his name . . . That's what you want to talk to me about, isn't it, Roland?'

'Yes,' said Kate.

He sat back and crossed his arms. 'Go on.'

'Why did you lie to us about not being in contact with Forrest?' asked Kate.

He looked between them, his eyes beady. 'How did you know I lied?'

'Forrest admitted to us today that he regularly sent money to Roland. Or Jon Chase, as he changed his name to. He also told us that he went to your mother's funeral and you spoke occasionally on the phone.'

'You have done your research,' he said, still sitting with crossed arms. Kate couldn't read him.

'Did Forrest tell you he was still in contact with Roland?'

'He did. Forrest has been good to both of us. He sends me

money, too.' Robert shrugged. 'I've got health problems, so I can't work.'

'Were you in contact with Roland?'

'No.'

'Why would Forrest send you money at the same time as cutting off contact?'

'It's a working-class thing. You'd understand that, wouldn't you?' he added to Tristan.

'May I ask how much Forrest sends you?' said Kate.

'No. You may not,' he said, imitating her voice. He swilled the last of his beer around the glass before knocking it back. He placed the glass down on the table.

'Forrest is an out-of-work actor. How can he afford to send you and Roland money every month?' asked Tristan.

Robert shrugged. 'You'd have to ask him. Although . . . was he still sending Roland money? Roland would often go off the radar and move around. I had no idea that he was living near Watford. The last I heard was that he was living in Morden down in South London.'

'When was this?'

'Couple of years ago.'

'Why did he move around?'

'He rented rooms in houses around London, and then he got on the council house list and they got him a flat in Morden. Although it took an age for him to get a place. They tend to give the more needy, like single mothers, houses first. I don't know why he left Morden.'

'Did you have direct contact with Roland?'

'No. Forrest told me.'

'Why didn't you just tell us all of this when we first spoke to you?' asked Tristan.

'Listen, mate. You knocked on my door, out of the blue. You're not law enforcement. You're just a fancy business card away from being nosy bastards. I have every right to tell you what I want to.'

'Why lie about it?' asked Kate. 'Don't you want us to find Janey, especially if you're innocent?'

Robert leant forward and jabbed his finger on the table. 'I *am* innocent.'

'How do we know you're not lying?'

Robert sighed, exasperated. 'I just want a quiet life! I don't need any of this. I have no interest in dredging up the past.'

'I don't understand why you and Forrest can't just be friends again? It seems ridiculous.'

'Oh, does it? Forrest is an actor. He's done some quite high-profile stuff . . . You know how many idiots there are out there who can't separate creative people from the fiction they create as part of their job? There will always be a grey area around me: *Did I do it? Did I kill Janey Macklin?*'

'And you were happy with this?' asked Kate. 'To have him reject your friendship, but send you money on the sly? Charity?'

'Do you know what it's like to be poor? Do you know what it's like to be registered disabled and have the government threaten to take away your benefits? I'm lucky that I own my flat, but even then, life isn't cheap. I took what Forrest offered me gratefully.'

'Don't you miss the friendship?' asked Tristan.

'Jeez. Mate. You didn't come all this way to ask me if I

missed our friendship? People change. We're not the same carefree lads we were back in the late eighties.'

Their drinks arrived, and Robert waited until the waitress was gone before he spoke again.

'We'll both be at Roland's funeral. Me and Forrest. No one deserved to die like that. Stabbed sixteen times in his own flat.'

'Who do you think killed him?'

'If I knew that, I'd tell you,' he said. Kate watched him as he sipped his drink. She almost believed him.

'We've had the chance to look at the police case file for the Janey Macklin disappearance. You gave Forrest, Fred as he was known then, an alibi the night of 23 December 1988. You said he was out clubbing at the Astoria?'

'Yeah. It was a long time ago.'

'And Roland was at home with his parents?'

'Er, yeah. I think that's what I said.'

'You did say that.'

'OK, why are you asking me if you've got it written down?'

'I just don't understand something,' said Kate. 'You three were close mates. Working-class close, as you've just said . . .' Robert squinted and nodded, taking another sip of his stout. 'The night Janey Macklin went missing was the last Friday before Christmas. Yet you all chose to spend it separately. Not only that, the two other lads left you to package up a load of murals from the youth club. You say that you dropped off Janey just before six thirty, and you then went to move the murals. Why didn't they help you?'

'Bloody hell. It was thirty years ago!'

'And if Roland hated his parents so much that he cut them off, why did he choose to spend the last Friday before Christmas at home?'

'You'd have to ask him. Oh, wait. You can't,' snapped Robert.

'Forrest wasn't able to give us much of an answer, either,' said Kate. 'You all seem to have one thing in common. Withholding the truth.'

She glanced over at Tristan, and they both got up. Kate took out a twenty-pound note and dropped it on the table.

'That's it?' said Robert.

'Yes. Thank you. We've got all we need.'

'What do you mean? All you need?' he said sharply.

'You've given us more than you think,' said Kate, and they walked out of the pub.

43

'It's those three guys,' said Kate, fiddling with the empty sandwich packet on the table.

After their meeting with Robert at The Jug, they'd gone back to the flat in Percy Circus to collect Jake and their things, and caught an early train back to Exeter, managing to get seats at a table by the window. The sun was just starting to set over the fields as they raced through the countryside.

'You think it's all three?' asked Tristan.

'They were this tight-knit group until Janey, and then, they all . . .' Kate mimed something blowing up with her hands. 'It was like an explosion went off.'

'I'm surprised he said he *didn't* see Peter Conway in The Jug in the weeks leading up to Janey going missing,' said Tristan.

'I think the only person we should take seriously is Maxine. I believe she saw him.' She shrugged. She bit her lip, and a thought came to her. 'Do you think it's weird that they didn't all go out together on that Friday before Christmas?'

'Who?' asked Tristan.

'Robert, Forrest, and Roland. You've got mates, haven't you?' said Kate to Jake. He was sitting opposite, hunched down in his chair with the hood up on his sweatshirt.

'Yeah. Four of us who met at uni,' he said.

'You go out drinking when it's a special occasion?'

'Mum. People don't do out on the lash like they do here.'

'What about you, Tris?' asked Kate, impatiently.

'Yeah. If it was the last Friday before Christmas, I'd be going out and meeting up with Ade, definitely.'

'Yes. And didn't Robert and Forrest say that Roland liked a drink? In my drinking days, my early drinking days, I used to love an excuse to go and get pissed. And what's more of an excuse than the Friday before Christmas? Why didn't Robert, Forrest, and Roland go out that night?'

Tristan and Jake were silent.

'Didn't Robert say he had to package up some murals for the youth club?' said Tristan.

'Yes, why did they leave him to do it himself?' said Kate.

'Yeah, but also, close mates sometimes can be honest with each other. Maybe they'd been partying a lot in the weeks running up to it and they all needed time to chill,' said Jake.

Kate rubbed her tired eyes. 'I don't know. Maybe I'm clutching at straws. Maybe it's unsolvable? If we sign that NDA, we gain our fee, but we'll lose any rights to finish or even talk about the case.'

'What if we went to Janey Macklin's mother and asked if she would like us to take over the case? She's just won the lottery. She could afford to pay us,' said Tristan.

Kate chewed her nails, thinking.

'I don't know. Didn't she say she just wants to move on? And people are supposed to hire us. It would feel wrong to go to her cap in hand.' Kate could see Jake wanted to say something else, but he hesitated. 'What is it? Speak.'

'You won't like it,' said Jake, sitting up in his chair and taking off his hood.

'Right now, we don't have many options. Try me.'

'Okay. You were both hired by this agency to investigate the case and they forgot to get you to sign an NDA, which is pretty basic, and right now as things stand, they have no rights over what you've discovered.'

'But they owe us a lot of money,' said Kate impatiently.

'You also told me that this Faloola—'

'Fidelis.'

'This Fidelis said that Audible and Apple were interested in the idea of a true crime project about Janey Macklin. Mum. I know you've never wanted to profit off the whole Peter Conway story, but—' Kate opened her mouth to protest. 'Let me finish. This could be something bigger that has nothing to do with Peter, beyond the fact he's a bit-part player.'

'We can't rule him out,' said Tristan. 'There's evidence to show he was in the area when Janey went missing.'

'Listen. I work at a huge talent agency. So many production companies are gagging for content like true crime drama, documentaries, podcasts, you name it. What if you and Tristan tried to sell the story of this investigation yourselves?'

'We don't know anything about making podcasts,' said Tristan.

'You wouldn't need to. You would be selling the story of your investigation. "The Lost Victim of Peter Conway." Or "The Case of Janey Macklin, the Missing Girl in King's Cross."'

'We haven't solved it yet,' said Kate, her interest piqued.

'The point is, this agent, Fidelis, is shopping something around she doesn't own outright.'

'Isn't a lot of it in the public domain?' said Tristan.

'Yes, but I think if we shopped the idea with the whole angle of your private detective agency investigating, and Mum, your link to Peter Conway. And with Peter dying, there's a huge amount of interest in his past, his present, and everything. I had a call from the solicitor who's administering Peter Conway's estate. I'm his sole heir. There's not much, but I do inherit the recorded interviews he made with the ghostwriter of *No Son of Mine*. Imagine the interest if there's a last victim that he could have killed. That's enough in itself. If you two solve it, then that's bankable content.'

'Listen to him. My son talking about bankable content,' said Kate, unsure of how to feel about this.

'That journalist wanted you to sign his copy of *No Son of Mine* because your signature made it more valuable,' said Jake. He leaned over and took Kate's hand. 'Mum. I respect that you haven't wanted to profit on anything to do with Peter Conway. But this is different. Imagine if you could be paid to solve the Janey Macklin disappearance on your own terms, in your own time, and you could put the agency, you and Tristan, on a secure financial footing for many years to come.'

Kate rubbed her forehead. She could feel a headache coming on at the base of her neck. The idea had a spark of attraction. And she cared more about Tristan being able to pay his mortgage than she did her own.

'Do you know how long I had to work at being anonymous? After I caught him?' she said.

'Mum, you would be selling the idea. You could remain in the background. They would hire actors and writers. You could even specify you don't want to be involved in its promotion. The story is strong enough in itself. Think about it.'

Kate looked out the window. The sun was setting, and she could just make out her tired refection looking back at her. Being fired from the case really stung, and now they were returning home with their tails between their legs. She had no money, and bills to pay. The water damage to the field in the caravan site still needed to be fixed.

She'd worked so hard to escape Peter Conway and her association to him. What if she stopped fighting it? Could this be the way forward?

44

It was dark when they arrived at Exeter St Davids. Tristan's car was parked in the overflow car park, a few minutes' walk from the train station, and they trudged through the icy, cold streets, dragging their luggage with their heads down. Just as they got to the car, Kate's phone began to ring in her pocket. She took it out, and her face went pale.

'What is it?' asked Tristan. She held up the screen. It was displaying **PETER CONWAY**.

'He's calling from the grave,' Jake said.

'No. It's the number he rang from. The stolen mobile phone,' Kate snapped.

'Yeah. I know that, Mum. I was joking,' Jake snapped back.

'Answer it,' said Tristan. Jake climbed in the back seat and slammed the door. Kate answered the call and put her phone on speaker.

'Hello. Is this Kate Marshall?' asked a croaky male voice.

'Yes.'

Tristan got his phone out and pressed record.

'My name is Thomas Black. I understand you've been very interested in my letters to Judith Leary, among other things.'

'How did you get this phone?' asked Kate.

'I was given it, just as Peter was given it. I've been speaking to a woman called Fidelis. I take it you know her?'

Tristan rolled his eyes and mouthed 'Jesus.'

'Yes.'

'Slippery, isn't she?'

'How so?'

'She told me that she'd spoken to the prison governor. She lied.'

'Why did she give you her name? Did Fidelis organise that phone to be smuggled into Peter Conway's cell?' asked Kate.

'Clever detective, putting two and two together. Yes, she did. She wanted to get a recording of Peter Conway's voice answering some questions about your case. Presumably, in the hope she could sell it.'

'Do you know if she got a recording?'

'If she did, I doubt she can use it. With all the swelling after his tooth surgery, Peter sounded like someone speaking Welsh with a mouthful of pencils.'

'Who gave you the phone?' asked Kate.

'Commerce, my dear. The original courier of said phone, who is of no real interest, realised he could increase his fee if the phone came to me.'

'Why are you now calling me?'

'Because Fidelis has lied to me. I'm here up north. She

outsourced her work to go- betweens. Peter Conway told me you are a woman who gets things done.'

Kate felt surprised by this, but doubted it was true.

'What do you want?' she asked.

There was a hissing sound as he tried to catch his breath.

'Peter is dead. But we shared certain information before he died. I want you to visit me. You and your associate.' Tristan's eyebrows shot up with alarm. 'I don't want to discuss any more on the telephone. You both have to come and see me in Wakefield.'

'Wakefield is a long way. Can't you just tell me over the phone?'

'No!' he growled with an almost demonic rumble. '*This is serious*. This will be worth it, I promise you.'

'I need more than just a cold call and a vague promise,' said Kate.

'I can tell you where the body of Janey Macklin is buried,' he said. There was a click, and the line went dead.

Tristan stopped his phone recording, and he started the engine.

'Fidelis was working Peter Conway,' said Kate. 'Trying to get a recording of his voice. Sneaky cow. And it's illegal to smuggle a phone in to a prisoner.'

'It sounds like she used a go-between,' said Tristan. They reached the exit, and he had to wait for a gap in the traffic.

'And you don't think this would make the most amazing true crime podcast?' said Jake. 'Two serial killers. Multiple suspects. A juicy mystery.'

'Thomas Black could be bluffing,' said Kate, still holding her phone in her hand.

'He's dying. It could be a confession,' said Tristan.

'Do you think he wants to confess?' asked Jake.

'If he does, why wait until now?'

'Maybe he just wants to get a few things off his chest?'

'I love that you're still naive.'

'Mum, I'm not naive.'

'It's a good thing,' said Kate, turning to him and putting out her hand. He rolled his eyes and looked out the window.

They arrived in Thurlow Bay twenty minutes later, and as Tristan pulled onto Kate's road, he slowed on the uneven tarmac. The soil run-off from the storm was still piled up on the road, and as they passed the caravan site, the car headlights illuminated the huge channel of earth which had been cut out by the rainwater.

'We're going to have to deal with that soon,' said Tristan. He pulled up outside Kate's front door.

She sighed. 'Okay.'

'Okay what?'

Kate turned to Jake. 'Okay, call your boss.'

'Seriously? I can call Jeremy?' said Jake. Tristan looked at her, surprised, too.

'Yes. We have no income on the horizon, a vast canyon in the caravan site, and I'm not signing that bloody NDA. Not after that phone call from Thomas Black. He might be confessing, he might not, but we should go and see him. Don't you think, Tris?'

'Yes. Yes to it all.'

'Good. Call him, Jake, and tell him about this whole idea of selling the story.'

45

Whilst they waited to hear back from Jake's boss, Kate and Tristan decided to go back to basics. The next morning they drove to Exeter Cathedral to examine the microfilm archives in the records department.

They requested microfilm of all the daily national and London local newspapers, of which there were many, between 23 December 1988 and 31 January 1989. They split the microfilm and spent the next few hours working through it on the microfilm viewers in the back of the records office.

The black-and-white newsprint whizzed past on the large grainy magnifying screens, and Kate was confronted by just how much had changed in the past thirty years, with lurid stories of the unrest in Northern Ireland, famous men being 'outed' as gay, and AIDS being the 'gay plague.' The Lockerbie air crash tragedy had happened on 21 December 1988, two days before Janey went missing, and all over that Christmas period, it was still dominating the headlines.

The story of Janey Macklin going missing hadn't made

national news headlines until early January, and even then, it was never splashed over the front pages. The pinnacle of the national coverage of the investigation had been when the *Crimewatch* reconstruction had been broadcast. In the weeks afterwards, the story remained prominent in *Camden New Journal* and the *Islington Gazette.*

'What the . . . ?' said Tristan after a long morning of silence. His hand moved back and forward on the wheel on the side of the microfilm machine. 'Kate, come and look at this.' She scooted her chair next to him. 'This is an article from the *Camden New Journal.*' They both read the article.

More than two dozen people have been treated for apparent carbon monoxide poisoning at the Astoria in Soho.

Fire engines responded to a call shortly before 7.30pm on Friday (December 23) regarding reports of people becoming ill when the club opened.

Officials from Camden Council say 23 people were treated at the scene for exposure to noxious fumes, and one other was taken to St Thomas' Hospital for treatment.

They say the source of the carbon monoxide was from a coin-operated drinks machine adjacent to the dance floor.

Camden Council says that the drinks machine has been removed, and a full inspection has been undertaken. An official commented, 'Emergency services responded to a call at the Astoria nightclub early on Friday evening, where a few patrons had become ill with breathing difficulties. The venue was immediately evacuated, and a full inspection was performed. A coin-operated drinks machine was found to be faulty and immediately removed. All patrons made a full

recovery, and we're glad to say that inspectors determined it's
safe to reopen the Astoria on Christmas Eve.

'Forrest's alibi. He told the police, and us, that he went out clubbing at the Astoria on the 23 December, the night that Janey went missing,' said Tristan.

'If the police responded to a call at 7.30pm, and evacuated the Astoria, then where was he for the rest of that evening?'

Kate and Tristan then turned their attention to the rest of the microfilm, looking for any mention of Fred Parker and Roland Hacker around the time of the *Crimewatch* reconstruction, but it seemed that the police very quickly saw Robert Driscoll as their prime suspect, and only he was named in relation to the case.

After another hour of whizzing through the microfilm, Kate found something that made her look twice. It was an article, again from the *Camden New Journal*, this time from late January, when the reconstruction work was completed on the courtyard out the front of Victoria House. The black-and-white photo showed a local councillor, Mary Morrison, unveiling a tiny plaque on the side of the building to say that the building was dedicated to the original architect, Sir John Moss. It also showed a photo of the pristine new paving in the courtyard and the statue on the plinth. The article itself was fairly dry, but a box of text next to the photo caught Kate's eye.

'Tris, look at this,' said Kate. He scooted his chair over and read the article and the caption underneath.

The statue in the courtyard at Victoria House is named Odgoad, and has been kept in storage and cleaned up by a local youth volunteer group during the Victoria House renovations. The statue is fashioned as an eight-sided dice and is meant to be a symbol of prosperity. It was sculpted by local artist Gaia Tindall (now deceased), using her signature style of cast concrete panels bolted together. Tindall has also produced artworks for Leeds City Council and the art museum in St Helier, Jersey, and many of her works in sculpture and watercolours are held by private collectors and galleries around the world. Fred Parker attended on behalf of the local volunteer group.

Kate thought of the statue as they'd seen it, with weeds growing out of the plinth at the bottom, and the graffiti which read 'FUCK OSTERITY.'

Kate and Tristan went to get some lunch in the cafeteria next to the records office, and they googled the artist Gaia Tindall.

There wasn't much online, and as Tristan scrolled through the results, it seemed that Gaia didn't make much of an impression on the internet. Then he found an article about a photo book she had contributed to, published in 1989 about graffiti in London in the 1980s.

Gaia Tindall had died in July 1988, and her death was mentioned in the short biography at the bottom.

Tindall was born in Birmingham in 1947 and moved to London in 1965, where she set up an artists' collective in King's Cross, and worked with several local youth clubs. She was a sculptor and briefly imprisoned in 1971 for possessing cocaine and again in 1985 for her political graffiti. Her sculptures are in several private collections worldwide.

'Private collections worldwide?' said Kate through a mouth of sandwich. Tristan googled 'Gaia Tindall sculptures' and found a catalogue with a list of ten sculptures held by private collectors in six different countries, but annoyingly, there were no photos or other details.

'Have you got the *Big Issue* article with Robert, Forrest, and Roland?' asked Tristan. Kate wiped her hands and took out her phone. Tristan took it, zooming in on the text. 'In the article, Robert talks about them working with a local artist on the mural. Look, here he says, *'We've been encouraged and helped by a local artist in making this mural, which represents the people in our borough.'*

'If there was an artists' collective in King's Cross, where was it? And on the night Janey went missing, Robert said he was moving some artworks,' said Kate.

'Forrest said he was at the Astoria nightclub, but if it was evacuated, did he go somewhere else? Did he meet Robert? And what about Roland?'

'What about Janey? What if her body was stashed in the pipe behind Reynolds newsagent and then moved four days later. Where else could it have been taken?'

46

On Monday morning, Kate and Tristan were back on the train, this time from Exeter St David's to Wakefield. They arrived at 11.30am, and the train station was right next to HMP Wakefield prison.

They were met at security by a woman in a boxy suit, who told them that their meeting would be recorded, and then they were shown to a private visiting room, where Thomas Black waited at a table in his wheelchair. Kate was shocked to see how much he had wasted away from the pictures they'd seen of him as a big, strapping, athletic man. He wore a thin sweater and tracksuit bottoms. Every bone in his face and chest protruded through his skin, and his teeth and eyes also seemed too big for his skull. His lips were chapped, and his skin now had a yellow tinge.

'Good morning,' he said imperiously. 'I'm Thomas.' He spoke with a rumbling growl. They shook his withered hand, and as they did, his sleeve rode up to show black bruises mottling his skin like ink-stains.

'Thank you for meeting with us,' said Kate.

'What happened to your head?' asked Thomas, pointing to the stitches still in Tristan's forehead.

'I fell and hit my head on the corner of a table,' said Tristan.

'He's rather pretty. Do you like younger men?' said Thomas to Kate.

'We're partners in the agency,' said Kate.

'How lovely. I was sorry to hear about Peter Conway. You were there for him on his deathbed?'

'Yes.'

'Are you going to the funeral?'

'I don't think so.'

'When is the funeral?'

'We're waiting to hear,' said Kate.

'Will you be burning him or burying him?'

'I believe he wanted to be cremated.'

'Yes, I assumed it's going to be a fairly generic burning in the crematorium oven. Where do you think his ashes will be scattered?'

'We're not here to talk about that.'

'Yes. I'll change the subject. How is your son?' Kate stared at him, trying not to take the bait. 'Just last week I read a news story about a lad from California who got amorous with a young lady who didn't want it, and she ended up choking on her rape whistle. Was it Jake? I hear he's living in California.' Thomas grinned and arched the skin above his left eye, where Kate presumed an eyebrow had once been. 'Do you worry that the apple hasn't fallen far from the tree?'

'I bet it's going to be really painful, and drawn out, how

you die,' said Tristan. Kate put up her hand. She was annoyed how easily Black had taken control of the conversation and needled them.

'Thomas. Let's start this again,' she said. 'Thank you for meeting with us. You have something you want to tell us?'

'Yes, I do,' he said. He pointed up to a camera in the corner of the room. 'This is all being recorded.'

Kate glanced at the camera. They were also being watched by a prison guard standing in the corner of the room.

'You wrote in your letters to Judith Leary that you saw Peter Conway in The Jug in King's Cross in the autumn of 1988.'

'Did more than see him. We *hung out*, as people say these days.'

'You hung out?'

Thomas nodded. 'Mooched around. Spent time in each other's company. Peter was training to be a police officer in Hendon. He was staying in shared accommodation, a real flop-house by all accounts. A couple of times, I invited him to stay at my flat in Golders Green. We went out for a few drinks. A couple of times we picked up girls. Once, there were no girls, so we had fun with each other.'

'Peter Conway has never said anything about having sexual relations with men,' said Kate.

'It was horseplay. I think he only did it once . . . and I had to be the lady. He was too tense, and I couldn't get my cock up his arse. He did have a lovely body. But you'd know that, Kate, wouldn't you?'

Kate kept her face neutral, but she could feel her cheeks flushing with embarrassment.

'How do you know where Janey Macklin's body is buried?' asked Tristan.

'Because I saw Peter kill her . . . We picked her up on the street the night she went missing.'

'How did you pick her up?' asked Kate.

'We were in my van. We were just arriving at The Jug. We saw her on the street.'

'Why would she let you pick her up?'

'She recognised Peter from The Jug. He'd been nice to her, stepped in when some bloke was being funny with her.'

'Funny how?'

'I don't know all the details, love. I just remember him saying that Janey knew him and she trusted him . . . Am I shocking you, sweetheart?' he added to Tristan.

'No.'

'Pity. Anyway. We saw Janey. Peter got out and said hello. She was standing at the door to The Jug. Freezing cold. And she saw the ice cream van.'

'You drove an ice cream van?' repeated Tristan.

'Yes. An old ice cream van, off brand. I wasn't Mr. Whippy.' He chuckled. 'Imagine, if I was Mr. Whippy? I got the van cheap from a bloke who'd gone bankrupt. The pictures were faded on the side, and it couldn't play the tune anymore. Peter asked Janey if she wanted some chocolate. He said it was too cold for ice cream but he had a box of flakes in the back.'

'And she believed him?'

'She was hungry, poor little bitch.'

'That's enough,' said Tristan.

'Oh, behave. It's just an expression. Janey came around to the side of the van, and Peter got the door open . . . It wasn't planned or nothing, but the road was empty. We saw an opportunity. It was like we were psychic. He hit her over the head, and I dragged her into the van. It was all over very quickly.'

'What did you hit her over the head with?' asked Kate.

'The soft-serve ice cream machine was broken, and it was in pieces. I used a big metal wrench that was sitting on top.'

'Then what happened?' asked Kate, feeling sick.

'We took her back to my flat in Whitechapel.'

'What's the address?'

'Surely you know? Didn't you teach me as part of your Criminal Icons course at that dead-end shit hole of a university? I heard that some people, some followers of mine, were lobbying to have it included in the Jack the Ripper tours.'

'Why would they do that? Jack the Ripper was smart enough never to get caught,' said Tristan.

'You shut your mouth, you little shit,' growled Thomas, slamming his hand down on the table and then wincing. Kate turned to Tristan and shook her head. 'That's right, listen to Mummy.'

Kate could see Tristan grit his teeth, and then wince at the stitches he still had in his forehead.

'You say Peter Conway knocked Janey Macklin unconscious and took her back to your flat?' said Kate.

'Yes. It was December 23, 1988. We picked her up around six or seven, but it might have been a bit later. We used to like starting to drink as soon as we finished work . . . Do you want to know what we did to her?'

'Is it relevant?'

'Well. Relevant to Janey dying. We broke her skull, but she didn't die right away.'

'Where did you bury her body?'

Thomas took a deep breath. 'Kensal Green Cemetery. North London.'

'You buried her in the cemetery yourselves?' said Tristan. He turned to Kate. 'He's wasting our time.'

'No. I'm not,' he said, tapping on the table with a long yellow fingernail. 'Malcolm Newton. He died December 18, 1988. He's buried in Kensal Green Cemetery. Janey Macklin's body is buried in the same grave, under his coffin,' said Thomas, sitting back triumphantly.

'And how did you manage that?' asked Kate.

'I knew a gravedigger, dear. He had a very particular fetish. He liked snuff films. You know what snuff films are?'

'Yes.'

'I knew someone in snuff films – well, not *in* them. He worked on acquiring them. I used to get this gravedigger copies of the films on video. Do you know much about the snuff industry?'

'I came across them working in vice in the Met. Very few are genuine,' said Kate.

'That's the problem with snuff films. I knew some people who made the real deal. And I used to get him drugs as well. He liked to get high watching them. Anyway. He owed me one. So, when Janey came to her demise in my flat, we had to move quickly. Malcolm Newton's funeral was on Boxing Day, so Christmas night, we drove Janey's body over to Kensal Green and waited until he'd dug the grave. He buried her a few feet deeper than the coffin. We wrapped her naked in a blue tarpaulin. You'll find her there.'

Kate looked across at Tristan, who was writing all this down.

'Why are you telling us this now?'

'In return for telling you this, I've been assured that I can move to a hospital for palliative care. I don't want to die here.'

Kate looked up at the prison guard, who was staring ahead impassively.

'You'll get to choose where you die. Unlike your victims.'

'Dig. You'll find her.'

Kate looked at what was left of Thomas Black after he'd been ravaged by disease, and she felt physically sick.

47

'He's telling us Janey Macklin's body is buried under the coffin of a man called Malcolm Newton. He died December 18, 1988, and he's buried in Kensal Green Cemetery,' said Kate. They were hurrying across the railway bridge back into Wakefield station, opposite the prison, and Kate was on the phone to Varia Campbell.

'We've got less than a minute. It's platform three,' said Tristan. They broke into a run as they reached the other side of the bridge and started down the stairs.

'You want me to exhume a body on the whim of a multiple murderer who isn't known for his honesty?' said Varia.

'This is a deal which has been set up with the prison governor. Thomas Black is desperate not to die in prison. What if this is real, and it's always been his trump card?' said Kate. They reached platform three, where the guard was outside the carriage blowing his whistle. Tristan boarded the first carriage and held his hand against the door. It beeped just as Kate stepped inside, and the doors closed.

'Okay, let me talk to my governor,' said Varia. Kate ended the call and tried to catch her breath. Even though it was expensive, they'd bought first-class tickets. The prospect of an eight-hour round trip in a crowded train or, worse, standing, was too much. The first-class carriage was almost empty, and they sank gratefully into their seats at a table. They'd spent a little over an hour at Wakefield prison, and Kate was glad they were speeding back down south.

When they were settled and ordered coffee from the buffet car, they discussed the case.

'Do you really think Janey Macklin's body is in that grave?' asked Tristan.

'I don't know. Thomas knew things about the case. I don't know if it's been made public that Peter Conway met Janey in The Jug. If she had seen Peter outside that night in an ice cream van, she could have remembered him as the nice guy who stuck up for her and Maxine on the *Space Invaders* machine.'

'I'm just trying to think if I would have fallen for that when I was fifteen, some bloke telling me he had chocolate in the back of his ice cream van?'

'I hope I wouldn't have fallen for it.'

'He said it was around six pm, maybe later, that they saw Janey. That would fit with Robert Driscoll's story of dropping her off outside The Jug after they went for chips near Golden Lane,' said Tristan.

'That information wasn't released to the public in the *Crimewatch* reconstruction.'

'But the Janey Macklin case was in the newspapers over the years. The details could have been repeated, and he picked up on them.'

They were silent for a moment. Their coffees arrived, along with a couple of cheese sandwiches. Kate sipped her black coffee but didn't feel like eating. The memory of Thomas Black, withered and sickly, in his wheelchair with the bags of bodily fluids hanging off, still made her feel queasy.

'If Thomas Black is telling the truth, then it would mean Robert, Forrest, and Roland had nothing to do with Janey going missing.'

They sat in silence contemplating this. Tristan ate his sandwiches. Kate's phone rang, and she saw it was Varia again, calling on FaceTime. Kate angled the phone around so she could see Tristan.

'Are you on a train with me on speaker?'

'We're in first class, and the carriage is empty,' said Tristan. Kate angled the phone around to show her.

'You two are very fancy,' said Varia. 'I just wanted to call you with some more information. The gravestone in Kensal Green Cemetery for Malcolm Newell checks out – it's real. As we've just reopened the Janey Macklin case, we're going to apply to have Malcolm Newell's grave opened and the coffin exhumed. He doesn't have any next of kin, which will make it a little easier.'

'How fast will that happen?'

'Hopefully in the next couple of days.' Varia's phone moved as she opened a file on her desk. 'We've also had the postmortem results back from the body of Jon Chase or

Roland Hacker. There was a high amount of benzodiazepine in his bloodstream. Three hundred and fifty milligrams. A regular dose would be between twenty or thirty milligrams. The forensic pathologist was also able to test the contents of the stomach. They found alcohol – red wine, to be specific – and benzodiazepine. He'd been dead just over forty-eight hours when you found him.'

'Have you spoken to the neighbours?' asked Kate.

'Yes. Quite a motley crew of substance abusers and some straight shooters who just keep themselves to themselves. No one apart from an old lady at the other end of the corridor can remember seeing him since September. She thought he'd moved out.'

'Someone gave him a drink of red wine laced with benzodiazepine?' said Tristan.

'That's one theory we're working on. Roland Hacker, or Jon Chase, as he's legally known, had severe liver damage from alcohol abuse, he was underweight, and had traces of cocaine and heroin in his body. Forensics also found traces of cocaine and heroin in the flat,' said Varia.

'Whoever killed him tried to knock him out with benzodiazepine, but he had a high tolerance and fought back?' asked Kate.

'That's another theory. Forensics think that his flat had been wiped down, there were virtually no prints, but it had been done in a hurry. They found a thumbprint on the wall in the hallway. It doesn't belong to Roland. We also ran the print through the National Crime Database, and there was no match. However, the print matches a thumbprint we lifted from the voice recorder you found in the Percy Circus flat.'

'Wow,' said Tristan.

'Forrest Parker was never officially arrested, so he was never fingerprinted,' said Kate.

'I know where you're going with this,' said Varia.

'Can you arrest Forrest?'

'On what charge? He lied to you about being in contact with Roland, but he was also helping him financially,' said Varia.

'You need to find out where he was when Roland died.'

Varia put up her hand. 'We've spoken to him already. His partner, Maddie, says that he was with her.'

'And you believe her? What about when the flat was broken into?'

'She also says Forrest was with her all night.'

'They're lying!' It came out louder than Kate wanted.

Varia sighed. 'I can't just arrest Forrest Parker on a whim. I'd need evidence, probable cause. Especially if I wanted to take fingerprints from him.'

'Could you ask him to give you his prints voluntarily?' asked Tristan.

'It doesn't work like that. Roland Hacker had a history of drug and alcohol abuse. He also owed money to several people on his housing estate. It's a rough estate, which experiences a lot of violence. The CPS are already pressuring me to pursue that avenue.'

'What about the flat in Percy Circus?' asked Tristan. 'Surely the same fingerprint popping up on a hidden voice recorder gives you probable cause to investigate?'

Varia nodded wearily. 'When we spoke to Forrest and his partner, they gave us access to all of the guests they have hosted at the Airbnb in the past three months. The list is long, and we're working our way through it.'

They were silent. Kate could feel the frustration bubbling up in her chest.

'I hear you, and I promise I am doing all that I can,' added Varia.

'Thank you. We really appreciate you keeping us in the loop,' said Kate.

'It works both ways, remember,' said Varia. 'I'm hoping that the information you've given me is correct, and not just a last wind-up from a sicko like Thomas Black. If we can find Janey Macklin and close this case, it will be quite a coup after thirty years.'

48

On Tuesday, Jake heard that Peter Conway would be cremated in two weeks time, so he decided to stay in the UK to attend the funeral.

Kate wasn't sure if she wanted to go to Peter's funeral. It was going to be held in a crematorium in North London, and the details were being kept quiet. The weather was bright, and Jake joined her for her early-morning swim in the sea, and it was wonderful for Kate to have some unexpected time with him. They talked and talked about Peter's death, and oddly how life changing it felt for them both, no longer having him as a presence in their lives. The investigation seemed to slow down, after what felt like a breakthrough with Thomas Black saying he knew the whereabouts of Janey Macklin's body, and Kate and Tristan had to wait to hear if the body Black had identified in Kensal Green Cemetery would be exhumed.

Tristan had tried to avoid seeing his sister on their return from London. He didn't want to have to discuss why he'd suddenly come home, when the plan had been to stay in London for at least a few weeks. Sarah seemed to sense that the agency's fortunes were perilous, when she brought Adam Manthorpe, her colleague from work, to come and look at Tristan's spare room. Adam was a nice guy, a very handsome nice guy, whom Tristan remembered from school. Adam Manthorpe had been a star on the school football team, and he was often teased with the nickname 'Madam Anthorpe.' Still, Tristan didn't want to have to commit to losing his privacy, so he told Sarah he needed a few days to think it over.

'What's to think about, Tris, when you have a mortgage and bills to pay?' she'd replied.

———

On Wednesday morning Kate and Tristan met in the agency office, and they were just settling down to work when Jake knocked on the office door with a look of triumph on his face.

'Guys. You know you asked me to talk to one of the agents I work with about your investigation? Jeffery has had an offer from a production company.' When he told them about the fee, Kate almost dropped the cup she was holding.

'Seriously?' said Tristan. 'That's . . .'

'Buy-a-house money,' said Kate.

'The most important thing is making sure that the deal is strong in your favour, and that you would have control over how the story is told,' said Jake.

'I can hear a *but* coming.'

'Yeah. There's just one thing,' said Jake. 'I've been sparse with the details I gave Jeff, my boss, but I did tell him that you're waiting for something that could solve the case, for the grave to be opened where you think Janey's body is buried . . . The long and the short of it is that he thinks it could be worth waiting for the results of this, until we made any decisions.'

'Are you telling me this as an agent or as my son?' asked Kate.

'A bit of both.'

'So do we have an offer, or is it pending us solving this case?'

'We have an offer, but we need it in writing to make it a concrete offer, and solving the case would really . . .'

'Help mix the concrete?' finished Tristan.

Jake laughed. 'Yeah. That's one way of putting it. Listen. I know things are a bit difficult now, but if you can hold on for a few more days . . .'

Tristan looked over at Kate.

'What's happening with Fidelis at Stafford-Clarke?' he asked.

'She sent a flurry of emails, but in the last couple of days she's gone quiet. I don't know if she's got wind of us talking to a US agent.'

'I'll let you two discuss this,' said Jake. 'I'm going to go for a walk on the beach.'

Kate and Tristan were silent for a moment.

'Do you think it's grubby of us, to pursue a "deal"? Especially when it's concerning a young girl who's still missing, and her family don't know what happened to her?' asked Kate.

'I think we would need to tell them about it, and to maybe get their consent. Doreen and Maxine,' said Tristan. Kate nodded. She got up and went to the window in the kitchen, and looked out at the long trench cut through the caravan site.

'In the short term, I've managed to get us a small overdraft on the business account. It's going to cost a couple of grand to get the soil filled in, if we want to open the caravan site in March.'

Tristan came to join her in the kitchen and put the kettle on. 'March seems such a long way away. I've been looking at Roland Hacker's history online under Jon Chase. He was on the council tax register for a couple of house-shares. One of them, the one in Morden, had the names of a couple of other people, and I found one of them last night. His name's Tony Carducci. He lived in the house for six months. I sent him a message on Facebook, and he just replied. He lives in South London and is happy to meet for a coffee and talk about Jon. Maybe there's something there, maybe not. What do you think?'

'That could be very interesting – we don't really have any background on Roland,' said Kate. 'I want to talk to Maxine again, and ask her about the time Janey went missing. I know it was a long time ago, but kids sometimes notice things that adults don't. And it would be good to talk to her on her own.'

Her phone rang, and she saw it was Varia Campbell.

'Hi, I'm here with Tristan,' said Kate, answering.

'We've just got the go-ahead to exhume the body of Malcolm Newton. It will be tomorrow morning,' said Varia.

Kate looked over at Tristan and he nodded.

'We've got some things we need to do in London, and we'll be coming up tomorrow morning. We can meet you there.'

49

Kate and Tristan had a very early start the following day, arriving at London Paddington station just before 10am, and they took a Bakerloo line Tube train up to Willesden Green. Kate had never visited Kensal Green Cemetery. It was vast, covering several acres, and as soon as they were through the gates, she felt cut off from the surrounding city. Tall trees lined the endless rows of Gothic headstones, some dating back to the 1800s, and there were rows of elaborate mausoleums and vaults. Varia had sent them a map, and Tristan guided them to a broad gravel pathway between the hundreds of headstones, some in terrible decay and some new and dressed with fresh flowers, to a small chapel amongst the trees. Here, the gravel path broadened into a road running from the other side of the cemetery, and another police car was waiting with a large forensics van.

Varia was waiting for them on the other side of the small chapel. She wore a black trouser suit, a thick winter coat, and a hat. She greeted them both with a hug. 'I'm blaming you

ROBERT BRYNDZA

both if it goes south,' she said wryly. 'It's just over the way here.'

They left the chapel and walked to the right, down another path forking away between rows of graves. They came to a large tree whose roots extended out amongst the headstones, and some of the older ones sat at odd angles where the roots were pushing up under them. The tree was very tall, and on the top, a crow sat with its black feathers glistening in the weak sun.

A small digger was parked in front of a newer grave of black quartz, and two men were waiting in high-visibility jackets with two police officers in uniform.

'Morning. I'm Superintendent Varia Campbell,' she said, holding up her warrant card. 'Are we all ready to go?'

One of the men went to the digger, and the other was on hand to guide him.

Kate and Tristan moved closer to the gravestone and saw that Malcolm Newton had been eighty when he died. An epitaph on his grave, under the date of his death on 18 December 1988, read:

'To live is the rarest thing in the world.
    Most people just exist.'
    – Oscar Wilde

Within twenty minutes, the digger had carefully carved out a deep hole. They were joined by three forensics officers, who had backed up a small truck with a winch lift on the back. When the digger reached the coffin, two of the forensics officers took over and stepped into the hole to clear away the mud. Kate and Tristan watched as the mud-caked coffin was slowly lifted out of the hole. A low mist hung around the gravestones, and the crow cawed in the tree. The quote on the gravestone suddenly held a deep meaning and simplicity to Kate. Slowly, with clods of mud falling off it onto the ground, the coffin was swung around and placed gently on the gravel path. She suddenly felt tears coming, and she searched for a tissue in her pockets.

'Are you okay?' asked Tristan, touching her arm.

'Yes,' she said, dabbing at her face. 'I suppose seeing this kind of thing makes you feel lucky.'

A police support van drove up to join the forensics van. The coffin was now steaming faintly in the freezing air.

'Guys. Would you like to warm up and grab a coffee?' asked Varia, indicating the police support van. It was warm inside, and Kate and Tristan talked about the case, and made small talk for the next hour. Kate felt on edge, and she could see it in Tristan and Varia.

An hour later, Varia's radio crackled, and a voice asked her to come back to the grave. Kate and Tristan followed. There was now a second forensics tent pitched next to the one over the grave. There were things that Kate could never forget from her time in the police, and that glow emanating from the white skin of a forensics tent on a gloomy day was one of them.

They were all asked to put on white coveralls, and the second tent was warm inside from the bright lights.

'Good morning,' said the forensic pathologist, a short, squat man with bushy eyebrows poking out from under the protective hood of his overalls. He was standing next to a blue mud-stained tarpaulin. On it lay a small skeleton.

'Thomas Black wasn't lying,' said Tristan, his voice cracking with emotion. Kate could immediately see that the skeleton's small skull was broken, caved in at the front, and when she looked closer, the jaw was badly smashed.

'But is it Janey Macklin?' Kate said. It was more of a rhetorical question.

'Whoever buried this person didn't want the body or skeleton identified,' said the forensic pathologist, leaning closer, his arm casting a shadow on the broken skull. 'The teeth have all been smashed, along with the lower and upper jaw. The hands have also been removed.'

'Can you tell if it's male or female?' asked Kate.

'Not at this stage. And unless we find any teeth deeper in the grave, we won't be able to make an identification using dental records.'

'Would it be possible to use blood DNA?' asked Varia.

'Possibly. At this advanced stage of decay, with decay almost complete, I want to try and extract DNA from the victim's bones.'

'How long will that take?'

'I can make it a priority.'

Varia nodded. 'We have the blood samples from Janey Macklin on file, taken from around the same time she went missing.'

'Did you find anything else wrapped inside the tarpaulin with the body?' asked Tristan. All they could see were bones.

'No. It's all very clean, outside of the soil. Don't quote me, but the body could have been buried naked or with the bare minimum of clothes. Jeans, shoes made with plastics, leather belts, particularly if they have a metal buckle, don't decay,' said the forensic pathologist.

Kate looked at the small skeleton. A clump of dark, matted hair still clung to the largest piece of skull, which looked like the top of the head. The tent felt clammy. Kate was sweating under her Tyvek suit, and the soil and smell of decay seemed to cling on with the damp. It was a horrible feeling she'd had before, and she wondered how many dead bodies this white tent had seen. How much residual death and fear the thin white canvas had absorbed.

'We need to clear this area and arrange for the remains to be moved,' said the forensic pathologist, breaking the silence.

'Yes, I need to leave,' said Kate, suddenly feeling as if she could breathe behind her face mask.

They came out of the tent and back into the gloomy cemetery, where the air was fresh and cold. They were silent as they took off their suits and handed them back to the forensics team, and Kate could see they were all fighting with their emotions.

'Are you guys okay?' asked Varia when they were back by the van.

'No,' said Tristan. 'I thought Thomas Black was lying. I hoped he was. He told us that they hit Janey over the head, and broke her skull.'

'He didn't say they chopped off her hands, and smashed her teeth,' said Kate, dabbing her eyes with a clump of tissue.

'Of course. I'll let you know as soon as I hear anything, if it's Janey Macklin,' said Varia. 'Good work. Either way, we've found a body. Even if it's not Janey. There could be loved ones out there looking for someone they thought was lost forever.'

The crow in the tree had been joined by two others, and they cawed against the grey sky. Kate wondered if the smell of death was more enticing than their fear of people.

————

Kate and Tristan walked slowly back to Willesden Green Tube station. The image of the small skeleton was hard to shake off.

'What time did you ask to meet Maxine?' asked Tristan.

'Three o'clock.'

'Are you hungry?'

'Not right now. I could drink something. Right now I could just go to a pub and sink a large whiskey . . . but I won't,' Kate added.

'What about coffee?'

'Yeah. Coffee will have to do.'

50

'My mum's out at the cinema. She enjoys her solitary afternoons.' Maxine's voice quivered with emotion. 'I'm relieved she's not here. I can't fathom how she'd cope with this news.'

Kate and Tristan were sitting in the living room of Doreen's flat. They had just told Maxine about the skeleton they found at Kensal Green Cemetery and who had informed them where to dig. They sat in silence for a moment. Silence seemed the most respectful response.

'The police don't know for sure if it's Janey?' added Maxine.

'No,' said Kate. 'They need to run DNA tests.'

Maxine closed her eyes.

'DNA tests. Oh my God,' she said quietly. She opened her eyes, got up and went to the window.

'The police will be in contact shortly. We asked if we could come and speak to you first. To tell you.' Maxine nodded, with her back to them. There was another long silence.

'How long are you staying in England?' asked Kate.

'I returned to help Mum with her move, and then we were planning to leave. But as the days pass, and the police just informed us that Janey's case has been reopened, I'm torn.' Maxine turned to face them, her eyes glistening. 'I have to go back soon. My husband, my children, my life are all in California.'

'Could we ask you some questions about the time Janey went missing?' asked Kate.

Maxine took out a tissue and dabbed her eyes. 'I'm not sure what else there's left to say.'

'What do you know about the youth club Robert, Fred, and Roland went to?' Tristan asked.

Maxine seemed surprised by the question.

'Gosh, er. I haven't been asked about that before . . . I know it was on Old Street, because Janey wanted to go there, but you had to be fifteen. She was only fourteen.'

'Did you ever go there?'

'A couple of times, when I was older. There were Ping-Pong tables, a coffee bar, and I think there was a *Pac-Man* machine. I remember Janey talking about that because she was mad about those old computer games. Well, they weren't old back then. I think it was the kind of place where teenagers could hook up.'

'Robert, Fred, and Roland did some spray-painting and murals at the youth club. Do you know anything about that?' Kate asked.

Maxine sat back and rubbed at her face. 'I think a local

artist went to the youth club and did some work with them. But they used to get all kinds of people to come in and talk to the kids. I remember they had a karate guy come in and sign kids up for lessons, and our dance school teacher, Miss La Froy, went there once, but I don't think those fifteen-year-old boys and girls wanted to go and do ballet, especially not the boys.'

'Do you know if Robert, Fred, and Roland were close with this local artist?' asked Kate.

Maxine had to think about it again.

'I'm sorry – so much of that time is patchy in my mind. Actually, now you mention it, I remember the woman who did the art stuff with them, she died of cancer a few months before Janey went missing, and I think there was some memorial service for her.'

'Do you remember her name?'

'Gabby, Gail?'

'Could it have been Gaia?' asked Tristan.

'Yeah. That was it. Gaia.'

'Did you ever meet her?'

'No, but this was quite a bohemian place to live in the late 1980s. It wasn't developed. It was full of artists and musicians, and hippies – especially in the warehouses down by the canal. There was so much . . .' Maxine sighed and went to the window.

'What?' asked Kate.

'I was going to say *wasteland*,' she said. She turned back to them. 'It's very fragmented, my memories, but I vividly remember standing here by the windows a few days or a week after Janey went missing and looking out here, over what was the old canal and gasworks before it was redeveloped at all of the police dogs and people they drafted in to do a search for her body. That was when I knew I would never hear her key in the lock again. She'd never come back through the front door . . . It used to take her ages to get the key in the lock. And I'd sit here and hear the scraping. Eventually I'd get up and open the door for her.'

Maxine wiped a tear from her eye.

'Are you okay to continue?' asked Tristan.

'Of course,' she said, taking out a tissue and blowing her nose. She took a deep breath and composed herself.

'We've read the police case file, and the police documented their search of Reynolds newsagent with the sniffer dog five days after Janey went missing. When was this big search that you saw from the window?'

'It was after the TV reconstruction.'

'How soon after?'

Maxine shrugged. 'Maybe a couple of days. I know it was close because the police were really focused on it, after it was on TV. That was weird, the reconstruction.'

'Because the girl looked so much like Janey?' asked Tristan.

'Yeah, and also because I almost ended up in it.'

'How do you mean?'

'They filmed the TV reconstruction right after the new year, and they originally did some filming at the dance school where me and Janey used to go. Looking back on it now, they probably wanted to give people watching on TV an idea of Janey's personality and what she liked to do, and to play on their emotions. The TV crew asked my dance teacher, Miss

La Froy, if they could film the real girls doing a dance class. And it happened to be my dance class, so the film crew came and filmed us for a bit with the actress who looked like Janey.'

'Were you there?'

Maxine nodded. 'Yeah. It was weird.'

'Didn't anyone think to protect you? Question it?' asked Tristan.

'It was a different time; people were less reactionary, and life was harsher, not that anyone was being harsh to me. There was a lot less focus on mental health. In hindsight, was it good that I was one of the dancers featured in the reconstruction? No. It doesn't matter, anyway, because they cut it out of the final broadcast, along with the sniffer dog stuff. I know that because they filmed the sniffer dog stuff the same morning as they came to film us at the dance school. That was also weird. They used the real sniffer dog, the same one who went in and found Janey's scent in the yard behind Reynolds newsagent.'

'Molly?' said Tristan.

'Yeah, Molly, how do you know that?' said Maxine, smiling.

'It's in the case file.'

'Of course. Yes. I suppose there wasn't time to audition a fake sniffer dog. And Molly remembered Janey's scent. When they brought her into the dance studio she went mad in one particular corner, by a fire escape, scrabbling at the floor. It must have been where Janey had been sitting during a class and her scent was still there. And then when they took Molly outside, she caught Janey's scent on the road outside and the bench. I had no idea that scent dogs were so sensitive. They had to take her away in the end. I think that's when everyone realised I shouldn't have been there that day, and Mum came and got me. I never told her all the details, and they never used the stuff from the dance school in the TV reconstruction. After that I stopped dancing. I didn't want to go back.'

'Was there anything odd you remember about Fred and Roland, after Robert Driscoll was arrested?'

'No. They seemed to vanish. I never saw them around. I was only twelve. I'd stopped dancing. I really concentrated on school, and Betty and Stan next door looked after me a lot when Mum couldn't keep it together. I buried myself in books for the next five or six years. I used to spend a lot of time at Stan's bookshop. I'd go there after school most nights and help out. I liked it there, it was so different from here.'

Maxine had been standing by the window the whole time, and she came back to her chair.

'I'm sorry I can't be more help,' she said, sadly. 'It was thirty years ago. I think I've blocked a lot of it out.'

'No, not at all, and thank you for talking to us,' said Kate. Inside she was feeling a little despair. If the skeleton in the grave wasn't Janey, then they had nothing.

'Your investigation has made me think, about human nature,' said Maxine. 'Since you were here last time, I kept running it through my mind. The time we saw Peter Conway in The Jug. I really thought he was being nice, and in reality, he could have been planning what to do with me, or Janey.'

'We don't know that for sure.'

'I saw the news that he's dead. Do you think he died knowing where Janey is, and he kept it from all of us?'

'I spoke to him shortly before he died. I don't know, I'm sorry,' said Kate.

'Don't be sorry. Not knowing has become a coping mechanism over the past thirty years. I'm more scared what will happen to me and my mum if we find out the truth.'

51

It was dark when Kate and Tristan left Victoria House. The courtyard was empty, and Kate had a strange sense of déjà vu as they passed the sad, crumbling eight-sided die statue, sitting on its plinth.

'*Odgoad.* It sounds like one of those ancient kings of England,' said Tristan.

'And Gaia Tindall designed it. It very geometric. Communistic. Unlike the kind of person she was. Does that make you think of prosperity?'

'No, but then look at this whole area. I wonder if the person who sprayed *fuck osterity* knew that the name of the statue, *Odgoad*, meant prosperity?'

A gloom seemed to descend over them, and the bleak January weather didn't do much to lift their spirits. Tristan had arranged to meet Tony Carducci, Roland's ex-flatmate, the next morning, and Kate was planning to visit the British Library to look up street maps for the King's Cross area before the regeneration work in the 1990s. They ate dinner in a passably good pizza restaurant, and then retired to a grubby budget hotel where they'd booked two rooms.

———

The next morning, after they both had a fractious night's sleep, they split up. Tristan took the train across the river to meet Tony Carducci, who lived in a quiet residential street close to Canary Wharf.

When he arrived at Tony's house, a woman pushed a pram containing a sleeping baby down the path to the gate. She didn't say hello to Tristan but looked back when he approached the front door.

Tony was olive skinned, with a bald patch that made him look older than his thirty-two years.

He answered the door carrying a tea-towel and seemed a little stressed out.

'All right, mate. Come in. You'll have to excuse the mess,' he said, leading Tristan through a living room littered with toys and into a small kitchen, where he was unloading a dishwasher. 'Do you want a cuppa?'

'I would, thank you,' said Tristan.

'Ah, shit, no milk,' Tony said, opening the fridge. 'Well, I've got breast milk.'

'Black coffee would be great.' Tristan went to the window and looked out at the road, where the woman was walking with the baby. 'New parents?'

'Yeah. We split up a few weeks ago, though, and then got back together. You got a family?'

'No.'

'Lucky bastard,' he said, grinning and filling the kettle. 'I'm kidding. It's amazing being a parent. Tough. Tiring. I've got two weeks' paternity leave, and they're almost up. I don't know how she's going to cope without me . . . Tish, she's had depression before.'

'If this is a bad time, I can come back,' said Tristan, standing up. 'I just saw your girlfriend with the baby.'

'No! She always takes her out in the morning. And it's nice to talk to another bloke. And you intrigued me with your phone call about Jon Chase.'

'You used to share a house with him in Morden?'

'Yeah. Are you from London?'

'No.'

'It's right at the bottom of the Northern line, as south as you can get while still being in London. It was a cheap old house with a dodgy landlord,' he said, taking out clean mugs. 'There were three of us: me, a girl, and Jon.'

'What did you do in London?'

'I work as a copywriter, I still do . . . Can I ask why there is a sudden interest in Jon? You just said you needed some background information on him regarding a case you're investigating? Are you a private investigator?'

'Yes.'

'Wow. I've never met one before.'

'I do need you to keep this confidential.'

Tony raised an eyebrow. 'Of course. Why?'

'Jon was found dead in his flat a few days ago.'

'Seriously?'

'Yes.'

'How did he die?'

Tristan had debated whether to give him details, but he decided it was worth it to see if it elicited any more information.

'He was murdered.'

'Shit. *Seriously*? Where?'

'In his flat near Watford. He lived alone.'

'I was never close to him, he was very odd, and he only lasted in our house-share for about five months.'

Tony was silent for a moment as he spooned coffee from a little ceramic jar into two mugs.

'Why did he leave your house-share?'

'We asked him to. His behaviour was erratic. He kept us awake most nights.'

'Loud music and partying?' asked Tristan.

'No. He'd have these weird night terrors, which I felt sympathy for, but he'd wake up screaming most nights. The house where we lived had three bedrooms upstairs off a small landing, so we were all packed in like sardines. But the thing that made us ask him to leave was that he used to switch off the fridge.'

'What do you mean? When it was full of food?'

'Yeah. Jon would stay up until, I dunno, midnight, then unplug the fridge. I'd find it unplugged when I got up for work. He said the noise gave him night terrors, and that it was okay because fridges are designed to go off if there's a power cut, and the food stays cold for a few hours. He did this night after night, and our food would defrost and go off. This went on for three months, and it was in the summer . . . And then there was the screaming and shouting in the night.'

'Tell me about his night terrors, did he ever get violent?'

The kettle boiled, and Tony filled up the cups.

'No. He'd shout out things like, "She's falling, one of you catch her!" or "Her skin is so cold!" and "Her eyes are open and she's watching me!"'

'Jeez.'

'I know, mate. Scary fucking stuff to wake up to in the night. And there's something about the sound of a bloke screaming like a banshee. Of course, it's hideous to hear a woman screaming, but Jon. He really curdled my blood.'

Tony handed Tristan one of the mugs.

'Thanks. There's some other things I should tell you,' said Tristan. He explained in broad terms about the Janey Macklin case, how Jon had been friends with Robert Driscoll, and that Jon Chase had previously been known as Roland Hacker.

'I knew there was something weird about that dude. In all the time he lived with us, he never had a visitor, never really had any post, never did anything.'

'Was there ever a time when someone made contact with him?'

'No. Never. Our landlord found him on Gumtree. We made sure that the girl who replaced him came through an agency.'

'I know this is a long time ago, but did Jon ever scream out a name when he woke from a bad dream?'

Tony thought about this for a moment.

'No. It was always something about a woman, a *her*, being cold or freezing. "Her eyes are open and she's watching me." That's the one that used to get to me the most.'

52

The following morning, Kate and Tristan met at the campsite in Thurlow Bay. They had returned from London late the previous evening to be there when the truckloads of soil were delivered to fill the vast crack across the grass. When the soil had been dumped in a massive pile at the bottom of the road, they left a team of builders to fill the land with a digger and returned to the office. They'd planned to revisit all the evidence from the case, but Tristan's phone rang just as Kate made them tea.

'It's Varia on FaceTime,' said Tristan. He answered the call, and they saw Varia was in her office. She didn't look happy.

'Morning. I'm glad it's both of you. Listen. We've had the postmortem results on the skeleton we found in Kensal Green Cemetery. It's not Janey Macklin. . .'

Kate and Tristan were silent for a long beat.

'Yeah, I know. I feel the same as you two look. We used the tiny DNA sample of Janey's blood taken from the original investigation, and also asked Janey's mother and her sister to give us a DNA and blood sample. The skeleton – it's not her; there's no match.'

'Then who did Thomas Black kill?' asked Tristan.

'We're going back to reinterview Black. It could be a murder he committed, or it could be that he knew about the body being buried there by another prisoner, or a contact on the outside when he was still a free man.'

'Does the forensic pathologist know if the skeleton is male or female?'

'Female, and he estimates from studying the bone density and the size that it's a girl of eleven or younger. Whoever she is, she hasn't yet been through puberty.'

Kate and Tristan were silent and didn't know what else to say. Varia went on, 'Listen. I have to say that from when we found the skeleton, I've been trying to work out how Janey's blood could have been in the pipe behind Reynolds newsagent if Peter Conway and Thomas Black had taken her off the street on the night of December 23, 1988, driven her south of the river, killed her and buried her on the twenty-sixth.'

Kate nodded. 'It troubled me, too.'

'Where does this leave the Janey Macklin case?' asked Tristan.

'I've just been assigned an expanded team, and we will revisit all of the evidence in the case file. Our first thing will be to reinterview everyone involved in the case. Roland Hacker's funeral is on Monday 21 January. He's going to be cremated, and there's going to be a wake for him at Victoria House. Oh, and I managed to get a copy of the rough footage filmed for the Janey Macklin *Crimewatch* reconstruction.'

Kate had asked Varia to send them the footage after they'd spoken to Maxine. They'd thought it was a long-shot request.

'How did you manage to get hold of it?' asked Tristan.

'The BBC archives keep everything, and we have special access to footage from *Crimewatch* reconstructions. It's been digitised, along with the original reconstruction. I've just sent the files to your email.'

'Brilliant,' said Kate.

'Can I ask, why do you want this footage?'

'It could be nothing. When we spoke to Maxine, she said that they filmed some stuff at Janey and Maxine's dance school which was cut from the final broadcast.'

'Let me know if you find anything,' said Varia, and she hung up.

When Kate and Tristan came off the phone, they were silent for a moment and listened to the wind whistling around the office, punctuated by the sounds of the digger working outside.

'Did you expect that skeleton to be Janey?' said Tristan.

'I had hope, but like Varia said, it didn't make sense that she would end up there.'

'I thought the same,' said Tristan, nodding. He went to the agency email and downloaded the video files from Varia.

Kate sat down beside Tristan, and they started to watch the footage. It was like a window through time, and the grimy streets of King's Cross were captured in daylight while they filmed rehearsals of the actress playing Janey walking along Pancras Road close to The Jug. There were several minutes of out-takes with Molly, the police sniffer dog. She was shown in the backyard of Reynolds newsagent, being led to the metal drain cover and then sniffing the ground.

'Why do you think they cut this from the reconstruction?' said Tristan.

'I know I worked on a case once where a *Crimewatch* reconstruction was made. The aim is always to present a clear message and to get the public to call in with information. Maybe the police didn't want the focus to be on Janey's body being in the pipe. After all, this sniffer dog traced her scent, but there was no body. And it's only now that the blood sample they found in the pipe has been positively identified as Janey's,' said Kate.

The screen went blank, and they watched the footage taken at the dance school. There were several minutes of the young actress playing Janey taking part in stretches at the barre in front of a mirror. The dance studio was a huge cavernous space, and the young girls in their pink leotards were presided over by an almost comical elderly dance teacher, a rail-thin lady, immaculately dressed with her hair in a jet-black bun, and she was moving down the line of girls, tapping her walking stick to the music.

'I wonder if that's Glenda La Froy, the dance teacher?'

'Which one do you think is Maxine?' asked Tristan, peering at the screen as a row of young girls stood patiently at the barre. In a disembodied voice, the director asked them to repeat the warm-up exercises they had just done and not look at the camera.

The final few minutes of the footage showed Molly, the

sniffer dog, being led into the empty dance studio on a lead. There were four takes of the same scene. In each one, Molly was brought in by her handler, and she started pulling on the lead and went straight to a spot in the corner of the dance studio where there was a door and started to bark. On the fourth take, Molly began to frantically dig at the floor in front of the door and was interrupted by a woman's voice, off camera.

'No! No, stop. I'm sorry. That dog is scratching my floor.'

They heard a voice say, 'Cut.' The camera moved slightly as a man with a clipboard entered the shot. The police dog handler came, gave Molly a treat, and pulled her away. Glenda moved into the shot with her stick, talking to the man with the clipboard.

'This is a very expensive sprung wooden floor,' she said, tapping it with her stick. 'I can't have that dog scratching at it with her claws.'

'Where does this door lead?' asked another voice. The camera moved to show the door, and the focus shifted slightly. The man with the clipboard walked over to the door. He crouched down and peered at the floor.

'There's no scratches,' he said, his voice echoing.

'There will be if you let that dog at it again,' said Glenda. 'Does the BBC have ten thousand pounds to spare?' There was silence. 'I didn't think so. That's what a new sprung wooden floor would cost.'

'What's through that door?' repeated the voice.

'That's storage. I do know that the girls sit against that door. Maybe the dog is picking up on it. On, er, Janey's scent.'

There was a little more muffled speech, and then the screen went blank.

Kate was sitting very still, frozen in thought.

'What?' asked Tristan. She got up and went to the case notes, which now covered the wall in the office.

They'd managed to get a large Ordinance Survey map from the British library of King's Cross in 1988, and it was pinned up next to another Ordinance Survey map of King's Cross from the previous year.

'Where was that dance school?'

Tristan moved over to the copies they'd printed of the Janey Macklin case files, and thumbed through until he found the right page.

'It was on Horner Mews, er, number 8,' he said. Kate moved to the Ordinance Survey map from 1988. It was huge, a metre square, and it had a lot of detail.

'Okay, so number 8 was at the end.' She tapped her finger on the small squares making up the buildings on Horner Mews. 'What was next door, at number 7?'

Tristan moved to his laptop and typed the details into Google. It took him a couple of minutes, and then he looked up at Kate. 'It was the warehouse belonging to Gaia Tindall, the artist who volunteered at the Old Street Youth Club.'

'That's the link! We need to go back over the three guys, Robert, Forrest, and Roland. Their dodgy alibis for the night of 23 December 1988. Then we need to look at their movements in the days after Janey went missing. If her blood, but no body was found in the pipe five days after she went missing, then it indicates her body could have been moved. Gaia Tindall died in July 1988, but what if the three guys still had access to that warehouse? Oh my God. I think I know where Janey Macklin's body is buried.'

53

On Monday, 21 January, Kate and Tristan travelled up to London.

They'd been working with Varia and her team on the results of their breakthrough from the *Crimewatch* TV footage. That morning, Roland Hacker's cremation was being held at the City of London Crematorium in Newham, East London, and the funeral party were due to return to the pub at Victoria House for the wake later that afternoon.

At 10am, Kate and Tristan arrived at Victoria House, feeling nervous and apprehensive. The statue, *Odgoad*, sat on its plinth, looking a little worse for wear in the grey January light. A large police support van was parked next to it, with a shiny black forensics van, and a police officer in a smart uniform and high-visibility vest was unfurling crime scene tape and creating a cordon around the plinth.

Varia arrived a moment later, parking her car next to the police van, and she got out with DI Sean Bentley and another younger woman, whom she introduced as her colleague Detective Layla Morris. A few building residents were already peering from their windows, and some people had stopped on the steps leading up to the entrance.

'How are you going to do this?' asked Kate, watching as two of the forensics officers, wearing plain clothes, set up a stepladder next to the statue on the plinth.

'First, we're going to check the statue using ground-penetrating radar. Just to be sure.'

'And what if we're right? What happens next?' asked Tristan.

Varia peered up at the grubby eight-sided die. 'I don't want to think that far. But that's why forensics are here.'

They watched as the ladder was adjusted and propped up against one of the panels of the eight-sided statue. It was taller than Kate had thought. Almost two metres off the ground. One of the forensics officers was ready with a small, flat metal box.

Kate, Tristan, Varia, Sean, and Layla went to the open side door of the forensics van, where one of the officers held an iPad that showed them the results of the scan.

The forensics officer, up on the ladder, ran the box over the three panels she could reach. They watched the screen as a block of grey remained solid. After a couple of minutes, the ladder was moved to the other side of the statue. The tension in Kate's chest was almost unbearable. She looked up and saw that more people had come to their windows in Victoria House and were peering out at the police below. The forensics officer began to scan the other side of the statue.

'Are we sure this bloody statue is hollow?' asked Varia, concern creasing her brow.

'Yes,' said Kate. 'We tracked down details of its commission. The artist Gaia Tindall constructed *Odgoad* using eight triangular panels of cast concrete. They're bolted together and then sealed with cement. If the statue had been solid and filled with cement, it would be too heavy to lift, and the plinth in the courtyard wouldn't support it.'

Despite the cold weather, Tristan wiped the sweat from his brow. The forensics officer continued to scan the panels on the other side of the statue, and then the officer watching on the iPad shouted.

'Go back. There's something inside, some kind of mass.' Suddenly, they saw a blurred, long shape, and the grey lines in the mass on the screen were distorted.

Varia looked at the screen and then back at the statue. 'Shit. . .' she muttered. Then louder, said, 'Okay. Let's get a forensics tent around it and open it up.'

As the large white tent began to take shape around the statue. A crowd began to gather on the steps behind the police cordon, and Kate saw Betty, Doreen Macklin's neighbour, pushing Stan in a wheelchair. They were both dressed in black.

'Hello!' shouted Betty, waving at them and beckoning them over. Kate and Tristan moved to the police cordon. 'What's happening?' she asked, her face creasing with concern.

'We can't say, I'm afraid,' said Tristan.

'That's a police forensics tent,' said Stan, his eyes also

concerned. His white eyebrows were very long and stuck up like peaks of meringue from under the brim of his black hat.

'We're going to the wake,' said Stan, pointing across the long, low building which housed the bar and social club. 'We've come to pay our respects to Roland.'

'The whole building has been invited. I stopped by to ask Doreen if she was coming. Maxine answered the door. Doreen was still in bed. Apparently, she's not sleeping,' said Betty. 'We heard about the remains of that young girl. I think it got Doreen's hopes up. Has that forensics tent got something to do with it?'

'Yes. Obviously, you think there's something forensic there, something which needs investigating,' said Stan, arching one of his spectacular eyebrows. They looked at Kate and Tristan keenly.

'I'm sorry. We'd better go,' said Kate. They ducked back under the police cordon. The tent was now entirely constructed, covering the statue and a sizeable area around it. They were given white forensics suits to wear. A screaming whirr began as two forensics officers in white suits used a stone cutter to slice open the first panels of the statue. A shower of sparks fell onto the stone floor.

The morning was very grey, and a floodlight was switched on; the bright light gave the impression that the statue was some kind of sci-fi film prop. With a loud crack, the panel of the statue, which read 'FUCK OSTERITY', came loose, and it took four forensics officers to support its weight as it was lowered to the ground. The stone cutter continued to scream, and as more sparks rained down, an odd smell permeated the air of burning metal and the faint scent of rancid bacon. The second panel came away more quickly, and when it was set down next to the first, the statue looked more prominent with the top panels removed. The silence rang out as the stone cutter fell silent. One of the forensics officers in white coveralls climbed higher on the ladder and looked down inside. He was handed a light.

'There's something in here,' he said, the glow from the light bouncing back and illuminating his face. 'It's covered in some kind of sticky resin, which looks like it's hardened over it.'

Kate glanced at Tristan, but they didn't dare say anything. Kate was about to ask if they could climb the ladder and look inside when a stretcher was called for. Using a pulley rope connected to a stand, a shape was slowly lifted from inside the statue. As it rose out and over the lip of the statue, it looked like a body in a shroud and coated in dust and dirt. It flexed and moved like rubber when it was lifted out by three forensics officers, guiding it on the pulley ropes above their heads. It brushed against the forensics tent's high ceiling, then lowered slowly down to the waiting stretcher.

Kate and Tristan moved closer. They could clearly see it had the shape of a body. The feet, both together and sticking up, were prominent, and so was the shape of the head. Up close, it frightened Kate. The shape looked like it was coated in amber or beeswax and slightly translucent. Varia knelt down beside it.

'It looks like some kind of rubber resin,' said Varia.

'It could be floor sealant,' said one of the forensics officers.

'It's coating the whole body. Is it a body?' asked Kate,

hearing the fear in her voice. Everyone stood back as a bright light was brought down and shone over the surface. Inside, like an animal in a cocoon, they could make out the curled fingers and arms of a small body, and when the torch moved up towards the bulbous end of the mass, they could clearly see the outline of a small skeletal face.

'It's Janey Macklin,' Kate said.

54

Kate and Tristan were shaking when they came out of the forensics tent. There were now several groups of people milling around the police cordon in the courtyard. It would take time for the forensics officers to break through the hardened resin surrounding the small body, but they were in no doubt that it was Janey Macklin.

They stripped off their overalls in silence and were going to wait in the police support van when they saw the funeral guests begin to arrive in a fleet of black taxis. The courtyard in front of Victoria House was built up, and it wasn't possible to see the courtyard from the road.

Kate didn't recognise the inhabitants of the first taxi, but when the second pulled up, she saw Robert Driscoll and Forrest Parker get out, followed by Maddie. They were all dressed in black mourning suits, and Maddie wore a diaphanous black coat with a small black hat and a veil over her face. In the eleven days since they'd had the meeting in the office, Maddie's pregnancy was now really showing, even with the oversized coat.

Varia and her colleagues were still talking with the forensics officer, but the two uniformed officers tasked with watching out for Forrest and Robert took note of their arrival. Within a few seconds, everything seemed to escalate.

Robert reached the top of the stairs leading up from the road first and saw the vans and the white forensics tent built over the statue. Forrest reached the top of the stairs a moment later. They both stared, and twin looks of panic crossed their faces. From where they stood a few feet away, Kate and Tristan could see down to the road, where two taxis were just unloading a group of mourners, who were all filling the staircase behind Forrest and Robert.

Forrest turned and seemed to debate running back down the stairs, but the police officers and Kate and Tristan were too close. He saw he was trapped by the police cordon on his left, running parallel to the social club building. In a panic, Forrest ran for the entrance to the Victoria House. Robert realised a second later, and he followed. Kate and Tristan were the closest, and they gave chase. They were on the other side of the police cordon, and they ducked under it. Robert and Forrest tried to exit the courtyard by going past the front entrance of Victoria House, circumventing the police cordon, but bystanders blocked their way. It was then that they made the fatal mistake of running into the social club where the wake had been set up.

'Two suspects have entered the Victoria House social club, and we're following on foot,' said one of the police officers into his radio. 'Requesting backup. We think suspects are unarmed, but we will proceed with caution.'

When Kate, Tristan and the two police officers reached the door to the social club, Robert and Forrest were standing stock still in the middle of the empty bar, arms by their sides, turning and staring, looking ready to fight or flight. The tables and chairs had all been pushed to the sides of the room. There was a bar at one end, where a confused-looking elderly man in a dark suit was polishing glasses. At the opposite end, a buffet of sandwiches and cake had been laid out on a long trestle table, and the room was flooded with light from the windows lining the two walls on either side.

'It's Janey, isn't it?' said Forrest, looking at Kate. Robert stood beside him in shock. Maddie appeared in the doorway and pushed her way inside. Varia let her come into the room, and she stopped between Kate and Tristan and Robert and Forrest. Her face was white with terror.

'Don't say a word, Forrest. You need a solicitor,' said Maddie, clutching her belly.

'You lied, Forrest,' said Kate. 'You said that you were at the Astoria nightclub on the night that Janey went missing. You repeated this to the police in your statement. The Astoria was closed that night, due to a gas leak.'

They both stared back at Kate, Tristan, Varia, and the two police officers. Maddie reached out to Forrest, clutching a tissue in her hand, but he ignored her and kept his eyes on Kate.

'And Robert, you did give Janey a lift in your van on the night she went missing, but you didn't take her back to The

Jug. You took her to the warehouse on Horner Mews . . . the warehouse belonging to Gaia Tindall,' said Kate.

Maddie moved closer to Forrest and put her hand on his arm. 'Darling. What's going on out there? Why did you run?' she asked, sounding confused.

'He ran because he helped to cover up a murder,' said Kate.

Forrest looked around and saw the buffet table behind him. He reached out and grabbed a long knife lying next to a cake. He grabbed Maddie, putting his arm around her throat, and he held the knife against her belly. Maddie screamed, and he put his hand over her mouth.

'Now let's all calm down,' said Varia, with panic in her voice.

'Fred. What the fuck are you doing?' said Robert.

'Leave me alone!' Forrest cried, his eyes wild and bloodshot. 'I'll do it. I swear to God, I'll stick this knife in her belly, and she'll lose the baby.'

They all froze. People from the courtyard were now looking in through the row of windows outside, and beyond them, the forensics tent glowed.

'You!' he said to Varia. 'You're in charge? You're going to get me a car, a taxi, whatever. The knife stays against her belly until we're safely out of here.' Forrest glanced around desperately. Maddie was now crying, her eyes red; she looked terrified. Kate glanced at Robert. He looked defeated. Weary.

'Robert. Tell us what happened to Janey,' said Kate.

'Fred. It's over. Just let her go,' said Robert.

'They don't know anything,' said Forrest. Maddie made a

333

moaning noise, his hand still over her mouth. The knife glinted silver against the black material of her coat.

'We know you had keys to Gaia's warehouse on Horner Mews. When she died in July 1988, it took almost a year for her will to go through probate before her brother inherited her estate. The warehouse was empty in December 1988. You told the police you had to package up some murals for the Old Street youth club, and when they spoke to the manager of the youth club, he confirmed that. What the police didn't know is that you had the keys to Gaia's warehouse, and you moved the murals there much later that night.' Forrest kept his grip on Maddie, and Robert just stared at Kate. She went on.

'You did pick up Janey in your van, and you did offer to take her for chips. But what happened? We know her body ended up inside that statue. Did you take her to the warehouse?'

'I liked her,' said Robert, who looked close to tears. 'I used to see her in her dance uniform sometimes. I knew so many girls who would have more fun with a drink inside them. So when I offered to give her a lift, I took her to the warehouse. When I got there, Fred and Roland had been drinking.'

'Shut your fucking mouth!' shouted Forrest. Kate could see that one of the police officers was out of Forrest's line of sight on the right and was inching closer to Maddie.

'No. I can't do this anymore, Fred. I'm sorry. When we arrived at the warehouse, there was Christmas music playing. And it was next to her dance school. I told her some other girls were coming and it was going to be a party. Janey calmed down and asked for a drink. Honest to God, she did. We gave her some cherry brandy, but I don't think she'd drunk much alcohol, and she got really drunk, really quickly. We had some weed. And then . . .'

'Robert. I swear to God, shut the fuck up!' shouted Forrest.

'NO! I can't live like this anymore! Can't you see? They've found her. Fred. It's over . . . It was an accident. Inside the warehouse, there was this sort of parapet or balcony that ran along the top a few stories up. We were all up there having a laugh and dancing. We were all fighting to dance with her, you know, like lads. And we were high, and we all lifted her up, and we were pulling her between us to try and be the one who got her. Then, suddenly, she went over the edge of the rail. It was high up, three stories down, and she landed on the concrete floor. We all went down to try and help her, but it was too late. She was still and very pale, and the front of her head was caved in.'

'Why did you move her body from the warehouse?' Kate asked. 'Why did you hide it in the pipe behind Reynolds newsagent?'

'We panicked 'cos all of Gaia's stuff was there. We knew that her brother had inherited everything, and was going to be given the deeds, and we didn't know if he might come at any time. So we put Janey in the back of my van and drove to Reynolds. I had keys, and I knew about the water tank and the pipe in the back.' At this point, his face screwed up as if he were in pain. 'Oh, God. When we put her in . . . she wasn't dead. She moved, and she was bleeding from this gash on the top of her head.'

'Stop crying! She was as good as dead!' shouted Forrest.

'Her back was broken. You could see her fucking brains poking through her head!'

Maddie's face was now stricken with panic, and his hand was clamped harder.

'Roland put her in the pipe,' said Robert. 'And that's when she came to. He suffocated her with his hand over her nose and mouth. It took a long time and she stared up at us . . . watching, judging.' He shook his head.

'How long did you keep her in the pipe?' asked Kate.

'Three days. And then the police took an interest in me when the witness from the Golden Fry said she'd seen Janey getting into my van. I knew they might search Reynolds 'cos I worked there. We changed the locks on the warehouse. Roland got a locksmith to do it in the quiet. We put Janey's body in a chest freezer in the warehouse.'

Forrest was now staring at Robert, and he seemed to be in a trance, holding the knife against Maddie's belly. The police officer who'd been inching around lunged at Forrest and managed to grab the knife. Maddie screamed, and the other police officer grabbed her and pulled her away. Forrest stood still, and all the anger seemed to leave his body. Maddie was led out of the social club.

There was a long pause, and then Robert picked up his thread.

'I kept telling the guys, "The police can't do anything to us if there's no body." And then we saw that the statue *Odgoad* was being stored in Gaia's warehouse. It was her statue, and before she died, she'd taken it back to clean it up for the council when they moved it to redo the courtyard out the front of Victoria House. When they arrested me and then charged me the following January, I was out of the way. I was in police custody, and they stopped trying to find a body. And I said to them again, "The police can't do anything to us if there's no body." I came up with the idea to use industrial floor sealant. Gaia used it in the warehouse on the floor. She'd done it a few years previously, and a big wasp got caught in it, perfectly preserved, like those insects in amber. I didn't know if the same would work for a body, but we were desperate. I was in custody, and that's when Fred and Roland hid her body in the statue.'

'Stop. Just stop,' said Forrest. He sank down to the floor.

'I never thought it would go to trial, but it did,' said Robert. 'And we knew that the police didn't know much about our link to Gaia. We'd got to know her from the youth club and used to go and help her out on Saturdays before she died. I thought the police would find Janey's body in the statue in the warehouse . . . and it would be a mystery that could never be linked back to us. But when they finished re-paving the courtyard, they put the fucking statue back up outside here,' he said, pointing out of the window. 'It was shortly before I went to trial. And the guys never said anything. 'Cos we kept thinking . . .'

'The police can't do anything to us if there's no body,' repeated Forrest, from his slumped position on the floor.

'When I was sent down, they never said anything, because I was more likely to get acquitted if there was no body. And I was acquitted. And as the years passed, the body remained hidden, and the police can't do anything to us if there's no body.'

'Roland went mad, didn't he?' said Tristan. 'Posttraumatic stress disorder. I spoke to his former housemate about his night terrors.'

'Yeah. Fred, Forrest kept an eye on him, and I did when I came out of jail . . . He changed his name because he wanted to escape it all, escape the past, but we were worried about him speaking out. He came close a couple of times and said he wanted to call the police and just confess. Tell them where the body was.'

'Forrest. Were the payments you made to him to buy his silence?' asked Kate.

'He was a drug addict, so the payments were his fix.'

'Which one of you drugged him?' asked Varia. Robert looked up at her. 'We found a partial print in Roland's flat. It doesn't belong to Robert. You're both under arrest. You need to cooperate.'

'Both of us drugged him,' said Robert, looking crushed. 'He was close to breaking.'

'Is that why you broke into the flat at Percy Circus and stole the page from the police file we had there, with Roland's full name?' asked Tristan.

'It's my fucking flat!' screamed Forrest.

'Which means you also planted the voice recorder. And you were in the flat the night I woke up.'

'Fuck you! Fuck you all!' Forrest put his head in his hands and started to weep.

'We did it the most humane way we could. Well, we tried with Roland,' said Robert. 'A little something in his favourite drink to make him sleep, and then . . .'

'But he had a high tolerance to drugs?' said Kate.

Robert nodded. 'He went mad. Attacked us both. I was closest to the kitchen and the knives.'

People were now looking into the windows from all angles. The barman had stopped work long before and was just staring, fascinated.

'How did we end up being hired to investigate this whole thing?' asked Tristan.

'Forrest's ego,' said Robert, his demeanour changing for the first time to bitterness. 'He always needs the spotlight. I don't know what was going through his mind when he wrote that article for the magazine. The whole Peter Conway and Thomas Black thing was a coincidence. Or, I don't know. I don't know why a serial killer would want to confess to a crime they didn't commit. Ego? And then, for once, Maddie took something Forrest did seriously and, along with her stupid boss, suddenly got the idea they could make some money out of it. And since then, it's all been fucking damage limitation!' Robert suddenly snapped and launched himself onto Forrest, punching and clawing at him.

Varia stepped in and nodded at the two police officers. They pulled Robert off Forrest, who had a long bleeding gouge down the side of his cheek, and they were both put in handcuffs.

'Robert Driscoll and Forrest Parker, we're arresting you for the murders of Janey Macklin and Roland Hacker,' she said. 'You do not have to say anything. But it may harm your defence if you do not mention, when questioned, something which you later rely on in court. Anything you do say may be given in evidence.'

EPILOGUE

When Kate and Tristan came back out into the courtyard, the forensics tent was glowing against the darkening sky. Forrest and Robert were being loaded, handcuffed, into the back of a waiting police car.

'Do you think all that will stand up in court?' asked Kate.

Varia raised an eyebrow. 'I don't know. Forensics managed to get to the body inside the resin. It's wearing the same clothes Janey was wearing the night she went missing, and the material, this industrial resin, could be quite the time capsule. There are hairs caught in the mix that are different to Janey Macklin's, and we've found fingerprints over the surface of the floor sealant . . . Back in 1988, people weren't so aware of DNA and fingerprints. And it happened in December when there were freezing temperatures. If they kept her body outside in that pipe and then moved it to an unheated warehouse before they entombed her in this stuff, there could be other DNA that's been preserved. Good work, you two.'

'Thanks,' said Tristan.

Kate looked at the crowds milling around the police cordon and then up at the towering façade of Victoria House and could see two figures in the window of Doreen's flat. Standing. Watching.

'We should go and talk to Doreen and Maxine. They need to hear the news before it makes the rounds in gossip form,' said Kate.

'Yes. And then, I need to talk to both of you and make an official statement. We need to put it on record how you came to the conclusion that Janey Macklin's body was hidden in the statue,' said Varia.

———

A week later, Kate, Jake, and Tristan returned to London for a strange day. In the morning, Kate and Jake went to Peter Conway's funeral, which was held at a crematorium in North London. Just Kate, Jake, and the chaplain of Wakefield prison were in attendance. The humanist ceremony was brief, and it seemed like such a strange, meek end to a man who, at one point, seemed to tower with a terrifying evil presence that threatened to destroy Kate.

No music played.

No one cried.

Kate breathed a sigh of relief when it was over, and the body of the Nine Elms Cannibal, Detective Chief Inspector Peter Conway, slid behind a set of fraying pale-blue curtains in his plywood coffin to be burned in an oven.

Kate hoped the heat was sufficient to prepare him for hell.

They only just made it back into Central London for Janey Macklin's funeral, which was joyful, sad and celebratory. It was held in the Holy Cross Church, close to Victoria House, and drew quite a crowd in the congregation. Everyone from Janey's past had turned out to finally say farewell and put her to rest. There were women from the Glenda La Froy dance school, neighbours from Victoria House, and friends from her childhood. Maxine's husband and their four children sat with Doreen in the front row, and Janey's coffin lay by the altar with a small bunch of daffodils, her favourite flower, placed on top. Varia sat with Kate, Tristan, and Jake at the back.

The congregation was encouraged to sing the hymns *All Things Bright and Beautiful* and *Amazing Grace* with gusto, and Janey's brief life was celebrated.

Kate, Jake, and Tristan wanted to leave quietly at the end of the service. It somehow didn't feel right for them to attend the wake, as they would probably be asked questions about the case. As they left the church, they found Doreen waiting outside.

'I just had to thank you before you go,' she said with tears in her eyes. 'Thank you for finding my Janey.' She embraced Kate and then Tristan.

'This is my son, Jake,' said Kate.

'He's so handsome,' said Doreen. 'You keep him close.' She bit her lip. 'I know it might sound morbid to say, but I'm having Janey cremated. I want to take her with me when I move to California. Maxine has a beautiful garden overlooking the mountains, and we'll find a special place to scatter her ashes.'

'It's not morbid at all,' said Kate.

'I spent years searching for Janey, and she was close by the whole time. Now, I can leave this place and start afresh without leaving her behind. God bless,' said Doreen. They embraced again, and she hurried back into the church.

Kate, Tristan, and Jake walked back through the smart piazzas of King's Cross, past bars and restaurants, and found themselves outside the Midland Hotel, now the St. Pancras Renaissance Hotel London. They stopped amongst the busy traffic and people hurrying past.

'I can't face getting the train home and coming back tomorrow morning for our meeting about this podcast project,' said Kate. 'We've probably earned a night in a decent bed each, and I want to look fresh and bankable.'

'Mum, it's a done deal. They just want to meet you both,' said Jake. 'But this hotel looks cool.'

'They filmed the Spice Girls video for "Wannabe" on the big staircase in the lobby,' said Tristan.

'The Spice Girls were a little before my time,' said Jake with a grin.

'That makes me feel old.'

'What do you think it makes me feel?' shrieked Kate with mock indignation. 'Come on, let's treat ourselves.'

They walked into the hotel lobby, where Kate asked for three rooms. When they checked in, the man behind the desk asked, 'Would you like a map?' He reached for a pen and a square paper map. 'This is a lovely area. It's been completely regenerated. And there's much to do and see at this time of year.'

As Kate looked out the door at the bright lights and the people rushing past, the phrase on Malcolm Newton's grave swam into her mind.

To live is the rarest thing in the world. Most people just exist.

'Do you think we need a map?' she asked Tristan.

'No, thank you,' he replied. 'I think we're all the type of people who like to find our own way in life.'

A NOTE FROM ROBERT

Thank you for picking up *The Lost Victim*. If you enjoyed it, please tell your friends and family. Word-of-mouth really is the best way for new readers to find my books.

When I started to write *The Lost Victim*, I wasn't planning for Kate and Tristan to travel to London. I've always thought of London being the home of my other detective, Erika Foster. I hope that one day, Kate Marshall and Erika Foster will meet; it could make for an exciting story. I wasn't quite ready for them to run into each other in *The Lost Victim*, so Kate and Tristan remained north of the river Thames for this story. South London is very much Erika Foster's territory. As with all of my books, I try to use as many real locations as possible. Victoria House is fictitious, but the Golden Lane Estate is real. I have a close connection to the Golden Lane Estate because it was the first place I lived when I moved to London. My grandad and step-grandma, Les and Heather, lived in Bayer House on the Golden Lane Estate for many years. I went to drama school in Guildford, and when it came time to make the big move to London, I was lucky to have grandparents who welcomed me in. I lived with them for my first few months, which made all the difference. I was, and still am, a small-town boy at heart, and moving to a big city in my early twenties was incredibly daunting. I will always be grateful to Heather and Les for giving me a home when I needed one, and this book is dedicated to them. I must also add that the Golden Lane Estate is a happy place with friendly residents and a strong sense of community. There aren't any murderous types living there. . . As far as I'm aware.

I'm already planning the next book in the series, and I want to keep writing more Private Investigator Kate Marshall novels for as long as you want to keep reading them. I'd like to ask you the question: What would you like to happen next? Kate is certainly moving on with her life, especially after the events in *The Lost Victim*. What kind of cases would you like to see Kate and Tristan solve? I have a clear idea of where I plan to take the story next, but it's always wonderful to hear feedback from you, dear reader.

A big hug and a thank-you, as ever, to my first reader, Janeken-Skywalker, and the rest of Team Bryndza/Raven Street Publishing: Maminko Vierka, Riky, and Lola. I love you all so much, and thank you for keeping me going with your love and support!

As I always say, many more books are to come, and I hope you stay with me for the ride! Stay tuned for more book news.

Rob

ROBERT'S EMAIL SIGNUP

If you would like to be the first to know when my next book is out, sign up for my mailing list below using the QR code or the web address. I typically send out 3 - 4 emails a year, your email will never be shared and you can unsubscribe at any time.

http://eepurl.com/duluLz

ABOUT THE AUTHOR

Robert Bryndza is best known for his page-turning crime and thriller novels, which have sold over six million copies in the English language. His crime debut, *The Girl in the Ice*, was published in February 2016, introducing Detective Chief Inspector Erika Foster. Within five months it sold one million copies, reaching number one in the Amazon UK, USA, and Australian charts. To date, *The Girl in the Ice* has sold over 2 million copies in the English language and has been sold into translation in 30 countries. It was nominated for the Goodreads Choice Award for Mystery & Thriller (2016); the Grand prix des lectrices de Elle in France (2018); and it won two reader voted awards, The Thrillzone Awards best debut thriller in The Netherlands (2018) and The Dead Good Papercut Award for best page turner at the Harrogate Crime Festival (2016).

Robert has released a further seven novels in the Erika Foster series: *The Night Stalker*, *Dark Water*, *Last Breath*, *Cold Blood*, *Deadly Secrets*, *Fatal Witness* and *Lethal Vengeance*, all of which have been global bestsellers, and in 2017 *Last Breath* was a Goodreads Choice Award nominee for Mystery & Thriller.

In 2019, Robert created a new crime thriller series based around the central character Kate Marshall, a police officer turned private detective. The first book, *Nine Elms*, was an Amazon USA #1 bestseller and an Amazon UK top five bestseller, and the series has been sold into translation in 19 countries. The second book in the series is the global bestselling *Shadow Sands*, the third book is *Darkness Falls* and the fourth *Devil's Way.* The fifth book in the series is, *The Lost Victim.*

Most recently, Robert published his first stand-alone crime thriller, *Fear The Silence,* which was an instant global bestseller in the English language, and won the Czech Bestseller of the Year award in the Czech Republic. The Dutch edition of *Fear The Silence* was nominated, along with the Erika Foster and Kate Marshall series, for The Netherlands prestigious De Gouden Vleermuis (The golden bat) award, which is awarded to an author for their entire body of work in the crime genre.

Robert was born in Lowestoft, on the east coast of England. He studied at Aberystwyth University, and the Guildford School of Acting, and was an actor for several years, but didn't find success until he took a play he'd written to the Edinburgh Festival. This led to the decision to change career and start writing. He self-published a bestselling series of romantic comedy novels before switching to writing crime. Robert lives with his husband in Slovakia, and is lucky enough to write full-time. You can find out more about Robert at www.robertbryndza.com.

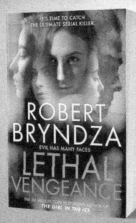

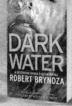

Read the first gripping thriller in the multi-million selling Kate Marshall series. . .

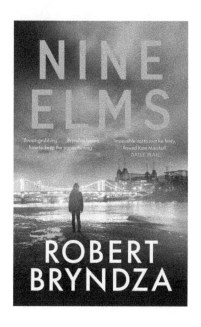

'Twisty dark and layered. . . A superb start to what promises to be another stand -out series.'

— M. W. CRAVEN, AUTHOR OF *THE PUPPET SHOW*

'Gripping from start to finish. I will wait with bated breath for the next Kate Marshall thriller.'

— RACHEL ABBOTT, AUTHOR OF *THE MURDER GAME*

Don't miss *Shadow Sands*, the second nail-biting thriller in the bestselling Kate Marshall series. . .

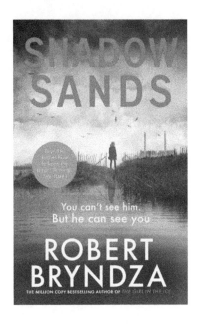

'A spine-tingling thriller from the master of suspense.'

— M. J. ARLIDGE, AUTHOR OF *EENY MEENY*

Taut, atmospheric and spooky, Shadow Sands is truly chilling

— JP DELANEY, AUTHOR OF *THE GIRL BEFORE*

Don't miss *Darkness Falls,* the third chilling instalment in the bestselling Kate Marshall series. . .

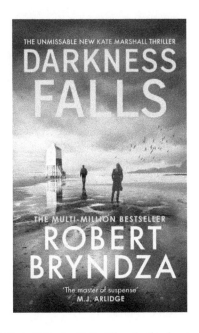

'The third Kate Marshall thriller, is the best one yet!'

— *THE TIMES*

'An exciting, riveting read from a master storyteller who never disappoints'

— RACHEL ABBOTT, AUTHOR OF *THE MURDER GAME*

Kate and Tristan's investigation into a young boy's disappearance sends them down an unexpectedly twisted path in *Devil's Way*, the fourth gripping instalment in the bestselling Kate Marshall series...

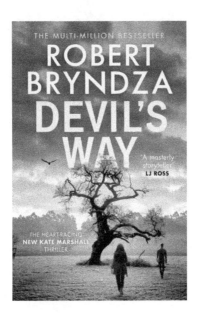

'A masterly storyteller.'

— LJ ROSS, AUTHOR OF *HOLY ISLAND*

Bryndza is my go-to guy for edge of the seat writing that keeps me hooked until the final page!

— AMANDA PROWSE, INTERNATIONAL
BESTSELLING AUTHOR

Printed in the USA
CPSIA information can be obtained
at www.ICGtesting.com
CBHW030507040724
11005CB00014B/285